THE *Duchess* GAMBLE

SOFIE DARLING

OLIVERHEBERBOOKS

❀ Created with Vellum

CHAPTER ONE

NEWMARKET RACECOURSE, MAY 1822

*T*he most beautiful woman in the room had nowhere to hide—except behind her smile.

Life had taught Celia that much—how to nod and smile and pretend.

A woman didn't reach her thirtieth year without having learned to do all three at once—convincingly.

What a useful hiding place was a smile. No one could see the nerves shimmering behind a pleasant curve of the mouth or an inviting crinkle of the eyes. The mechanics were simple.

And her smile was that good.

Take the lord presently pontificating at her. Oh, what was his name? Perhaps it began with *D*?

Anyway, even with all Lord D's banging on about a coffee farm on the other side of the world, today Celia's smile was genuine for two very good reasons.

First, her filly Light Skirt was the favorite to win the One Thousand Guineas, the second race of the popular Newmarket weekend that attracted the cream of society, dressed in their most fashionable silk and superfine, dripping in their most sparkling jewels and smiles.

1

And Light Skirt would win.

Celia knew it in her bones.

The second reason for Celia's smile was the proposal of marriage from the eminently eligible and eminently wealthy Duke of Rakesley that she would be receiving any day now.

And her stables would be saved.

It had been years—more than a decade—since she'd had so much to smile about.

Her gaze shifted discreetly away from Lord D, beyond the second floor of the grandstand where all the *haut ton* were congregated, and toward the racecourse. Truly, the day was a beautiful one for a race. The sky was clear, and the air possessed of the right amount of nip for horses and spectators alike. And the turf, green with spring and ready for the action it would see within the hour, was perfection. The rains had stopped a week ago, so the Ditch Mile held a firm spring.

Celia's heart tapped out a few extra beats as it always did at the races—especially when she had a horse in the running.

Nothing could touch her smile today.

Lord D stumbled over his words, and she couldn't help wondering if her eyes appeared as glazed over as they felt. Possibly, she was being rude. *Probably.* But it was a very mild rudeness, and she was a duchess.

A dowager duchess, a small voice reminded her.

As if it needed to.

Besides, the man's conversation bordered on the soporific. In recent years, it had occurred to her that society was structured to protect the delicate feelings of men. After the death of her husband a year ago, however, a mildly rebellious thought had lifted its head—what about her feelings?

Then the thought gained momentum and carried a step further—who in all her life had ever given her feelings a lick of consideration?

No one—not even herself.

"But, oh, poor Lady Artemis," came a feminine voice behind Celia.

Her ears perked up, even as her gaze remained fixed sightlessly on Lord D, his fleshy mouth still going on and on and *on* about coffee, and she listened to the gossip.

"Did you ever hear such a wail?" asked a second lady, distaste evident. "Over a *horse*?"

The first lady's voice lowered to a whisper. "So common."

And there it was—Lady Artemis's sin: to show feeling—*over a horse*.

No matter that Lady Artemis was the daughter of one Duke of Rakesley and the sister of another Duke of Rakesley—Celia's soon-to-be fiancé. It was a small world occupied by the *ton*.

Celia's hands wanted to clench into fists, but she didn't allow them the luxury. Her smile slipped not a notch. In fact, it might've broadened and sent entirely the wrong message to Lord D, who stepped closer, emboldened by her appearance of renewed interest.

Celia took an instinctive two steps back.

Smiles had their limits.

All the talk today—except Lord D's, of course—was about Lady Artemis and the death of her filly Dido during yesterday's race, the Two Thousand Guineas. Just as the filly had been on the verge of winning, she stumbled and fell in the final furlong. But it had been no mere stumble. It had been a total collapse from which the filly never recovered. As Dido drew her final breath on the turf, Lady Artemis had been inconsolable.

Emotion still clogged Celia's throat at the memory.

Not that her smile showed it.

Lady Artemis, on the other hand, had never learned Celia's smile. She'd never needed to. Though almost thirty herself and unmarried, the lady had never in her life once smiled for anyone she hadn't wanted to.

Celia couldn't imagine such freedom.

She gave herself a mental shake and reminded herself of the two reasons for her optimistic mood. Light Skirt about to win the One Thousand Guineas and Rakesley would be proposing any day now.

"Ah, there you are, Celia," came a most welcome lady's voice. A hand slipped into the crook of her arm, accompanied by the familiar scent of lily of the valley, and Celia felt tense muscles relax with relief.

Mrs. Eloise Fairfax—simply *Eloise* to Celia—had come to her rescue. Eloise was both Celia's cousin and bosom friend, as their ages were only five years apart.

"My apologies, Lord Derwin," said Eloise smoothly, "but I must steal my cousin away, and I make no promise to return her."

The last was spoken with a charming wink meant to assuage Derwin's feelings. Petite with luminous dark eyes that exuded warmth, Eloise had the gift of making men feel large and generous and like everything was their idea.

Celia could learn something from her cousin—if only she just would.

Out of earshot from Derwin, Celia couldn't help venting her irritation. "I thought widowhood afforded a lady the luxury of avoiding droning men."

"I've found widowhood affords no lady any such luxury," said Eloise, her voice even as ever. "But, oh, how on earth did you find yourself stuck in conversation with that lout?"

"Attracting louts is my special gift," returned Celia. "Haven't you heard?"

Going by Celia's disastrous marriage, everyone had.

Eloise squeezed Celia's arm with affection.

Celia loved Eloise. It had always been so, with Eloise assuming the role of older sister who knew best. Never once had Celia felt stifled by her cousin, but rather loved. And some years—an entire decade of them, in fact—love had been in short supply.

Together, Celia and Eloise moved through the intensifying crowd. With her natural friendliness and curiosity, Eloise greeted friends and acquaintances—she ever collected more and more of them—while Celia nodded distantly. She was known to be a cool duchess, one who held herself at a remove. She'd never minded all that much.

"Is Rakesley about?" Leave it to Eloise to cut directly to the subject occupying half the space in Celia's mind.

"He followed Lady Artemis to London yesterday."

Eloise nodded approvingly. "Like a good brother should."

"Indeed."

Of course, Rakesley wouldn't have been able to allow his sister to grieve alone. So, he'd cut short his own celebration for his colt Hannibal having won the Two Thousand Guineas. Like the caring, responsible brother he was.

Celia liked him the better for it.

"Still," began Eloise.

Though a single word spoken, Celia detected the note of worry within. She knew what Eloise was about to say—and she wished her cousin wouldn't.

"It would be a relief," continued Eloise, "if he would ask the question and have it done."

An objective truth.

All they had to do was be in the same room together, and nature would take its course. Rakesley would ask, and Celia would say *yes*. Wasn't it only natural for a duke to marry a duchess? The laws of the universe all but decreed it so.

"Oh, these delays," fretted her cousin. Eloise was a worrier.

Celia allowed that worry no entry. After Light Skirt won today's race, she would follow Rakesley to London, and send her condolences to Lady Artemis. In a separate note, she would invite the duke to join her for tea at her late husband's St. James's Square mansion. Then she would arrange herself appealingly on the chaise longue opposite his and agree to make him the happiest man on earth.

She would be saved.

More accurately, her stables would be saved.

Rakesley—arrogant duke that he was—thought his stables the best in the land, but Celia knew hers to be. And her deceased, wastrel of a husband had nearly squandered them away.

No.

She wouldn't think of her deceased, wastrel of a husband.

Not today.

Not when she had two very good reasons to smile.

Celia and Eloise settled into their box seats, front row, nothing impeding the view of the turf. Though Celia had found few pleasures in her life as a duchess, a front-row box at Newmarket was one.

The weigh-in now completed, horses and riders began taking their places at the start, all arrayed in a rainbow of colorful silks. Celia leaned forward and held her fan to her forehead as a shield against the sun, searching the scrum for her colors. Pink and white livery shouldn't be too difficult to locate, particularly when the shirt was bright pink with large and small white polka dots. She'd designed the pattern herself.

Her heart lifted in her chest. *There.* A flash of pink and white as Light Skirt and her jockey Ames jostled to the front of the starting line. A filly of even temperament, Light Skirt took no issue with being at the center of two dozen high-spirited Thoroughbreds. And, oh, was she a beauty with her shiny chestnut coat, white socks showing her elegant fetlocks to advantage, and braided black mane. Further, the filly's name suited her. When she ran, she possessed a lightness of step Celia had never encountered in another horse.

Anticipation had Celia's palms slicked with perspiration.

"By the by, Celia," began Eloise, angling in her chair so they could've been mistaken for conspirators.

Celia knew that tone. Whatever Eloise was about to say, it wouldn't touch her smile.

She was determined.

"I've heard a rumor about the title."

Celia didn't need to ask which title. Her late husband's title, of course. *Duke of Acaster.* The title that would go extinct if an heir wasn't found. She flicked a dismissive wrist. "There have been rumors about the title since Edwin exhaled his final breath."

Eloise gave a firm shake of the head. "This rumor isn't precisely a rumor, Celia. A line of inquiry appears to be bearing out."

"And let me guess." Celia couldn't resist a tease in her voice. "You have this on the good authority of Mr. Lancaster?"

A light blush pinked Eloise's cheeks. "As it happens, I do."

A widow these last seven years, Eloise had developed a special, *erm*, friendship with Mr. Lancaster during the last three, a discreet arrangement that suited both. Further, Mr. Lancaster was a barrister in Lincoln's Inn, and as such, he was privy to solid information and wild rumor both. This latest would prove to be the latter, of course.

"I appreciate your help, my dear." She squeezed Eloise's hand. Her cousin was only trying to help. "But it's been a year. If there were an Acaster heir, one would've been discovered by now."

The courts had given it nine months before they'd been satisfied she wasn't carrying Acaster's heir. Then they'd discreetly expanded the search, which looked doubtful as no family had been located.

It mattered not to Celia one whit. She cared about two things in this world—the woman sitting beside her and her horses. For the ten years of her marriage, she'd poured all her affection into her horses. They'd saved her at her lowest point, and now it was her turn to save them.

She would do anything.

Even marry again.

Eloise's seriousness didn't relent. "I think you should be prepared for the possibility, Celia."

Celia was saved from having to further engage on the subject, when she noticed the man with the starting gun taking his place. "Oh, look," she said, pointing. "The race is almost underway."

"We'll see," said Eloise, with a doubtful lift of an eyebrow.

False starts were a known strategy of the Ring's blacklegs to rattle horses at the starting line.

In the two decades since the blacklegs had secured near total control of betting in horse racing—laying odds and making the books—their brazen corruption knew no bounds, from false starts to bribing jockeys to poisoning rival horses to secure their favored horse a win. In 1818, the Jockey Club attempted to rein in the power of the blacklegs by opening the Subscription Room at Tattersall's, where bets were to be struck. But it was a mostly ineffectual attempt, for the scale of betting had ballooned well beyond the power of the Jockey Club.

On any given racing weekend, the hundreds of thousands of pounds just waiting to be plucked as if from thin air by the wiliest opportunists was too great a temptation for many to resist. When the spooking of a favored horse at the starting line could make a fortune for a blackleg overnight, the stakes couldn't be higher for the desperate chancer.

As the horses jostled into position, Celia's mind wandered in an unwelcome direction.

It was all this talk of Acaster.

A debauched lecher for most of his life, it only occurred to him at the young age of five-and-seventy that he could expire without a legitimate heir. He'd needed a wife.

One wasn't difficult to find. He was a duke, after all, and Celia's father was a wealthy merchant with a beautiful, obedient daughter and on the hunt for a title in the family.

Everyone got what they wanted.

Everyone, except Celia.

The duke had been serious in his intention to father an heir.

A clammy shudder traced through her at the remembered feel of the duke's hands on her skin... clamped around her wrists... clamped around her throat...

She swallowed the memory down. She couldn't think of the particulars of that life and maintain the smile on her face.

"My dear, are you alright?" asked Eloise, her gaze searching. "Do you need the ladies' retiring room?"

Celia shook her head. "It's only nerves."

Her smile had slipped.

She returned it to its place.

Her lech of a husband had, at least, done one thing right: He'd left her the horses in his will. They belonged to her outright—as long as she was able to keep them, for one rather sizeable problem remained.

Acaster had left her with no money for their upkeep—only debts. A new bill arrived every day.

Even a year after his death.

How like Edwin not to think or care about the practicalities. If—*when*—Light Skirt won today, the thousand pounds in prize money wouldn't take Celia very far. Every last farthing of it needed to go toward the buy-in for the Race of the Century in September, as tempting as it was to keep it and forego that race. But the Race of the Century carried a £10,000 purse, which would be enough to keep her afloat while she established the Thoroughbred stud she'd put in motion.

She simply had to keep her head above water for the next few months.

Perhaps Rakesley would agree to a quick wedding—a special license or a trip up to Scotland.

Then all her troubles would be over.

Another concerned crease formed on Eloise's brow.

Celia's smile had slipped—*again*.

She couldn't think about marriage and not think about the

marriage bed she'd been subjected to with Acaster—not if she was to proceed with her plan and marry again.

While Rakesley was all arrogant duke, he wasn't a bad sort—as men went. He knew his duties and responsibilities and took them seriously. He would make her the only sort of husband she would be able to tolerate: One whose life wouldn't much intersect with hers. For here was the most important consideration for marriage with him.

He didn't gaze upon her possessively or with hot lust.

He viewed her in a dispassionate, respectful way that suited her perfectly. She intuited he wanted the same sort of marriage as she—one not tangled up in emotion.

She would do her duty and give him an heir and two spares.

And he would save her stable.

Her ears picked up a snippet of whispered conversation from a passing couple. "...and soon to be the Duchess of Rakesley, by all accounts."

Good.

Gossip was spreading about her and Rakesley, and the feeling of safety, the feeling she'd been holding at arm's length until he'd officially asked the question—*Will you marry me?*—began to take on a tangible feel within her.

The life she wanted—*security... freedom*—was within reach.

Eloise tapped her hand and jutted her chin. The man with the starting gun had lifted the weapon into the air.

Even as Celia's heart thumped into an all-out gallop, her gaze caught on one horse and rider, the colors of purple and black unmistakable. *Little Wicked.* From the moment of her birth, she'd been proclaimed the most promising filly of her year. High expectations had followed. Lord Clifford, however, lost her in a card game to a chancer named Deverill, a man known in society for his mountains of blunt.

Celia didn't give a toss about the gossip. But she did care what happened to Little Wicked.

"Why is Little Wicked running today?" she hissed. The filly had run in yesterday's race, placing third and showing herself to be a contender for the rest of the racing season. "It isn't right that she's here. It shouldn't be allowed."

Eloise placed a calming hand on Celia's knee. "The Jockey Club has trouble enough enforcing their existing rules without adding one more."

Celia glanced around. It didn't take a second to find Deverill, surrounded as he was by a scrum of married ladies and their husbands.

"He has a few admirers, it appears," said Eloise.

"Oh, those lords want his mountains of blunt." Celia was feeling ungenerous.

Eloise gave a dry laugh. "And the ladies want in his bed."

Celia ignored that last bit.

Lord Devil was the moniker society had bestowed upon the man. With blue eyes that could pierce a soul and hair the black of a raven's wing, he possessed a male beauty severe in its intensity.

And he had not the slightest effect on her.

What did have an effect on her was that he was running Little Wicked on two consecutive days. "Deverill has no business owning a Thoroughbred like Little Wicked."

"How unexpectedly snobbish of you, cousin."

Celia shook her head, impatient. "Thoroughbreds are a touchy breed. They need to be run and worked, but they also require coddling. Just because someone has the money to keep a stable and train a Thoroughbred doesn't mean they should. Little Wicked deserves more than to be treated like a rich man's toy," Celia finished with more passion than was strictly necessary.

Eloise watched her calmly. "But her future isn't yours to decide, Celia. Besides, she certainly appears to be full of vim and vigor."

As if to illustrate Eloise's observation, Little Wicked gave a restless stamp of her hoof and toss of her head. A note of portent crept through Celia. Little Wicked was about to give Light Skirt a run for the money. She could feel it.

Starting line and stands alike went still and eerily quiet. The next sound would be the firing of the gun.

A sudden plume of gray smoke puffed into the air, followed the next instant by the crack of the shot.

The horses were off.

Light Skirt jumped to her usual fast start and would've been in the lead if it weren't for Little Wicked beside her, living up to her promise and acclaim. Both fillies possessed blistering speed on the flat that ran alongside Devil's Ditch, making it apparent in the first furlong that this would be a two-horse race.

Heart pounding in her throat, Celia shifted forward, her hands gripping the railing, knuckles gone white. Little Wicked showed no signs of exhaustion from yesterday's race. In fact, she was running today like yesterday had been a warm-up amble.

By the third furlong, the horses stretched out, and Celia waited for Light Skirt to transition into her signature cadence. The filly had the rare ability to hold the length of her stride while increasing her turnover. It was this quality that made her so light on her feet.

But, today, Light Skirt was running tight in the shoulders.

Without a thought, Celia was on her feet, hands clenched into fists, her mouth silently repeating, "Come on... come on... come on..."

A possibility occurred to her. A possibility she couldn't face—not if she was to keep her breath and hold her nerve. But this possibility pushed through, anyway.

Light Skirt could lose.

Which meant...

Celia could lose.

All her plans gone up like a cloud of dust in the horses' wake.

A vision flashed in her mind—of herself in London, *begging* the Duke of Rakesley for his hand in marriage.

No.

It couldn't happen.

Didn't life owe her better than that?

Hadn't she earned it?

Then, in the fifth furlong, a shift occurred.

Light Skirt's shoulders relaxed, and her cadence increased. The breath caught in Celia's throat. Here it was—the filly's special magic revealing itself.

By the sixth furlong, she'd nosed half a length ahead of Little Wicked. Only two furlongs to hold...

Celia's nails dug red crescents into her palms.

Into the seventh furlong, Light Skirt extended her lead another half a length, the finish line in sight.

In an instant, Celia's despair inverted into utter, effervescent joy. Hands clapping, she began shouting and hopping up and down as her brilliant filly crossed the finish line ahead of her adversary, who had regained some ground, but too late. If the race had been a furlong longer, it was possible Little Wicked would've taken the prize. That filly would be one to watch in the remaining races of the season, since she was a latecomer and those courses were longer.

But that didn't matter now, as pure, unadulterated joy streaked through Celia. She threw her arms around Eloise, tears streaming down her face in equal parts exhilaration and relief, as she received congratulations from all around. She was certainly making a *common* spectacle of herself.

But it mattered not.

Light Skirt had just won the One Thousand Guineas and its £1,000 purse. She'd secured her place in the Race of the Century —and a chance at its £10,000 purse.

Her stable was safe.

For now.

Long enough for her to obtain a discreet line of credit to float her through the short term—until her wedding to Rakesley.

While it was true she would have to smile at another man for the rest of her days—another husband... another *duke*, no less—she wouldn't mind smiling at the man who had saved her stables and secured her future.

This last decade had put her through the mangle, but—*at last*—she'd come out the other side.

How very close she was to the past never mattering again.

CHAPTER TWO

LONDON, A WEEK LATER

$\mathcal{I}$t was an ordinary Wednesday night at The Archangel.

The gentlemen and lords had finished their supper and drinks at their respective clubs—Brooks's, Boodle's, or White's. Some had toddled off home to their virtuous beds. Others had stumbled in the direction of the rookeries and the various flavors of vice on offer there. And yet others were presently ambling into The Archangel, filling its four walls with the familiar scent of cigar mingled with whiskey and the familiar sounds of elation mingled with despair. Such was the character of a gaming hell, no matter its exclusivity.

And no mistake, The Archangel was exclusive.

Gabriel Siren had no interest in touching money unless it ranged in the hundreds to thousands of pounds. It only followed that the stakes ran high on his hazard and roulette tables. The card tables, too. And while the gaming aspect of The Archangel was necessary to attract the lords who spent nights begun at dusk and ended at dawn—and even paid a monthly fee to indulge the extravagance—it wasn't the part of his business that interested Gabriel. Rather, it was a necessary evil.

Luckily, he had the very person to manage the gaming hell

side of the business—his older sister and right hand, Tessa, who was now determinedly climbing the stairs to join him on the second-floor gallery.

"Tessa," he said in greeting.

Nearly of a height with Gabriel, she barely had to lift eyes the crystalline blue of a Swedish fjord—precisely the same blue as his own, along with those of their two younger sisters, Saskia and Viveca. "Brumley is demanding to see you," was her returned greeting.

"I take it he's losing at hazard." Gabriel wasn't surprised. The man had a special talent for losing.

Tessa exhaled an irritated sigh. "He's saying it's all a big misunderstanding and his old school chum Siren will straighten out the confusion."

"What is the big misunderstanding?"

It seemed fairly straightforward. In a gaming hell, one lost money—and one paid for the privilege.

"That he lost one hundred pounds in two minutes. Give or take a minute."

"Why else would anyone play hazard?"

"He would rather lose the hundred pounds over the course of the evening. His words."

A wry smile twitched about Tessa's mouth, which was as big a smile as one was likely to see from her. His sister was the most serious person Gabriel had ever known—and possessed of the most brilliant mind of his acquaintance, including his own.

"It's only sporting, old chap," she continued, perfectly imitating Brumley's posh Eton intonation. "Again, his words."

Gabriel understood he might as well get the inevitable over and done. "I'll take care of it."

Two steps later, he heard, "Oh, and that solicitor is back."

Gabriel half turned. "Send him on his way again."

He only met with solicitors he knew. Otherwise, he would be subjected to a deluge of swindlers and cheats.

Tessa didn't budge. "This time, he comes bearing a letter stamped with a royal seal."

"A fake, no doubt."

"No doubt," she agreed. "He's waiting in your office."

"Tessa—"

She held up a staying hand. "He won't take *no* from anyone but you."

With other matters to attend, Tessa set off on her own business. As it was the top of the hour, that would be a first accounting of the evening's take. Even in an establishment as efficiently run as The Archangel, light-fingered croupiers and dealers abounded.

Gabriel continued down the stairs to see about Brumley, his *old school chum*. Even in his mind, the words sounded ironic. In the technical sense, they had attended Eton and Cambridge at the same time.

But—and this was the important part—Gabriel had done so on scholarship.

And hadn't those sons of dukes, marquesses, earls, viscounts, barons, and knights let him know it?

Until, of course, Gabriel had become useful to them by assisting them with their maths revision.

Then it was on to assisting them with their vices.

It had been but a small step once Gabriel discovered he could take a little money and make more from it.

Of course, not everyone was a winner every time—except Gabriel.

The house always won.

His foot hit the bottom step, and an irritable shout cut through the din. "Siren!"

From the far side of the room that housed four hazard tables and four roulette tables, Brumley waved frantically. Gabriel nodded and made his unhurried way across the floor, greeting patrons as he went. He knew precisely how to handle this *old school chum.*

It had been a year or so since he'd last spoken to Brumley, as Gabriel spent little time on the floor. Though of an age at four-and-twenty, Brumley had acquired a good three stone. The natural consequence when one's only physical activity was throwing dice and lifting tumblers of whiskey to one's mouth. Ironically, Gabriel had little use for either pursuit.

"Enjoying the evening?" he asked in his low, ever-even voice.

"But that's exactly my point, old chap," said Brumley. For a night barely started, the man was deep in his cups.

Further, Brumley was laboring under a severe delusion if he thought he was having those hundred pounds returned. The Archangel was neither a charity nor a place for lords still in need of leading strings. Still, Gabriel could meet him some of the way. "I'll make a note that your subscription fee is to be waived for the next quarter."

The dark cloud over Brumley's face lightened, but didn't entirely recede.

Too bad.

Gabriel offered a slight bow before pivoting on his heel. He caught a glimpse of the Duke of Richmond entering the card room and followed, finding Richmond settled into a plush leather armchair and snapping open a turf rag.

"Richmond," he said, taking the chair opposite.

"Siren," said the duke.

A few years ago, Gabriel had expanded his business into a diversity of interests that ranged well beyond the four walls of The Archangel, holding stakes in ventures that looked to the future. His investment in the manufacturing of steam engines was close to outearning The Archangel, in fact. But his investment with the Duke of Richmond represented a new sort of venture.

Horse racing.

He'd never given much thought to that shadowy world. Too

much uncertainty. Too much corruption. Then Richmond, a true aficionado of the sport, had approached Gabriel with an intriguing idea. They would hold a racing meeting at the end of the 1822 season that would run only five horses—the winners of the season's five major races: the Two Thousand Guineas, the One Thousand Guineas, the Oaks, the Derby, and the St. Leger.

The Race of the Century.

Richmond set his turf rag aside and cut to their business. "How were ticket sales during the Newmarket weekend?"

"We took in six hundred and thirty-one pounds." Gabriel could tell him down to the penny if he asked.

Not that dukes counted pennies.

Scholarship lads did, though.

Richmond lifted an impressed eyebrow. "A good start."

"Decent," countered Gabriel.

With a £10,000 purse and the costs associated with using Epsom Downs as the venue, there was quite a bit more to recoup, but they were on their way. Of course, each race entrant was required to pay the £1,000 buy-in for their horse, which put him and Richmond £5,000 closer to recovering their costs and running in the black.

"We're in the process of setting up stalls across town to sell tickets."

Skepticism etched Richmond's features. "That seems an unlikely avenue for sales."

Gabriel didn't betray himself with a snort or roll of the eyes or any other movement that would indicate what he thought of the duke's view. Instead, he explained, level and cool. "We aren't actually selling tickets to a horse race. We're selling tickets to a dream. To see the fastest three-year-old colt or filly in England."

"Speaking of," continued the duke, undeterred. Dukes were notoriously difficult to deter. "The tickets are too cheap."

"They're not."

Gabriel wasn't easily deterred, either.

He'd been standing this ground since the beginning and would continue to do so. This race would attract the high of society and the low. It was a chance for the masses to see the best horses of their day run, instead of the sway-backed nags on their local courses.

This was the angle.

This was the attraction.

Gabriel didn't expect a duke to understand it.

Richmond cocked his head and narrowed his gaze. "They say you're four-and-twenty."

"Aye," returned Gabriel.

The duke shook his head on a scoff and reached for the turf rag. "The youth today."

Gabriel understood what Richmond was about. He encountered it on a near daily basis. The duke was using Gabriel's age to diminish him and his accomplishments.

"Will that be all, Your Grace?" he asked, rising.

Richmond gave a nod of dismissal and absent wave of his hand.

As Gabriel made his way through the club and up the stairs to his office, he ran the numbers through his mind again. *£10,000.* That was the winner's purse. Subtract the £1,000 buy-in for each of the five entrants. *£5,000.* That left the ticket sales. A £631 take at the Newmarket races. *£4,369.* Between sales at other races, around London, then on race day, Gabriel fully expected to close in on that number all the way to £0.

Yet the point of the ticket sales wasn't about the money they brought in. Ticket sales were about the *people* they brought in— people who liked to bet on the horses. Therein lay the real money Gabriel was after, for it was no great secret that hundreds of thousands of pounds changed hands during the Derby and all the other major racing weekends.

The Race of the Century would be no different—except in one crucial way.

The Ring's blacklegs wouldn't be running the betting post on race day, for Gabriel was leaving nothing to chance.

The Race of the Century was a one-off race that wasn't bound by the rules of the Jockey Club, Tattersall's or the Ring's blacklegs. So, The Archangel would be handling all the odds laying and book making themselves. He and Richmond stood to become even richer men than they were already.

Here was the secret to success Gabriel had discovered at Eton. He kept his head down, his nose clean, and he worked the numbers.

He strode into his office and was halfway to his desk when he noticed the still figure seated in the corner, satchel on lap, hands folded on top. Neat as a pin, this bespectacled man.

And Gabriel remembered—*the solicitor.*

If he could be called such.

A chancer, more like.

Gabriel didn't acknowledge the man until he reached his sturdy oak desk and stood before it. "You have business with me?" He consulted his pocket watch and didn't wait for an answer. "You have two minutes."

Without a word, the man stood and crossed the room to the chair nearest Gabriel, but didn't sit. Instead, he placed his satchel on the seat and began efficiently removing papers. Gabriel cocked a hip onto the desk and watched, no small bit nonplussed. This man certainly possessed the efficient manner of someone who knew his business, not a whiff of the chancer about him.

A square of parchment emerged from the depths of the satchel. With its elaborate folding, fluttery ribbons, and bold stamp, the missive certainly bore the look of a royal seal. With great reverence, the man held it out.

Gabriel crossed his arms over his chest. He was under no obligation to accept anything this man offered.

The man's brow gathered. "You're Gabriel Siren, yes?"

"I am."

"This is for you."

Gabriel remained as he was. "What is it I can help you with?"

"You may want to sit down."

Gabriel made no such move.

"Have you heard of the Duke of Acaster?"

"He'd darken the doorstep of The Archangel on occasion."

Multiple occasions.

The solicitor laughed. When Gabriel lifted an eyebrow, the laugh turned into a throat-clearing cough. "You must know he drew his last earthly breath a year ago."

"Without settling his debts here," said Gabriel. "I'm aware."

"Well, you're not alone in that regard."

Gabriel let a few beats of silence lengthen. "Can I send for someone to escort you to the door?" he asked. "I've a night to get on with."

The solicitor didn't move. "And no heir."

"Pardon?"

"Acaster died without an heir."

Gabriel had enough. He shifted forward, intending to the take the barmy man by the arm and personally walk him from the premises. The man began waving the sealed letter. "Read this."

Gabriel decided the most expedient course would be to humor the man. So, he accepted the letter and broke the seal with an efficient swipe of his penknife. He gave the contents a quick scan.

Deep grooves dug into his forehead.

The words refused to penetrate.

He took the second read at a slower pace—words like *Gabriel Siren* and *duke* jumped out at him—but, still, they rolled off his brain like water from a duck's back.

By the third pass, words began finding fissures in his mind and seeping through.

Words that presented a logic that didn't hold.

At least, not in the combination and sequence they appeared.

He thrust the paper toward the man. "Is this a jape?"

The solicitor sat with the unbothered mien of a man at peace with how very right he was. "I can assure you it isn't."

"This says—" Gabriel began reading. *"Henceforth, the man known as Gabriel Siren is His Grace Gabriel Calthorp, Seventh Duke of Acaster."* His gaze lifted. "This cannot be."

"Oh, but it is, Your Grace. It even has a stamp direct from the king's very own signet." He pointed out said stamp.

Gabriel went still, his mind searching for a thread of logic. "What is your name?"

"Mr. Mossley."

"Who put you up to this, Mr. Mossley?"

His mind did a quick calculation. It could've been any number of people. One didn't start a successful gaming establishment in London without ruffling a few feathers and gaining a few enemies.

Mr. Mossley's hands spread before him as if helpless to the situation. "It's a royal decree."

Gabriel wasn't having it. "I am not descended from dukes. My father was a law clerk killed by a dray horse while crossing Fleet Street."

The solicitor's head canted with curiosity. "What do you know of your grandfather?"

"He was a clerk before my father. A man who worked hard and expected it of others."

"And what do you know of your grandfather's father?"

Gabriel shifted in sudden discomfort. "Grandpapa wouldn't speak of his father."

"And his brother?"

Brother?

Though he hadn't asked the question aloud, Mr. Mossley seemed to hear it. "Your grandfather married a Swedish woman, yes?"

"Gran was Swedish," Gabriel said, wary. "How do you know all this?"

"Took months, I can tell you."

"That doesn't answer my question."

"You see, your grandfather took his wife's surname."

Gabriel waited.

"That was how he was lost." Mr. Mossley spoke as if he stated the obvious. "But now you're found."

A humorless laugh escaped Gabriel. "Funny, I didn't feel lost."

"Oh, but you were." Mr. Mossley's dull gray eyes went bright behind his spectacles. "You see, your grandfather was the younger son of the Fifth Duke of Acaster. By all accounts, he didn't get along with his family. So, he decided to make his own way in the world. It was when he wed your grandmother that he became lost."

"And how is that?"

"Her last name was Siren. It's a Swedish name, not English at all."

The man thumbed through his stack of papers until he found the one he sought. Gabriel took it gingerly, as if it might burst into flame. He'd become wary of papers offered by this man.

After a cursory scan, he glanced up. "A certificate of marriage?"

Unable to contain his excitement, Mr. Mossley tapped the paper. "See? George Calthorp—that's your grandfather—and Ebba Siren—your grandmother."

"Yes, they married," said Gabriel. "What is it you're seeing that I'm not?"

Being caught on the back foot happened to him rarely—and he liked it not one bit.

"The marriage is legitimate."

"I never doubted it."

"Well, the courts are tougher to convince, and it makes all the difference in this case."

"Why is that?" Gabriel asked, but the answer was already making itself known.

"Because it makes you legitimate issue." Mr. Mossley's smile of triumph wouldn't be contained. "It makes *you* the Seventh Duke of Acaster."

The words refused to sink into Gabriel's brain all at once, but in slow increments.

Him... a... *duke.*

"Your great-grandfather was the fifth duke and your great-uncle the sixth."

An utter absurdity occurred to Gabriel... "The Duke of Acaster who came shambling into The Archangel twice a week was my *uncle?*"

"Great-uncle, yes. And when he died without legitimate issue, you became the seventh duke." Now firmly in his area of expertise, Mr. Mossley was only too happy to explain. The man bordered on the giddy. "How fortuitous that you managed to get yourself educated at Eton and Cambridge, instead of becoming a—"

"*Guttersnipe?*" Gabriel finished for him, dry. "How fortuitous."

The solicitor's smile fell a chastened increment. "You know this new world you'll occupy and its rules. Dukes and such folk are decided in their notions about rules, Your Grace."

Your Grace.

The man kept saying it—wouldn't stop, in fact.

"I don't give a toss about the *ton*'s rules."

It needed to be said—and understood.

Mr. Mossley smiled. "Spoken like a true duke."

Gabriel wasn't a man given to displays of frustration, but the feeling that was now building inside him felt fit to burst.

The door swung open, admitting both the roar of downstairs gaming and Tessa, who was two strides into the office when she suddenly stopped, only now registering the scene before her. "Oh, you're still here," she said to Mr. Mossley. Her gaze met Gabriel's. "I thought you would've sent him packing by now."

"Sister," he said, "you may want to sit down."

Recent experience had taught him as much.

Tessa's shrewd gaze flicked back and forth between the two men. "I'll stand, thank you."

Gabriel saw that no good could come from beating about the bush. "It appears I'm a duke."

"You are, Your Grace." With a satisfied smile, Mr. Mossley turned toward Tessa. "And *you* are Lady Tessa, I presume."

She snorted, but when everyone else in the room remained serious, her mouth fell agape. "Gabriel," she began, "say it isn't so."

He remained quiet.

He could only presume the sequence of emotions marching across her face precisely mirrored those that had played out on his own only minutes ago.

Disbelief... befuddlement... bewilderment... horror...

She shook her head, ever stubborn. "That cannot be."

As Mr. Mossley began explaining everything to Tessa, showing her the relevant papers when she dismissed or doubted, Gabriel kept an eye on his sister.

The solicitor finished, and unquiet silence descended on the room—and Gabriel continued watching Tessa.

Then it flickered across her face.

The final emotion—the inevitable one.

Acceptance.

Gabriel was the Seventh Duke of Acaster, and she was Lady Tessa.

And all the nobs presently circulating through the gaming rooms of The Archangel on the floor below, the nobs whose blunt they didn't mind in the least pocketing...

Well, she was one of them.

As was he.

Unsavory realization struck Gabriel. Until this moment, he'd been free to fashion the life he wanted, his only impediment his own imagination.

But, now, he felt bound—bound to a life not of his choosing.

A life that didn't suit him.

A spark of rebellion fired through him. *No.* He'd never been a victim of his circumstances.

And he wasn't about to start now.

Even as a duke, he would have the life he wanted.

He was determined.

And never once had he been determined to have what he wanted and not attained it.

If he was to be a duke, so be it.

But he would do it his way.

CHAPTER THREE

ASHCOTE HALL, SUFFOLK, A WEEK LATER

*P*ale pink bedroom curtains swept open, allowing sunlight to stream through the bow window that over-looked the rose garden, and Celia dragged a pillow across her face.

"Must you, Mrs. Davies?" she mumbled into dense goose down.

"A gent has arrived," said Ashcote Hall's redoubtable housekeeper.

Celia peeked from beneath the pillow. "*A gent?*"

Mrs. Davies sniffed. "From London by the sound of him."

Celia's brow creased. "Has Mr. Murdoch arrived already? What is the time?"

"Eight of the clock, Your Grace."

That didn't sound right. Why would the horse painter she'd sent for arrive at such an early hour? Unless... "Have I slept through the day?"

In anticipation of this meeting, she'd gone through an entire bottle of plonk last night in a fruitless attempt to drown her sorrows.

In other words, it was possible she'd slept through the day.

Mrs. Davies dropped a lump of sugar into Celia's morning tea and stirred, the spoon an efficient, ear-piercing *ting-ting-ting* against porcelain. "Eight in the *morning*."

Celia groaned, and last night's sorrows were upon her—still floating on the surface, ever buoyant and unsinkable. Today, she would have to face what she'd set into motion by necessity—the selling of her beloved stable.

Honestly, it defied belief how her life had all gone so horribly wrong, so incredibly fast.

One moment, Light Skirt was winning the One Thousand Guineas and Celia was on the verge of receiving a proposal of marriage from the Duke of Rakesley...

The next moment—well, a week later—Rakesley was asking Celia if she would mind very much *not* marrying him. The enthusiastic *yes* perched on the tip of her tongue turned to dust as the import of the question sank in.

She wasn't to marry him.

Her life was in shambles—*yet again*.

A day later, as if the universe was keen to add insult to injury, a letter had arrived. An official one. The one Eloise had warned her to expect.

A new Duke of Acaster had been located.

From its place on her bedside table, the letter pulled at her gaze like a magnet. Since its arrival, she'd read it three or four times a day, though it was no longer necessary. She'd memorized its contents word for word. She'd even dashed off a note to Eloise's Mr. Lancaster to verify it wasn't some sort of jape.

Impossibly, it wasn't.

There was a new Duke of Acaster.

He would be a wastrel, of course.

It was in the Acaster blood.

But that didn't concern her. What did concern her was that she was in trouble. It was only a matter of time before this new duke turfed her out into a dower house at the Acaster family seat in Kent.

Which wouldn't be the worst of it.

Her horses would be turfed out, too.

She was about to lose the one thing she cared about.

So, she'd made a necessary decision—sell off two of her beloved Thoroughbreds. Not at a Tattersall's dispersal sale, but rather by putting a discreet word about that two mares from the Godolphin line were on offer. That would drum up some excitement in turf circles and perhaps see her through the next few months of operating costs.

Horses were no inexpensive love.

Yet one silver lining lay within all this. Her dead husband's mountain of debt? It would—*blessedly*—transfer to this new duke.

She snorted, drawing a chastising lift of the brow from Mrs. Davies as she pulled the coverlet back for Celia. Mrs. Davies had been her one concession from the late duke, who had allowed her to set up her former governess as Ashcote's housekeeper. But Celia hadn't been many weeks married before she understood it wasn't concession so much as necessity. Acaster hadn't been able to retain female staff for longer than a handful of months.

For the obvious reasons.

The man had been an unapologetic lech.

"Has any correspondence arrived this morning?" Celia shrugged on her dressing gown.

"Nothing yet," said Mrs. Davies, her attention divided as she signaled for the scullery maid to stoke the wood in the fireplace.

Celia tried not to wallow in her troubles—truly, she tried—but a full week had passed since she'd received news of the new duke, and there was still no sign of the man. So, she'd kept herself busy. The day after receiving Mr. Lancaster's confirmation, she'd dashed off a letter to the renowned horse painter, Mr. Silas Murdoch. A faithful rendering of her two mares was the necessary first step toward their sale.

Three days ago, she received a reply from the painter that he would arrive at Ashcote three days hence.

Today.

Hence, last night's bottle of plonk—and today's aching head.

"Mrs. Davies," she groused. "Is all that sunlight strictly necessary?"

The housekeeper cast an assessing eye over Celia. "Yes," she said, firm. "Now, drink this." She wasn't referring to the tea, but rather a concoction that held a shade of green, a sheen of slime, and a scent of egg.

"Are you trying to murder me?" Celia squeezed her eyes shut against an errant shaft of sunlight. She wasn't sure she would mind being put out of her misery all that much.

"You'll come to no harm from anything my mam swore by."

And that was that.

Mrs. Davies' mam was the final word on any subject.

Like a good soldier, Celia took the glass, held her breath, and drank the surprisingly bland contents in three large gulps. Mrs. Davies gave a nod of approval, which was her highest praise.

Half an hour later, Celia was dressed in a drab woolen dress fit for a morning in the stables and braced for the day—whatever it would bring. She ran through the meeting ahead of her. As duchess, she would have the upper hand over Mr. Murdoch—in the beginning. During this time, she would lay out her requirements for the painter. That was the simple part. The complex— and delicate—part of discussion would be when it turned to money. Namely, his price. There, she could lose the upper hand and be reduced to begging, for she had no intention of paying a farthing more than she had to.

As she descended the loose coil of Ashcote's grand curved staircase into the receiving hall, she caught a glimpse of a man's back, his gold-streaked brown hair touching the top of his collar. Her gaze followed the width of square shoulders, down the length of his coat of charcoal gray. The fabric was fine—too fine for a horse painter.

It meant he was paid well for his work.

Which Celia couldn't do.

And tall, was her next thought.

Of a sudden, his head cocked. He must've heard her. He pivoted, his gaze immediately landing on her. Celia's step faltered, and the breath caught in her throat. *Handsome.* Cheekbones defined and chin dimpled. A mouth with lips not full or thin, either.

Men shouldn't be this handsome, especially not horse painters.

It upset the balance of the universe.

Men never affected Celia in this way. Perhaps it was like when she'd viewed the Parthenon Marbles at the British Museum or the first time she'd heard Herr Beethoven's *Moonlight Sonata.* A thing of beauty ever had such an effect on her.

It so happened the thing of beauty twenty feet away from her was a man.

A *young* man.

It was his eyes, however, that drew her in and held her in place. Not a striking blue, but a hue the clarity and changeable quality of the sea on a sunny day. They held more within, too. Intelligence—and a hint of irony.

This man might be young and a thing of beauty, but brainless he wasn't.

Irritation streaked through her. This handsome, intelligent, young man wasn't Mr. Murdoch.

He couldn't be.

The illustrious horse painter had sent an apprentice.

"Duchess," he said with a shallow bow.

His voice wasn't particularly deep, but it brushed across her with the consistency of crushed velvet. Further, she detected that ironic quality, again. This man wasn't all that impressed by her title.

Or her, for that matter.

Celia wasn't accustomed to that.

She might not have been dressed in the first stare of fashion for a morning in the stables, but men stopped and took notice of her—to a one.

It was simply her effect on men.

But within this man's clear, ironic eyes, she detected none of that appreciation.

She gave a regal nod of acknowledgement and continued down the stairs. Several feet away, she stopped and held out her hand. The expectation was clear: He was to give it a courtly kiss.

Instead, he offered a slight—*ironic*—bow.

Celia's hand fell to her side. The cheek of the man and his irony. How dare he gaze upon her with that look in his eye?

As if he knew something she didn't.

"And your name?" she asked—demanded, really.

"Gabriel Siren." A flicker of uncertainty flashed behind his eyes. "At least, that was—"

"I appreciate your promptness in calling, Mr. Siren," she said, intentionally cutting him off. She didn't need to know anything more.

Yet... she experienced a ping of recognition. *Gabriel Siren.* She'd heard the name somewhere, but couldn't quite place it...

Gabriel.

He certainly looked like an artist's rendering of an angel—until one met his eyes.

One didn't find sweetness and light in those cerulean depths.

Unusual for a man who couldn't be all that many years removed from university.

Bewildered dark eyebrows drew together. "You were expecting me?"

"Why wouldn't I?"

A lopsided smile tipped at one corner of his mouth. "I, *erm*, honestly don't know."

What a strange young man.

Well, he was an artist, and artists were known to be entities unto themselves.

Celia gestured toward the door. Best to get on with it. "Shall I take you to them?"

Mr. Siren made no move to follow. *"Them?"*

"Cleopatra and Lady Fanny."

"Your... *daughters?*" He looked genuinely perplexed.

Was the man altogether daft?

"The mares."

His brow released. "Ah." He shrugged. "Why not?"

Annoyance bristled up Celia's spine. He acted as if he were granting her an allowance rather than the other way around. Not only did this young man have no business being as handsome as he was, but he had no business being as confident, either.

"Follow me," she said with no small amount of imperiousness. She was the duchess here, and the perplexing Mr. Siren would know it.

In silence, she led him through the house. She'd thought to put him in his place by making him trail three steps behind her like a servant. But she found she didn't like him at her back. It made her feel strangely exposed.

Deemed a beauty from the moment of her birth, Celia had always accepted her place as the object of an enraptured gaze.

But with this man it felt... different.

He wasn't enraptured.

Then she heard it—the absence of footsteps behind her.

She threw a glance over her shoulder and found the confounding man wasn't gazing upon her at all, but rather standing in fascination before a musty old portrait. She supposed a painter would be interested in paintings. "Mr. Siren?"

He spared her a quick glance. "Who is this?"

Celia ruffled at the demand. "My husband's father."

"The Fifth Duke of Acaster?"

"That's right."

He stared for another solid minute. Then turned to her. "We may go now."

Celia's eyebrows lifted. "May we, now?" No small amount of sarcasm laced the question.

He nodded his assent.

The cheek of this man!

And Celia found herself leading the way—*again*.

Upon their entrance into the stables, her first genuine smile of the day dawned. Here was where she came to return to her real life and real self. In truth, she didn't allow interlopers easily. She had a trusted head groom, multiple stable lads, and a trainer for the season. All knew their places and ran the stables accordingly. As the clock was near to striking nine, they'd arrived in time to find Light Skirt being led into the stable yard on her way to the paddock. Celia reached out to run her hand across the filly's velvety nose. She squinted up at the stable lad on her back. "How is our girl this morning?"

"Right as rain, she is," said the lad.

Celia nodded, and the lad was on his way. They didn't stand on formality in the stables.

She glanced over to find Mr. Siren quietly observing her. *Unsettling.*

She turned on her heel and marched straight down the center aisle of the stable, tossing over her shoulder, "Cleopatra and Lady Fanny are this way."

"An impressive operation you have here," came Mr. Siren's voice at her back.

Celia supposed she should slow her pace and allow the man to walk by her side. "Not as impressive as some."

Mr. Siren glanced around. "No?"

"Ashcote houses twenty Thoroughbreds," she said. "The Duke of Rakesley has fifty or so at Somerton."

The serious, lopsided smile curved about Mr. Siren's mouth. "Only twenty?"

"However," continued Celia. She couldn't help herself. "What we lack in quantity at Ashcote, we more than make up for in quality."

"I believe it."

Celia blinked.

I believe it.

Strangely, she believed him.

Mr. Siren didn't deal in flattery.

Which was why she continued talking to this man who unsettled her no small bit. "At Ashcote, we don't only breed from winners, unlike Rakesley. We pay attention to other qualities, as well. Take temperament, for example. A foul-tempered stallion is likely to sire foul-tempered offspring, though they may never live in the same stable. Thoroughbreds are a tricky breed and have to be managed with thought and care."

She stopped before a box, and a docile chestnut mare with a black mane poked her head over the gate. "Take Lady Fanny here. On the small side, but she's a real goer on the turf and has been known to bite other horses. But to humans she's as sweet as can be." The mare nosed Celia's arm, demanding the attention she rightly deserved. "Alright, girl," she said, stroking the mare's nose. "And there—" She pointed across the aisle. "There is Cleopatra. A little more high of spirits, but containable, and able to focus on the turf."

As Celia spoke, she realized something unusual. Mr. Siren let her talk, uninterrupted.

It was that quality which unsettled her.

Most men interrupted—often.

Most men only waited for her to finish talking, so they could start talking.

Not this man.

He listened.

And took in every word.

She wasn't sure she liked that better.

"Was your late husband involved in the running of the stables?"

An un-duchess-like snort that wouldn't be suppressed sounded from her nose. "Of course not."

Mr. Siren lifted his eyebrows and said nothing.

She'd revealed too much.

"This stable is your life's work." He made the observation with genuine interest.

Celia had to swallow against the sudden surge of tears that constricted her throat. She'd told herself she wouldn't cry, and she wouldn't.

However, with a single, simple sentence, this young and too-handsome horse painter had spoken her pride and her shame.

This stable *was* her life's work.

She'd built it—and now she was stripping it for parts.

And this man saw because he listened to her as if she were an equal.

Not a social equal, but a human equal.

Celia had never encountered that in a man.

She might be powerless against such treatment.

She might be powerless against this man she'd known for less than half an hour.

CHAPTER FOUR

*T*he duchess surprised Gabriel.

While waiting for her in the receiving hall, he'd gone over the few facts he knew about her. Fifty-six years younger than the late duke. Numbers generally stuck in his mind, and that one was no exception.

What had a young lady of late teen years been doing marrying a duke in his eighth decade?

A question with an easy answer.

Title hunting.

A woman willing to do anything to get what she wanted.

The logic only followed.

Yet when he'd seen her descending Ashcote's staircase, he realized he'd formed preconceived ideas of her, as well. That she would possess a hard, shifty eye on the lookout for the angle. A woman with a tall pink powdered wig dressed in silks, possibly from the last century. He might've been expecting Marie Antoinette to walk down the stairs. After all, his great-uncle had never stopped dressing in colorful silk breeches from the last century, complete with a smudge of rouge on each cheek.

But the reality of the duchess—clad in plain wool dress—had Gabriel reevaluating his assumptions about her.

She might not be that sort of woman.

Then he understood what tempted him to think as much.

It was her beauty.

Hers was the sort of beauty that could take the linear flow of one's thoughts and whip them into a scramble with no effort at all on her part.

The duchess was no mere wisp of a woman, but rather statuesque and curvaceous. A woman whose form held substance, along with curves too numerous to count. Surely, they were quantifiable—of course they were—but it wouldn't be gentlemanly to stand here and enumerate them.

Besides, her curves weren't pertinent to the conversation ahead.

His gaze wouldn't linger on her porcelain skin or rosebud lips the hue of ripe cherries. So, he concentrated on her eyes—a honey amber that glowed from within. Her sable hair parted down the middle and pulled back into a loose chignon at the nape of her neck only amplified their luminosity.

Gabriel would do well to give this woman's beauty a wide berth. In nature, beauty was used to obfuscate and confuse. He sensed it was no different with this woman.

In other words, her beauty was a trap.

One he wouldn't fall into.

When she'd extended her hand for him to bow over, Gabriel's brain had, at last, unscrambled. How very aware was this woman of her position. She hadn't even allowed him to finish a sentence. Which had been to his benefit, in truth, for she was clearly laboring under a misunderstanding about his identity.

A misunderstanding he was in no hurry to correct.

She seemed to think he would be interested in her horses.

He wasn't—not in the least.

However, if following her into the stables meant she would

keep talking, it was only to his advantage. People revealed themselves when given free rein over a conversation. He was learning about more than horses from the duchess. He was learning about her—where her passion lay.

Horses.

It wasn't a mere or passing interest. Gabriel concluded these animals were her life—and he'd said as much.

This stable is your life's work.

It had been simple statement of fact.

Yet as they stood now, eyes locked, there was nothing simple about the raw emotion that passed behind her eyes.

Emotion Gabriel would need to understand, if he were ever to understand her.

He gave himself a mental shake. He didn't need to understand this woman. He'd only ventured from London to the wilds of Suffolk to take stock of one of the few estates his great-uncle had managed not to gamble away. As the property was unentailed, Gabriel was at liberty to sell it and use the proceeds to bite a chunk out of the debt held by the duchy.

The duchess broke contact with a shift of her amber eyes. "Yes, well, we duchesses must find ways of filling the idle hours of our days."

Gabriel didn't know this woman—had no intention of knowing this woman—but he knew a lie when he heard it. Before him stood no idle duchess.

The lie intrigued him.

Why lie?

Specifically, why lie when the truth held no risk?

When her gaze again met his, it no longer held raw emotion. Instead, she was impenetrable with imperiousness once again. "I believe you've seen all you need to start." Her voice was clear, but it didn't carry far. A voice accustomed to making itself small. "Shall we take tea and discuss the particulars?"

"As you like."

She swept past him and led the way, this time in reverse through the stables and manor house. The sitting room where they were to take tea lacked any semblance of comfort—all chipped gilt furniture and threadbare watered silks, which was only in line with what he knew of the former duke. With the duchy's debt, there would have been no money to spare for refurbishment—not with the stable operation he'd just viewed.

Another example of how this duchess might not be the duchess he kept expecting.

She'd picked horses over new furnishings. Few duchesses would make that choice, not when appearances were everything in the *ton*.

She perched on the edge of the opposite settee, the elegant arranging of her skirts like second nature, and looked everywhere but at him. Gabriel took his seat and waited. Eventually, she would have to acknowledge the fact of him.

At last, she inhaled and met his gaze. "Was your journey to your satisfaction?"

"It was but a few hours' ride from London."

Gabriel wasn't much for small talk, but neither was the duchess.

Again, he waited.

She appeared to have something to say to him—and was having difficulty saying it. Her hands lay clasped on her lap, the knuckles showing white. At last, she said, "It's but two horses."

"Are we speaking of Cleopatra and Lady Fanny?" Gabriel could hardly get the second name out of his mouth. Racehorse names never ceased to shock.

The duchess blinked. "Of course."

Tea service arrived with the housekeeper, who kept casting an eye that could only be described as baleful in his direction.

"That will be all, Mrs. Davies," said the duchess.

The housekeeper looked in no mood to vacate the room, but she'd been dismissed and therefore was left with no choice.

And Gabriel was alone with the duchess again.

She brought fine porcelain to her mouth and blew a cooling breath across the tea's surface. "I was thinking that since there are two of them—"

"The horses?"

She gave a curt nod. "So, perhaps an accommodation could be made." Her cheeks had gone pink. "On price."

Undoubtedly, it would be ungentlemanly to allow her to continue under the misapprehension that he was someone else, but his curiosity was fully drummed up.

What service was he to provide her?

Further, and with great difficulty, she was attempting to haggle with him.

If his time spent in a public boarding school and as owner of a London gaming hell had taught him nothing else, it was that people revealed themselves in times of distress, and he found he wanted this duchess to reveal more of herself.

Silence was his best tool.

So, again, he waited.

Her throat cleared awkwardly. "The first painting at your going rate? And the second at half?"

Gabriel's gaze lowered a fraction to her throat, where the hard beat of her pulse was visible. "You would like me to paint your horses?"

Her blush drained away until she was pale as a sheet. "I have cash."

It was time. He must reveal his identity. To go on like this seemed cruel. "About that," he began.

"Unless it's Mr. Murdoch who makes such decisions?"

"I'm not acquainted with any Mr. Murdoch."

Two heavy beats of silence thudded past. Her brow crinkled, and her head canted. "Who are you?" Her teacup and saucer clattered to the table. "What have I gotten wrong?"

A throat cleared at the door, drawing her gaze and preventing

Gabriel from providing the long overdue truth. "You have a visitor, ma'am," said Mrs. Davies.

"Oh?" asked the duchess. "And his name?"

The baleful glare Mrs. Davies directed toward Gabriel was now undeniable. "Mr. Murdoch."

The duchess's gaze shifted and met Gabriel's. "Please show him in."

The intervening ten seconds might've been the slowest of Gabriel's life as the duchess watched him as if she dare not allow him out of her sight. At last, she spoke. "Who are you?"

At that moment, Mrs. Davies arrived with the visitor. "Mr. Murdoch, Your Grace."

A man of middling height entered the room. When his bespectacled gaze landed on the duchess, he gave a low, obsequious bow. A broad smile lifted the ends of his bushy mustache as he straightened. "Your Grace."

She inclined her head like the duchess she was. "Mr. Murdoch, I've just finished introducing your apprentice to my mares, Cleopatra and Lady Fanny."

Mr. Murdoch's wiry eyebrows met in the middle of his forehead. "My apprentice?" He shot Gabriel a thunderous look. "I don't have an apprentice."

"Of course, you do." She pointed at Gabriel. "He's there—Mr. Siren."

"I've never seen this man in my life," blustered Mr. Murdoch, bristling with genuine affront. "Besides, I would never send an apprentice to service the Duchess of Acaster."

The duchess blinked and her cheeks flamed scarlet—whether from the fact of the mistaken identity or Mr. Murdoch's interesting choice of words, Gabriel couldn't know.

"Of course, Mr. Murdoch, you must be exhausted from your journey." She reached for the bell. Mrs. Davies returned not two seconds later. "Will you show Mr. Murdoch to his rooms?" Her gaze returned to the bewildered painter. "You must be in need of a lie-down."

Though couched in a gentle tone of concern, Gabriel heard the duchess's words for what they were—a command.

While a flummoxed Mr. Murdoch searched for a reply, she continued, "You and I shall reconvene later to discuss our business."

She nodded for Mrs. Davies to lead Mr. Murdoch from the room.

The door clicked shut behind them, and once again, Gabriel was alone with the duchess.

He caught a flash of her stormy gaze before she shot to her feet and strode to a window overlooking a cheerful rose garden with its colorful riots of early-summer blooms.

Back propped against a window casement, she crossed her arms at her waist. It wasn't that Gabriel wanted to notice, but the pose foregrounded the generosity of her bosom.

No one would mistake him for a poet.

"*Again*," she began, the storm in her amber eyes not having abated one whit, "who are you?"

Gabriel supposed the question had been inevitable. "A mathematician, I suppose."

"You suppose?"

"That was my area of study at Cambridge."

Confusion shone in her eyes. "Have I spent my morning with a bedlamite?"

"It's beside the point."

"Which you'll be getting to presently?"

"I shall."

Her head canted. "Aren't you too young to be a mathematician? What are you? Twenty?"

He shifted. "Four-and-twenty."

"So young."

"Six years younger than you, in fact."

She gasped, indignation shimmering about her. "Who taught you your manners, anyway?" But his words appeared to catch up with her, and suspicion entered her eyes. "How do you know my age?" But before he could answer, she cut him off. "What was the *was*?"

"Pardon?"

"The *was*," she repeated. "Earlier, in the receiving hall, you said your name was Gabriel Siren, then you said it *was* your name. As in the past tense."

"Ah."

This duchess possessed intelligence. A good thing to know about a person.

"You like drawing out a moment, don't you?"

She was also impatient.

He smiled. "It's in the stretch of a drawn-out moment that a person will reveal herself."

"And who have I revealed myself to be?"

"Not precisely who I thought you were."

A dry laugh escaped her. "Well, you have the advantage of me there, for I haven't the faintest idea who *you* are." The laugh was gone in an instant. "If you *were* Mr. Gabriel Siren, then who are you *now*?"

And here it was—the pointed end of the question.

"A duke, apparently." The statement didn't emerge with the strength of conviction.

"You're either a duke or you aren't." A deep line formed between her delicately arched eyebrows. "There is no *apparently*."

"I'm a duke."

"Of?"

"*Of?*"

"The Duke *of...*?"

The time had arrived. He'd avoided this moment for days, understanding the instant he spoke the fact aloud, it would be true—forever.

"Acaster."

A skeptical eyebrow lifted. "My husband was the Duke of Acaster."

"*Was.*"

The line between her eyebrows deepened. "You... *are...*"

"The Duke of Acaster."

She reached for the chair beside her, as if her legs had given a sudden wobble. "*Siren,*" she said, slowly, consideringly. "*You* are Gabriel Siren."

"*Was.*"

"You own a gaming hell—The Archangel, correct?"

"I do."

"And you're an investor in the Race of the Century?"

"I am."

"And..." She shook her head as if attempting to shake an idea loose—one that had grown stubborn roots. "*You* are the Duke of Acaster."

She slid sideways into the chair, a dazed look in her eyes.

At least she was taking the news well.

"I'd assumed you'd been informed."

She shook her head. "I had, but I wasn't given details. Like..." She waved her hand up and down in his direction, as if the gesture were sufficient to complete her thought. "*You.*"

"I wasn't aware you were in residence at Ashcote Hall." He felt the need to explain himself in the face of her utter bewilderment.

That got her attention. "Why wouldn't you be?"

"I would've thought as duchess you would divide your time between the St. James's Square mansion in London and the Acaster family seat in Kent."

"Ashcote is my main residence." Her gaze sharpened. "Why are *you* here? Shouldn't *you* be making yourself at home in the St. James's Square mansion or the family seat in Kent?"

"I needed a firsthand look at Ashcote Hall."

Her gaze narrowed. "Why?"

He supposed only the truth would do. "I shall be selling Ashcote Hall."

Her skin turned the shade of papery ash. *"Selling?* To whom?"

Here, Gabriel found comfortable territory. "To the highest bidder, presumably."

"Selling... *Ashcote?"* she stammered, outrage in every syllable. "To the highest bidder?"

"It's how matters proceed in business."

"Business," she spat. "That's all you see when you look at Ashcote? But you've seen the stables."

"A selling point to be sure," he said evenly... reasonably.

The glint in her eyes turned fierce. "The horses are mine. Acaster left them to me in his will."

"I'm aware."

"Then you'll know you can't sell them."

"I was speaking of the structure of the stables."

Some of the wind knocked out of her sails. But she wasn't finished. Her gaze roved over him, assessing. "You're a very precise young man, aren't you?"

Young.

That word again.

A putting of him in his place.

An unexpected surge of anger stirred within him.

A powerful urge demanded he prove to this woman how young he wasn't.

An urge that felt oddly new.

Primal.

Medieval forebears likely had similar urges. Urges that were to be fought against and contained in a civilized society.

The urge affected him in another way, as well.

Physically.

A physical stirring that similarly must be fought against.

So as not to allow that stirring to ignite into flame, he shot to

47

his feet. This conversation was better ended now. "If that will be all, Duchess?"

She'd gone as cold as a north wind in January. "As pleases you, *Duke*."

No small amount of irony dripped from that last word.

No matter. Within three minutes, he was ensconced inside his coach-and-four and on the road back to London. He'd seen all he'd needed. Ashcote Hall was in good condition and ready to sell to the highest bidder.

Even so, it was the duchess, not the potential numbers of that sale, that occupied his mind.

The fact was he had little experience with women who weren't his sisters. His world was one of men. Since Eton, it had ever been so, and after Cambridge, he'd done nothing to change that status quo. It suited him. He'd always been drawn to numbers and the structure they provided. The opposite sex seemed too dicey a proposition. That way lay chaos—and insatiable need. He'd seen it happen to too many men.

And Celia Calthorp...

Within the passionate, luminous depths of her eyes he sensed an ability to unleash a whirlwind of chaos into his life.

He wouldn't give a moment's consideration to the possibility of insatiable need.

Simply, he would let none of it happen.

He wasn't a man given to sudden primal urges, particularly those brought on by troublesome women.

He was a man of logic and reason. Those were the tenets of his life.

In truth, he and she never had to occupy the same room again.

A satisfied smile traced about his mouth.

In life, as in numbers, a solution neatly arrived at ever pleased him and set his world to rights.

CHAPTER FIVE

LONDON, ONE WEEK LATER

*C*loak hood lifted to conceal her identity, Celia stood on one side of Bennet Street, glowering at the townhouse opposite.

The building she'd been attempting to muster the nerve to enter for the last hour.

The Archangel.

In the row of Mayfair townhouses, it was one of many. With its unassuming brown brick and black trim, it wouldn't draw the eye if one didn't know where to look. One wouldn't know it for a gaming hell. And seeing how it was around the corner from the popular gentlemen's clubs, it was smartly placed for those only getting started with their nights after dining at their respective clubs.

This new Duke of Acaster was an intelligent man.

An intelligent *young* man.

The shock at meeting him a week ago still hadn't subsided. She'd never considered the possibility that a Duke of Acaster could be under the age of seventy years—much less four-and-twenty.

The fact of the matter was this—she was well and truly in the suds.

This new Duke of Acaster was young, but he was no young man who could be wrapped around her finger. He possessed a sharp edge in his eye that could slice through blancmange. How else did one establish the most exclusive gaming hell in London?

She needed to take a step.

Then she needed to put another step in front of that one, and another and another, until she'd crossed the street and the threshold of the unassuming building that saw two or three gentlemen enter every quarter hour or so. It was early enough in the evening that more patrons were arriving than exiting.

A quiver of anxiety shot through her. She'd never been inside a gaming hell, but that wasn't what had arrows of nerves flying through her veins. She'd come to London, to this gaming hell for one reason.

To beg.

If necessary, she was fully prepared to sink to her knees and plead with this new duke to hold off on the sale of Ashcote Hall and let her keep her horses there through the Race of the Century. He didn't give two figs about Ashcote or her horses.

It would cost him nothing.

She would do anything.

Anything?

She could use her body. A tactic that had been done before by women the world over—and herself specifically.

No.

Those instances had been others using her body for their wants and ends.

Which was a whole other matter entirely.

And something that would never happen to her again.

But her problem remained. In fact, it had tripled in size. This new duke was determined to sell the roof from over her beloved horses' heads.

She didn't yet know how, but she couldn't let it happen.

Right.

She squared her shoulders and began putting one foot in front of the other.

Then it was up the five steps to the door and a few taps of the knocker, her exterior composed, her palms damp, and her heart a racehorse in her chest.

She was at The Archangel.

She was doing this.

The door swung open on silent hinges and a large form filled the doorway. *Massive* was a more accurate descriptor for the form as the doorman's shoulders threatened to touch either side of the doorframe. "Is madame lost?" he asked, his French accent light.

"This is The Archangel, correct?" Celia set her tone at mildly imperious. She would only go full duchess if absolutely necessary.

"It is."

"Then I am not lost."

He remained, unmoved. "This is a gentlemen's club."

"I'm aware."

In locked silence, they stood, neither willing to cede an inch of ground. Celia understood it couldn't hold and any moment the door would slam in her face.

"*Ricard?*" came a feminine voice from behind him. "Is something amiss?"

Celia lifted an eyebrow. "One of your gentlemen?"

Ricard didn't look inclined to answer, as a woman swept around him unlike any Celia had ever seen. Tall and striking, she wasn't dressed exactly like a man—she was wearing a skirt— but not like a woman, either. Women simply didn't wear white silk cravats and teal watered silk waistcoats.

Further, this unusual woman possessed authority at The Archangel.

Sharp blue eyes that meant business fixed on Celia and assessed her from tip to toe, drawing conclusions and holding them to herself. "Ricard," said the woman, at last, her conclusion drawn. "Allow the lady inside."

Ricard gave a nod and stood aside.

Celia had only taken a few steps before she felt a hand at her shoulder. "Your cloak," said the woman.

Celia shrugged off the garment and allowed it to be taken.

Then it was through a black velvet curtain and into The Archangel. Celia hadn't known what to expect of a gaming hell, but it wasn't this. *Tasteful.* That was the first word that sprang to mind. *Male.* All rich woods and subdued brown and burgundy, The Archangel was a tasteful, masculine establishment. And while the gentlemen at various gaming tables were obviously enjoying their evening, it wasn't the raucous atmosphere she'd assumed it would be.

The woman turned toward Celia. "I take it you're here to see Mr.—" The woman bit off the next word.

And Celia knew why.

The owner of this establishment was no longer Mr. Siren.

He was the Duke of Acaster.

"I am here to have a word with the duke, yes."

Something unreadable and complex passed behind the woman's eyes. "I trust you can keep yourself entertained while I see if the duke is in?"

Celia glanced around. A few lordly eyes had already landed on her and taken note. "Of course." She hardly recognized her own voice for how tight it had gone.

All she wanted to do was reclaim the last few minutes and turn her feet in the opposite direction and be far, far away from this place.

Which would get her nowhere.

Actually, that wasn't true.

It would see her and her stable turfed out of Ashcote.

She squared her shoulders. Here, she would remain.

The other woman nodded and set off.

Celia spotted a chaise longue against the nearest wall and settled onto it, alone.

Nay, not entirely alone.

A buzz was building through The Archangel. It had to do with a woman's presence.

And not any woman's presence in this decidedly masculine domain.

The Duchess of Acaster's presence.

From various groupings of gentlemen scattered through the club, she sensed a gathering—of intention.

Soon, one lord, then another, broke free and ambled in her direction to bid her a good evening, a question in their eyes. *What in the blazes was the Duchess of Acaster doing in The Archangel, anyway?*

Celia's mouth curved into its practiced smile—the one meant to dazzle—and she batted the couched inquiries away.

These lords weren't gathering around her as they would a young unmarried lady, with honorable intentions. The glint in these men's eyes told of an altogether different motive regarding the widowed Duchess of Acaster.

In the domain of The Archangel, she wasn't wife material.

She was a potential conquest.

She was *mistress* material.

"*Duchess?*" came a voice to her right.

She directed her smile toward a lord with the eager look of an excitable puppy, his bland handsomeness holding no threat. A safe, young lord. "And you are?"

"Lord Wrexford at your service," he said on a deep bow, gratification pinking his cheeks.

"Pleased to make your acquaintance, Lord Wrexford." Her smile tipped into the genuine. Wrexford had a bit of sweetness about him. "And are you a habitué of The Archangel?" she asked as if they were in the most proper drawing room in London rather than a risqué gaming den.

"I'm afraid not." His blush spread to his scalp. "This is my first time, actually."

"Oh? Why is that?"

"I'm not much for gaming, in truth."

"That only speaks well for you, my lord." She had to say it.

His blush intensified, offering a radish red contrast to his coppery hair. "But I had to see."

"Had to see what?"

"The gaming hell run by the Duke of Acaster."

Celia's brow lifted. So focused had she been on her goals, she hadn't considered that a duke who owned a gaming hell would be a matter of some curiosity for the *ton*.

"The duke and I have known each other since school," continued Wrexford.

"Is that so?"

"Of course, he wasn't a duke then."

"No, he wouldn't have been."

"What a come up, eh?"

"Certainly is."

Was she the only person in London for whom this story held little fascination? A question occurred to her as she took in Wrexford. Oh, how she didn't want to ask it... "So, you and the duke are the same year?"

"Actually, I'm a year below him."

Celia only just didn't gasp. "You're... *younger?*" Which meant...

This lord who was flirting and blushing madly at her couldn't have more than three and twenty years on him, not if Acaster had four and twenty.

A feeling whispered across Celia's skin—of being watched.

Unerringly, her gaze lifted toward the source. There, on the gallery above, stood the duke, his intense gaze upon her. The whispery feeling penetrated skin and shivered through to dark interior places within her.

Her smile slipped.

Wrexford's puppy eyes went wide with concern. "Is all right with you, Your Grace?"

Celia gave a vague nod and reminded her mouth of its one job —to smile.

Then it happened.

The crowd parted like the Red Sea, making way for the Duke of Acaster, a man now one of them.

Nay, not merely one of them, but a cut above them in the social hierarchy—a *duke*.

Across the closing distance, their eyes locked. He was a mystery, this new Duke of Acaster.

But more of a mystery was her response to him.

She'd dismissed it a week ago as an anomaly brought on by shock.

It was more than he was handsome.

It was something else.

Sitting here, her gaze left with no choice but to meet his, the mysterious *it* revealed itself.

Simply put, the man lit a little thrill through her veins.

And she liked it not one bit.

But trivialities such as *like* or *dislike* held no power here.

It felt like an inevitability.

CHAPTER SIX

*A*s Gabriel's gaze held the duchess's captive, a few quick reactions flicked through him.

Surprise.

He hadn't thought her so bold as to venture into The Archangel.

Curiosity.

What was she doing here, anyway? Their business with one another had reached its natural conclusion.

And yet another reaction coursed through him, one not easily identifiable. A novel reaction.

A *need.*

The need to pull her away from the besotted group of men gathered around her and claim her as...

What?

Ridiculous thought for two very solid reasons.

He wasn't the sort of man who *claimed* a woman.

And she was his great uncle's title-chasing widow.

That fact alone was enough to dampen any needs he might have in relation to this woman.

Still, it couldn't be denied that his memory of her a week ago was a dull shadow of the woman before him tonight. Gone was the woolen dress of practical drab brown, and in its place was blush silk nearly the shade of her skin, cut low over a generous décolletage that possessed a gravitational force all its own, pulling the eye, demanding a full accounting of every supple curve.

He resisted the pull—unlike the men around him. How reductive to simplify a woman into parts. He made it a rule never to succumb to thoughts that reduced one to the animal side of humanity—and he wasn't about to start now.

"You aren't going to steal her away, are you?" came a voice accompanied by a few light-hearted grumbles.

"Family business," said Gabriel, his gaze refusing to release the duchess.

That got a laugh from the crowd of lords who still couldn't quite believe their favorite gaming hell was now owned and run by the newly-minted Seventh Duke of Acaster. Word had spread like wildfire.

For Gabriel, nothing had palpably changed. A few more responsibilities, that was all.

The duchess came to her feet and stood, unmoving. She was waiting—for him. As a gentleman, he should extend his arm for her to take while he escorted her to his office. Propriety demanded it.

But The Archangel wasn't proper society.

It was a gaming hell.

Different rules applied.

Except that was only the excuse.

The fact was he didn't want to touch her—*couldn't* touch her. For he sensed something inside him. The flicker of a small flame.

To touch her would be putting tinder to fire.

A risk best avoided.

He pivoted and trusted the duchess to follow. At the office door, he stood aside and allowed her to enter first, the scent of jasmine and bergamot trailing in her wake. He supposed he should offer her a seat.

He didn't.

He didn't want her to sit.

He wanted her to leave.

He cocked a hip against his desk, crossed his arms over his chest, and waited. His first rule of conversation was never to speak first—and then only as little as possible. Given room, people generally talked themselves out and into a better state of mind. He could only hope that would be the case with the duchess.

An armchair between them, she rested elegant fingers on the leather back. Her tongue swiped across her pouty bottom lip. A nervous habit of hers. He'd noticed it on their first meeting. He found it irritatingly difficult to remove his gaze from that pouty bottom lip and sheen of moisture.

At last, she opened the conversation. "I'm shocked Edwin wasn't a member of your little club."

"Oh, he was." Gabriel saw no reason to withhold that information from her.

Luminous amber eyes blinked. "Of course, he was." A cynical little laugh followed. "And racked up a mountain of debt, too, no doubt."

"He did." Gabriel kept his tone carefully neutral.

"Debt accrual was Edwin's one skill in this world." She gave a shrug. "At least, there's one debt you won't have to repay."

"Every debt requires payment, Duchess."

The words emerged hard and low. He didn't want this woman thinking she had free rein over him, like she held over the men downstairs.

The remainder of her smile fell away.

Only now that they floated in the air did Gabriel hear another possible meaning embedded within his words. They hinted at a gray area—an area where payment could take other forms beyond blunt. Perhaps he hadn't meant to speak them in such a way, but now that he had, he didn't want to take them back, for they were having such an effect on the duchess. Her skin had gone flush, and her amber eyes, bright. Her cherry-red lips parted, as if she were in desperate need of a deep breath.

He might like having that effect on this woman.

Which he didn't like—at all.

"Why are you here?" The question teetered on the offensive.

Her fingers drummed the seatback, nails a light *click-click* against leather. "I was curious."

"*Curiosity* brought you into The Archangel?"

He didn't believe it for an instant. The place would've inspired intrigue, to be sure, but mere inquisitiveness wouldn't have pushed her this far beyond the bounds of propriety.

She offered no answer with her mouth, but her eyes held a different story. She'd come here with purpose.

"I'll ask again—"

"Don't sell Ashcote," she said in a sudden rush, words tumbling over themselves in a hasty jumble.

Now, he understood what he saw in her eyes—*desperation*.

"It's my home."

Gabriel uncrossed his arms and planted them on the desk to either side of his hips. "Other homes can be attained. As dowager duchess, you're entitled to the dower house at Acaster Castle in Kent."

Her brow gathered in distress. "*Acaster Castle?* That drafty old pile of rocks?"

"Then use a portion of your dowry to find a place to your liking."

"Ashcote is to my liking."

"Would you like to make an offer?"

"I can't."

That math didn't add up. In going through his great uncle's papers, he'd come across the marriage contract. Generous didn't begin to describe the terms. How desperate this woman and her family must have been for a title within their ranks. "Wasn't half your dowry returned to you upon Acaster's death?" Such a financial arrangement in the event of widowhood was only standard practice.

She gave her head a tight shake. "It would have been."

Gabriel almost didn't want to ask… *"Would have been?"*

"If any of my dowry was left."

Of course. "Acaster gambled it away." It wasn't a question.

Another tight shake of her head. "I spent it."

Gabriel felt his brow lift with disbelief. And he'd thought this woman possessed of a modicum of good sense… "You spent it?"

She nodded. "On my stable."

"You spent your widow's portion on *horses?*"

"I don't expect you to understand." Her chin lifted to a stubborn angle. "Horses are expensive."

The duchess presented a problem. He saw that now. However, Gabriel liked to solve problems, and fortunately a solution to this duchess arrived readily.

"As a widow, you can return to your family."

The luminous amber of her eyes went flat and hard. "That isn't an option."

"Why not?"

"That's my business, and none of yours."

The duchess may have thought that was him put in his place, but she didn't know him. There was no problem Gabriel couldn't solve.

And when the solution arrived to him, he almost laughed aloud at its elegance.

Of course.

Though, judging by the narrowing of her eyes, the duchess would require some convincing.

"What do you want most in the world?" He knew the answer, but he wanted her to speak it aloud.

"Why would I tell you?"

"We might be able to help each other."

Interest sparked in her eyes, but she remained cautious. "How so?"

"Should I tell you what I want most in the world?"

"I'm not sure."

And Gabriel understood what she expected him to say—*your body.*

How many times had she heard that line?

Well, he hated to disappoint... "To see my sisters accepted into society and assume their rightful place."

The duchess's brow gathered. "*Sisters?*"

"I have three sisters." He spread his hands wide before him. "Two of them need to make their debut in society." A strange rule that still baffled him. "Saskia and Viveca are impressionable and young."

The duchess blinked, and a flummoxed line formed between her eyebrows. "*You* are young."

"Would you like me to prove exactly how young I'm not?" he said as coolly as if they were discussing the weather.

The duchess's mouth snapped shut.

In one sense, Gabriel regretted the words. He'd allowed his irritation to get the better of him.

But in another sense, one more visceral, he didn't.

He spent so much of his time inside his own mind, but somehow, this duchess pulled him out of his head and into his body.

And he didn't like that—not at all.

No.

He should definitely regret speaking such words to her—if only he could.

"And the third sister?" asked the duchess "Is she—"

"Deceased?" He shook his head. "You've already met her."

"I have?"

He jutted his chin, indicating The Archangel beyond his office. "Out there."

Sudden realization dawned across the duchess's face. "*That* was your sister?"

"Tessa."

"*Lady* Tessa."

"Pardon?"

"As the sister of a duke, she's Lady Tessa."

Gabriel snorted. "Don't remind her."

The duchess canted her head. "She doesn't wish to be a lady?"

"You needn't concern yourself with Tessa." They were veering off course. "Only Saskia and Viveca."

"*Ladies* Saskia and Viveca."

"They are, as yet, unmarried and will need a place in society."

The duchess remained unmoved. "What has that to do with me?"

Gabriel could smile. He had her. She simply didn't know it yet. "It has to do with what you want most in the world."

"It most assuredly doesn't," she scoffed, so sure of herself.

"Oh, but it does," Gabriel assured her. "How would you feel about a little gamble?"

"You seem to have mistaken me for my deceased husband." Even as she refused to relent, her curiosity was piqued. He saw it in her eyes.

"I can assure you no one would mistake you for an octogenarian wastrel, but..." Gabriel let a few meaningful beats of time elapse. "You *are* a dowager duchess."

Sudden umbrage glittered about her. "Are you saying I'm aged?"

He kept his even keel. "I'm saying you could be useful."

"How so?" Dread snaked through the question.

"You could be their chaperone into society."

Her mouth fell slightly agape with shock. "You are definitely calling me old."

"I can offer you what you want most in the world."

She went wary as a skittish cat. "Precisely like a man to over-promise."

"To save your horses," he said. "Isn't that what you want most in the world?"

"You presume to know me so well?" She wasn't giving in—*yet*.

"One doesn't run a gaming hell without understanding what lights a fire inside a person."

"And you understand what lights a fire inside me?"

"I do."

Disbelief marched across her face, then she laughed. "Oh, you are *such* a young man."

Gabriel's back teeth ground together. Her condescension… her certainty…

She was attempting to put him in his place.

She was trying not to take him seriously.

His determination solidified into steel.

She would.

"You don't have two farthings to rub together," he stated, no longer inclined to coat the conversation with sugar.

Her fingers ceased drumming the seatback. "Light Skirt won the One Thousand Guineas and the one-thousand-pound purse."

"And you need that prize money to enter her in the Race of the Century. It's why you sent for a horse painter—to raise fast money."

Her jaw went tight, and twin scarlet patches blossomed across her cheeks. He'd humiliated her. Gabriel almost felt guilty. *Almost.* For here was his leverage, and he would use it.

"You take Saskia and Viveca around society, introduce them, and see them fitted into your world, and I'll finance your stables through the racing season."

Her mind immediately set to work on the proposition, he could see that from where he stood. But he could also see she didn't trust him. He would have to state everything explicitly and possibly sign with blood before she would agree.

"Five seasons."

She was making a counteroffer.

A penniless woman with zero leverage.

He respected the attempt.

"You want me to finance your stables for five years?"

The duchess's demeanor shifted incrementally—enough that humiliation no longer hung about her. A new light shone in her eyes. The light of challenge. Gabriel much preferred it.

"You want to see your sisters made welcome in society?" she asked, incredulous. "What I want is only money. What you want is nigh impossible."

"I appreciate the challenges."

She canted her head. "Do you?" Doubt laced every edge of the question.

"I was on scholarship at Eton and Cambridge. I appreciate the challenges," he repeated.

She spread her hands wide, helpless to the facts. "Then you understand what you're asking. Until a few weeks ago, they were simply the unremarkable sisters of a gaming hell owner. As such, you can appreciate the whiff of scandal that will yet linger about them."

"Three years," he countered. "And a cut."

"*A cut?*"

"Of race winnings and stud fees," he said. "Half." A thought occurred to him. "In fact, why do you have to race at all? It seems like an unnecessary risk to your Thoroughbred stock."

She shook her head. "You can't have one without the other. One needs winners in a stud. Races demonstrate the product, so it's essential to keep racing—and to keep winning."

"And you believe you can?"

"I know I can."

And looking into her eyes, Gabriel believed her.

Or, at least, he believed she believed her words. Only time would prove them out.

Gabriel found himself genuinely hoping she would agree to his terms, for at hand was his favorite sort of investment opportunity. He'd been given a tour of this woman's private domain. He'd seen with his eyes her skill and talent for horses. Even more, he'd seen her passion.

He wanted to invest in her operation.

This woman had everything it took to make the stud successful—talent, brains, grit—but she lacked the one thing he possessed in abundance…

Money.

Really, he'd be a fool not to invest in her.

"I'll agree on one condition," she said, her mind still working angles.

"Which is?" he prodded.

"You don't sell Ashcote until our bargain is complete."

He wanted to get the estate off his hands, it was a fact, but he saw no harm in keeping it for a few years. The duchess was clearly attached to the place, and if by agreeing he could gain his sisters entry into the highest circles of society, then it was no sacrifice at all, for he wouldn't see them shunned or snubbed— even if he himself had little use for society beyond the blunt they gamed away in The Archangel.

"It's a bargain."

Though the duchess was positioned ten feet away behind a chair, he held out his hand. They were to shake on their bargain, his extended hand said. He sensed her hesitation. Duchesses didn't shake hands—but gaming hell owners did. Once, there had even been spit involved. A handshake he wasn't keen to repeat.

The point was he shouldn't be asking to shake her hand. But something in him couldn't resist—as if he needed to test her.

Something in him wanted this woman to know they were equals—and to acknowledge it.

So, his hand remained extended and waiting.

It was she who would have to bridge the distance.

Would she do it? How badly did she want to save her stables?

She inhaled and squared her shoulders, resolve strengthening around her as she stepped around the chair, step by hesitant step. Her tongue gave her bottom lip a nervous swipe. She wasn't a small woman—standing above average height and possessed of above average curves—but she was smaller than he remembered.

Or might it be that she'd begun to loom large in his mind?

He found he very much wanted to shake her hand…

To touch her.

To feel the substance of her.

The flame inside him demanded it.

Honey amber eyes lifted as, uncertainly, she extended her hand and pressed it to his. Though encased in a glove, he felt her heat and substance through white silk. She wasn't the goddess the lords in the club proclaimed her to be, but a woman composed of flesh and blood.

An unsettled feeling stirred inside him, and he understood which was the more dangerous of the two—by far.

Driven by instinct to preserve himself, he pulled his hand away first. Her eyes went wide with surprise.

He needed her gone.

Toward that end, he swept around her and crossed the room, unceremoniously grabbing the door handle and jerking it open.

An inscrutable expression on her face, she made slow progress toward the door. "Tomorrow."

"*Tomorrow?*"

"We start tomorrow. Bring your sisters to Madame Dubois's shop on Bond Street."

"And she is?"

"London's top modiste."

Gabriel nodded. "It's a deal."

"It's a gamble is what it is."

"All of life is a gamble."

"Then why risk more?"

"Because one can't help oneself."

Her eyebrow arched at a skeptical angle. "Is that true for you?"

Then she stepped through the open doorway and was gone.

Leaving Gabriel alone with thoughts that would surely plague him long into the night.

By demanding they shake hands to seal their bargain, he'd thought to rattle her, but it was he who was left shaken by the contact, the sudden awareness of the proximity of their bodies.

And he'd thought himself in control?

Except the handshake hadn't been a stratagem borne of power or control, but rather base feeling.

He'd needed to touch her—to know if her touch would give oxygen to the flame inside him and spark it into a conflagration.

And now he had his answer.

Yes.

CHAPTER SEVEN

NEXT DAY

"*We* shall save your stable, Celia, and that's a fact," Eloise stated with the absolute certainty borne of life having always fallen into step with her wishes.

Celia and life had rubbed along together very differently.

So, she nodded and sipped her tea and kept her doubts to herself.

The tea was a surprisingly delicious brew considering they were tucked away in a modiste's private sitting room. Then again, Madame Dubois always knew precisely how to cater to a customer's needs. For now, the need was privacy and tea while Celia and Eloise awaited the arrival of the Ladies Saskia and Viveca Calthorp, the younger sisters of the new Duke of Acaster.

For no reason Celia could understand, nerves skittered through her at the prospect of meeting the duke's sisters. So much depended upon those two young ladies.

"I have a little dosh put by," continued Eloise.

The vein of sympathy running through her cousin's words was nearly enough to undo Celia. She shook her head, definite. "Fairfax left that for you and your future." Unlike Celia, Eloise had enjoyed a happy marriage with a man who loved her to bits.

"But Celia—"

Celia held up a firm hand. "The funding of a duchess's stable is a folly you shouldn't become entangled with."

"Pish, you don't truly think your stable a folly?"

"Most days I don't, but some days I wonder." Celia shrugged, helpless. "Why does love have to exact such a high price?"

A pensive smile lifted Eloise's mouth. "After Fairfax's death, I gave that very question some consideration, and I've decided it's a scarcity issue."

"*Scarcity?*"

Eloise nodded. "Love is a precious commodity. There are only so many opportunities to give and receive it. It only follows that the price of love is prohibitively high."

Eloise always did have the right words.

"It was hard on me," continued Eloise, "having loved Fairfax so and lost him. Our marriage didn't start off as a love match, you know."

Celia reached across the table for her cousin's hand.

Wistfulness hung about Eloise. "Then, a few months after the wedding, he brought me my tea in bed for the tenth morning in a row, and I realized I loved that man."

Celia knew the story—and she also knew her cousin had to keep telling it.

Tears shone in Eloise's eyes. "Any man can put a shiny bauble on your finger, but not every man knows how many lumps of sugar to stir into your tea. It's the care a man shows you in the small things that illustrates his love." A tear broke free and rolled down her cheek, which she immediately swiped away. "We had ten happy years."

In companionable silence, the cousins sipped their tea, each considering their histories—histories that couldn't have been any more different, though Celia begrudged Eloise none of her past happiness.

The small sitting room door creaked open, and a head popped

in. "Might you be needing anything?" asked a small woman, impeccably dressed in crisp black bombazine.

Celia smiled. "This is lovely, Madame Dubois. We appreciate that you were able to accommodate us for a fitting on such short notice."

The modiste inclined her head. "It is my pleasure that you chose my shop for your wardrobe requirements, Your Grace."

That was certainly a diplomatic way of putting it, as Celia hadn't purchased a new dress in ten years. But today was a different story. Today, they were going to see the Duke of Acaster's sisters fitted with a new wardrobe, courtesy of the duke's deep coffers. Celia found a mean little delight at the prospect of spending the duke's blunt.

"Please send the Ladies Saskia and Viveca through when they arrive."

Madame Dubois nodded and closed the door behind her.

Last night, once the whirlwind of The Archangel had worn off and she was lying in bed and staring sightlessly at the ceiling, Celia's mind had finally begun functioning logically, and she was able to devise the beginnings of a plan.

First thing this morning, she'd sent the duke a note, providing him with Madame Dubois's Bond Street address and instructing him to have his sisters here at three o'clock. Two birds would be killed with one stone. They would take a light tea together and become acquainted. Then the young ladies would be fitted for their new wardrobe—from day dresses to riding habits to ballgowns, and everything in between.

However, the plan couldn't succeed without help. Eloise's, specifically—for both moral support and her eye for fashion. Besides, it would be no imposition, as her cousin enjoyed this sort of venture and challenge. Eloise loved a project.

"Have you met Acaster's sisters?" Eloise idly swirled cream into her tea.

"No." Celia reconsidered her answer, as it wasn't precisely

true. "Well, one of them. From what I could gather, Lady Tessa helps run The Archangel. She's not our concern."

And thank heavens for that. Lady Tessa knew her own mind only too well. As the Ladies Saskia and Viveca were younger, Celia clung to the hope that they were more moldable.

Eloise's eyebrows threatened to lift off her forehead. "A *woman* runs the most exclusive gaming hell in London?"

"Alongside her brother, yes."

"Her brother, the *duke*," said Eloise, seeking clarification on the point.

"Yes, he's the only brother in the family."

Eloise sipped her tea and let this new information soak in. "This is a different sort of family."

"Indeed."

And, strangely, though the new duke wasn't as manageable as she would prefer, Celia thought she might like that difference when it came to these siblings who were now Calthorps and no longer Sirens.

"About last night," began Eloise.

"What about it?"

Celia felt herself grow tense. She'd related to Eloise only the necessary facts of last night, leaving out immaterial information —like the intelligence contained within the new duke's eyes or the sheer physicality of him or that when they'd shaken hands, the touch of him had sent a spark of lightning through her veins.

Immaterial information.

"But, Celia," pressed Eloise. "Did you have to agree to Acaster's terms so quickly?"

Celia didn't hesitate. "Yes."

On this point, she was unequivocal.

She'd been desperate and would've agreed to almost anything. That was the material fact Acaster's sharp eye had caught.

Further, their agreement bought her time. A few years, in fact, to rebound from the disasters of her marriage and the loss of

Rakesley. Time to find a horse-mad husband—one with the blunt to support her stables.

Then she could tell this new Duke of Acaster to sod off.

But a third reason was why she'd agreed so quickly and was meeting with the duke's sisters less than twenty-four hours later.

It was the handshake.

Or, more accurately, his reaction to it.

For the flick of a second, he'd looked as if he very much regretted their bargain—and in the next flick of a second, Celia decided. She must bind him to it as soon as possible. Hence, a visit to the modiste with his sisters today.

He wouldn't wiggle out of it.

She wouldn't let him.

"And this new Duke of Acaster...?" asked Eloise, leadingly.

Celia knew what her cousin wasn't asking. "What of him?"

"What's he like?"

"He's, *erm*..." Celia searched her mind for a word and seized upon a suitable one. "Direct."

Eloise lifted a skeptical eyebrow. "*Direct?*"

"And..."

"*And?*"

"Young."

"How young?" asked Eloise. "I mean, almost everyone is younger than the late duke."

"Four and twenty years young."

Eloise's eyes went wide. "That is young." She tapped her forefinger against pursed lips. "So, not an old lech."

"No."

"A *young* lech?" Eloise shrugged. "He runs a gaming hell, after all."

Celia hesitated. "I don't think he's that, either."

She knew next to nothing about this new Duke of Acaster, but she didn't think him dissolute. In fact, she suspected he might be the very opposite.

"And what does he look like?" Eloise popped a strawberry into her mouth.

"He's, *erm*, tall."

Celia didn't want to think or talk about Acaster's looks. But Eloise would see the man for herself soon enough, then wonder why Celia hadn't mentioned the obvious. So, she might as well say... "He's quite possibly the most beautiful man one is likely ever to see."

There.

She'd said what must be said.

The obvious.

"Objectively speaking, of course."

"Well." Eloise's eyebrows would have to be peeled from the ceiling. "Since it's objective."

"Now, about the sisters," Celia plowed forward, hoping to distract her cousin.

"*The sisters?*" huffed Eloise. "But we aren't finished discussing the brother."

"Yes, we are."

Eloise shifted forward, a terrier with a rat between her teeth. "There's more, isn't there?" Her bright eyes begged to be scandalized.

Celia most definitely could not discuss the *more* of the new Duke of Acaster with her cousin. She couldn't even discuss it with herself.

The shiver was why.

The shiver that had sizzled through every nook and cranny of her body when Acaster had taken her hand into his firm grip.

The truth was she'd never experienced a shiver like it. And when she'd met his intense gaze she saw reflected an awareness—of her shiver or of his own, she couldn't be sure, but either way, it wasn't good.

And, even now, just thinking of the shiver, a trace of it yet echoed through her.

A light tap sounded on the door before it swung open and admitted a pair of young ladies. As was her usual instinct, Eloise sat forward and introduced herself, in the process making everyone comfortable, while Celia observed the proceedings with a bland smile. Though her smile indicated otherwise, Celia was, in truth, a shy duchess.

The Ladies Saskia and Viveca Calthorp made a striking pair of young beauties—one with strawberry blonde hair, like her sister Lady Tessa, and the other with light brown hair streaked with gold, like her brother. They must've been very small when they lost their parents. An observation which gave Celia insight into their family of four. The duke and Lady Tessa would be protective of these two.

Further, Acaster had been correct that these sisters were impressionable, though not in the way Celia had expected. The impression they'd formed was apparent from their squared shoulders, unsmiling eyes, and the challenging lift of their chins.

The Ladies Saskia and Viveca didn't want to be here.

Eloise shot Celia a quick glance, a world of meaning in her eyes. She'd arrived at the same conclusion. But Eloise being Eloise, she immediately set about making the sisters welcome. "How many lumps of sugar do you take in your tea?"

"One," said a sister. She would be the elder of the two—*Lady Saskia.*

"None," said the other. *Lady Viveca.* "But a dollop of cream, if you would."

As Eloise happily set to, Celia continued to observe them—and they were only too content to observe her directly back. Though aged nineteen and eighteen years respectively, this was no flighty pair of young ladies. They knew their own minds.

Right.

"Please call me Celia," she said, hoping to reduce the intensity of those supremely composed gazes.

"Oh, yes, call me Eloise, if you please," chimed her cousin, concentrating on the wobbly task of transferring a thick slice of cake to a plate.

"And you are Lady Saskia?" At the affirmative nod, Celia said to the other, "Which makes you Lady Viveca."

"And you're the dowager duchess," said Lady Saskia.

Celia's recently swallowed sip of tea went down the wrong pipe and nearly all came sputtering out. As she dabbed her chin with a napkin, she was fairly certain she'd been called *old* by a young lady. The little smile curving one side of Lady Saskia's mouth said that was precisely her intention.

The cheek!

"Now," began Eloise, the look in her eyes all business, "you're here for a new wardrobe, which is the fun part of this new life you're now part of."

"It is?"

The skeptical lift of Lady Saskia's eyebrow spoke of harbored doubts. Lady Viveca snickered.

Eloise wasn't having it. "It is." She let that settle for a moment. "You are clearly bright young ladies, but you weren't brought up to occupy the world you now inhabit. So, before we can introduce you into society, there will be lessons."

"Oh, we like lessons," said Lady Viveca, brightening.

Eloise nodded her approval. "Also, there will be your debut ball, of course."

Lady Saskia shifted forward. "So we're clear. *Lady* Viveca and I have no intention of entering the *ton*'s marriage mart." She planted a definite fingertip into the table. "*Ever.*"

"Not at all," chimed Lady Viveca, as if her sister hadn't made their point of view abundantly clear.

Ah... "But, you see, it's not that simple," said Celia. Now she had an angle from which to approach these sisters.

"You're ladies now," said Eloise. She would see it, too.

"We don't care about that."

"You might not, but others do."

Eloise was trying to soften the facts, but Celia wouldn't—for the sisters' own good. "Tell me, does your brother have money?" She knew the answer, but she had a point to make and these young ladies would hear it.

Lady Saskia crossed her arms over her chest. "More than King Midas."

"And who knows it?"

Lady Viveca waved an airy hand. "Everyone, I would presume."

"*Lords*," said Celia. "That's who."

The sisters stared at her, unmoved.

"Here's the thing. You aren't only ladies now, you are heiresses, and every young buck and old lech in London knows it."

Celia's words were met with a shrug.

"We simply don't give a fig."

"I don't even like figs," said Lady Viveca. "Too many seeds."

Celia experienced a niggle of worry for these formidable sisters. Now that they were the sisters of a duke, they no longer had the luxury of not giving a toss about society. They needed to be made ready for the slings and arrows heading their way, for like it or not, they were now part of the *ton*.

Celia realized something else, too. She liked the Ladies Saskia and Celia. They had spirit and intelligence.

Sudden determination seized her. She would see these two young ladies ready to navigate society on their terms, but in keeping with the rules. It was a fine line, but achievable.

"These lords will be persistent," continued Celia. "They will try to win your affections. Then your hand. Then your dowry. And the odds are one of them will cut through your defenses."

The stubborn set of the sisters' jaws softened not a bit. In fact, they looked slightly insulted.

Celia went on, undeterred. "And you need to be ready."

As one, their heads canted to the side.

At last, Celia had piqued their interest.

"I think you've formed the wrong impression of my goal," she continued. "I'm not going to teach you how to enter into matrimony with the first lord who shows a speck of interest. Or be manipulated into a match you don't want by some ruthless fortune hunter or by family pressure. I'm going to help you avoid that fate."

This was met with three lifted pairs of eyebrows.

"Your brother is rich." Celia was warming to her blunt manner of speech. This must be how men felt all the time. "And he's a duke. You can marry who you like." She spread her hands. "Or don't marry at all. But here's the thing to know—a bad marriage is worse than no marriage."

"Oh, yes," said Eloise, "you should heed Celia's words. She knows about bad marriages."

"Eloise," said Celia, no mistaking the note of warning in her voice. She understood her cousin only meant well, but she had no intention of holding her marriage up to the light as an example.

Eloise, however, either didn't hear—or didn't care to hear. "Your marriage was a crime, Celia. Everyone knows it."

This certainly got the attention of the sisters. "A crime!" exclaimed the younger.

"He was fifty-six years older." Eloise was only getting started. "It was unconscionable."

The sisters gasped.

And so did Celia.

But for an altogether different reason.

There, in the open doorway, stood the Duke of Acaster. The look in his eyes said he'd heard everything that had been said over the last thirty or so seconds—which were thirty seconds too many.

An unsettled feeling sheared through her. She wasn't sure how to feel about this man knowing a truth about her beyond the untruths that everyone thought they knew about her.

Soon, the direction of her gaze caught the room's attention, and greetings were had all around as the duke took a seat beside his sisters. Celia felt the heat of Eloise's gaze on the side of her face. Within her cousin's eyes she found precisely what she'd expected—a question.

About the duke.

Nay, not *a* question.

A flurry of questions.

Well, Eloise had been warned about the obvious.

As the duke conversed with his sisters in muted tones, Celia took in his profile and tried to view him as Eloise might—not as duke or horse painter or gaming hell owner.

As a man.

This man was more than young and beautiful. More than the sum total of his physical qualities or his age. He was intelligent and capable. It was in the way he listened to others when they spoke. *Confident.* Nothing to prove to anyone other than himself.

Attractive... magnetic.

This man was all those things and one thing more.

A temptation.

That was the knowledge shining in her cousin's eyes—an understanding of that last quality.

And this temptation was to be her business partner for the next three years...

What had she done?

CHAPTER EIGHT

*T*he duchess wasn't best pleased to see him.

In fact, the heat of her gaze threatened to bore a hole into the side of Gabriel's face.

No matter.

It had always been his intention to disrupt this meeting after about twenty or so minutes. A tactic he often employed in business dealings to jar an opponent or even a partner out of a sense of complacency.

This meeting was about Saskia and Viveca, but no decision would be made without his express consent. That was what his presence said and what he would have the duchess understand.

Beneath hooded eyes, his gaze shifted to the woman seated beside the duchess. A relation, he would guess with her sable hair and large dark eyes. Except this woman's eyes held openness where the duchess's held wariness.

A crime.

That was what the woman had said about the duchess's marriage to Acaster.

Unconscionable.

That would explain the guarded quality that ever hung about the duchess, except…

A marriage was a choice. She'd chosen to chase a title and marry one in the form of an old lech. *That* was who the duchess was at her core.

Lest he forget.

A conversational lull occurred, and silence descended upon the room. The woman beside the duchess cleared her throat and nudged an elbow for good measure.

The duchess blinked and appeared to snap to. "*Erm*, Your Grace, may I introduce my cousin, Mrs. Fairfax, to you?"

Unsure about what a duke would do, Gabriel stood and hesitated before offering an awkward bow. Saskia snorted, and Viveca snickered, but Mrs. Fairfax accepted his greeting graciously. The duchess watched—ever wary, ever guarded.

"The pleasure is mine, Mrs. Fairfax." It seemed like what a duke would say.

"Please, call me Eloise."

This woman had a way of putting one at ease—unlike the woman beside her, who produced much the opposite effect. "And I much prefer Gabriel to any of the other names currently in my possession."

This pulled a charmed laugh from Mrs. Fairfax—he wouldn't be calling the duchess's cousin by her given name. He shot a glance at his sisters, who offered him teenage smirks.

Mrs. Fairfax clasped her hands together. "Oh, I know what we need to discuss now that the duke is here."

Gabriel tried not to wince. Every time someone called him *the duke*, a noxious feeling churned through his gut. Not unlike the sensation that overcame one in the final few seconds before one retched.

"We're already here for new gowns, so that's one item ticked off the list." Efficient energy vibrated off Mrs. Fairfax. "Now, we must secure vouchers for Almack's. But before that, we must engage a dancing master. And a—" She interrupted herself. "Do you speak French, perchance?"

"We know a bit of Swedish," offered Viveca.

"Mostly swear words," said Saskia.

Mrs. Fairfax didn't bat an eyelash. "It would be useful to have a smidge of French, so a French master, too."

Gabriel stole a glance at the duchess, who was watching the proceedings with a distant smile. Nay, not distant. *Impenetrable.* A fortress of a smile she could hide behind. A smile he very much wanted to penetrate.

Penetrate.

Gabriel stopped himself there.

"And there must be a ball," Mrs. Fairfax carried on. "There's nothing else for it. Attended by all your family."

This got Gabriel's attention. "I have no intention of attending a ball."

The duchess's eyes narrowed. "I thought the goal is to see your sisters established in society."

"It is."

"You're the duke." The duchess's smile was no longer merely impenetrable, but adamantine. "You will throw a ball. You will attend the ball. And you will successfully launch your sisters into the *ton* by demonstrating how important they are to you. Everything else we're doing is laying the foundation for that moment."

"And in doing so," said Mrs. Fairfax, the twinkle in her eye unmistakable, "you will become the most eligible man in society."

"I don't wish to become the most eligible man in society."

Mrs. Fairfax gave a helpless shrug. "I'm afraid you haven't a choice. You're a duke. You're wealthy. And you're—" She blinked, and a blush stained her cheeks. *"You."*

Into the uncomfortable silence that followed, the duchess said, "But first, you must move into the ducal mansion at St. James's Square."

Of a sudden, Gabriel's sisters were a bundle of protest,

expressing displeasure with their words and pleading with Gabriel with their eyes. However, he was relieved the duchess had broached the subject. For it was the reality of their new elevated status in the world—they would, of course, live in the ducal mansion.

"But our townhouse in Knightsbridge is fashionable enough." Saskia wouldn't give in easily.

The duchess shrugged a helpless shoulder, little sympathy in her eyes. "Dukes don't reside in Knightsbridge."

"All our books are there," said Viveca.

"Of course they'll be brought with you, my dear," said Mrs. Fairfax with genuine compassion. "Do you enjoy reading?"

Viveca's head canted. "Do lungs enjoy breathing?"

"Ah," said Mrs. Fairfax with an understanding smile. "It's a necessity. And what sorts of books do you read?"

"Novels," said Viveca. "Saskia likes the Greeks."

"And *The Aeneid*, too," said Saskia. Into the blank silence that followed, she added, "It's a Roman work."

Mrs. Fairfax responded with a lift of her eyebrows.

Though Gabriel and Tessa were mathematically inclined, their younger sisters were no less rigorous in their intellectual pursuits, only they veered in a different direction toward the written word.

Saskia shifted her attention toward the duchess. "Is the St. James's mansion where you live?" She was the most questioning and precise of Gabriel's sisters.

The duchess flicked a glance toward Gabriel. That simple flash of contact had the blood pumping through his veins. What was it about her?

"When I'm in London," she replied. "But I've moved into the east wing." She emphasized her next words. "Your family will occupy the west."

"Imagine, a house with wings," mused Viveca. "Where shall we fly?"

And Viveca was the most whimsical sister. The one who could be counted on for a bit of levity. The Siren siblings could be a serious bunch.

Now, even the duchess was smiling.

The first genuine smile he'd seen from her. It would be Viveca who charmed it out.

"After you move to St. James's Square," said the duchess, "you will begin to receive calling cards and invitations. Society will be most curious about you. Like it or not, you're the sisters of a duke, and you will be entering society."

"We didn't ask for this," said Saskia.

And there it was—the truth he and his sisters had been ramming against since they'd learned of their new identity. A lack of choice that burrowed beneath the skin like a sharp, insidious nettle.

"Unfortunately, it matters not." A measure of sympathy now shone in the duchess's honey amber eyes. "But there are benefits. The musicales and soirees. The balls are fun. So, here's how it will go. You will attend a few events in the company of myself and Eloise. Then, in July, we shall throw your debut ball." At last, she met Gabriel's gaze. "And see that Lady Tessa attends."

"I can only ask," he said. "Tessa does as she pleases."

"It's true," supplied Viveca.

"I've had a thought, Celia," interjected Mrs. Fairfax. "The Derby is in a week's time."

The duchess—*Celia*—began to nod, considering. "It could work."

"What is *it*?" Gabriel had the distinct feeling the two women were conspiring between the words spoken.

"That we all attend Derby Day together as a light introduction," the duchess said, as if it were the most ordinary thing in the world.

Gabriel blinked, flummoxed. "You wish to introduce my sisters to society at a *horse race*?"

"Not any horse race," said Mrs. Fairfax.

"The *Derby*," supplied the duchess.

"Everyone of note will be there." Mrs. Fairfax appeared to speak her thoughts as they came to her. "We shall attend for the day only. Not the night, *erm*, festivities."

Bacchanalia, from everything Gabriel had heard and never cared to endure.

The duchess caught his irritation. "They aren't yet out, but it will be to their advantage to show the *ton* that they have minds and interests of their own."

"Won't they be compromised in some way?"

The duchess shook her head. "Not unless they wander off with some dandy." She cut Saskia and Viveca a stern look. "Don't do that."

Viveca giggled, and even Saskia snorted.

"Don't they need to be seen as proper young ladies to be accepted?"

Even as the question escaped his mouth, Gabriel felt his resistance slipping. Strangely, he trusted the duchess. She had the experience of such matters, and she appeared to have taken to his sisters.

The duchess wasn't ceding an inch of ground. "Forgive my unladylike bluntness, but by every account, you're a duke who sleeps on piles of gold. Society won't take much convincing."

"Now," said Mrs. Fairfax, rising, "the time has arrived for you to go, Your Grace, and leave us ladies to the rest of the afternoon." She directed a warm smile toward Viveca. "What's your favorite color?"

"The blue of winter's first frost, but—" She glanced uncertainly toward Gabriel.

He gave a barely perceptible nod. He wasn't sure there was any denying the force that was Mrs. Fairfax's amiable will.

"That settles it, then." The woman clapped her hands together in delight. "You shall be dressed in frost blue for the Derby. Let's pick fabrics, shall we?"

Mrs. Fairfax stepped between his sisters and led them from the room. As they passed through the doorway, a question directed at Saskia floated in their wake. "And your favorite color, my dear?"

"Old shoe brown."

Mrs. Fairfax's laugh didn't miss a beat. "I'll have to keep my eye on you."

Saskia shot Gabriel a pleading glance over her shoulder. He suspected his sister might be outmatched by the formidably cheerful Mrs. Fairfax.

That left Gabriel alone with the duchess, who was coming to a stand herself.

"I believe that's all for now. As you can see, my cousin and I have the matter of your younger sisters well in hand." She hesitated. "As per last night's agreement."

Last night.

She was still discomfited about last night.

She wasn't the only one.

But it wasn't his discomfort that interested him—it was hers.

Was it possible he discomfited her in the way she discomfited him?

She made to step around him, and he was tempted to block the doorway.

He allowed the temptation to pass.

No good could come of it.

As she moved past, he caught a hint of jasmine and bergamot —her scent.

Right.

He bowed a curt farewell, pivoted, and strode through the modiste shop out to Bond Street—and into a spring shower, a sheet of rain slamming directly into his face the instant he stepped onto slick cobbles. Reactively, he jumped back into the shop and began shaking raindrops off his person, not unlike a wet dog.

Alone in the foyer of the shop, muted women's voices drifting from the back, Gabriel recognized he was bothered. It had naught to do with the rain or that somehow he'd become soaked to the skin in a matter of three seconds.

It was the duchess—and her cousin.

Not Mrs. Fairfax herself. She was a perfectly amiable woman. Rather, it was the fact of her very presence, and the longer he stood in the entryway, stewing in rainwater and his own juices, the more certain he was that he required a private word with the duchess.

Now.

To that end, he pivoted and strode with undeterrable purpose through the shop. Predictably, Mrs. Fairfax had Saskia and Viveca sorting through colorful bolts of silk. Even Saskia looked begrudgingly won over.

But no duchess.

He poked his head into the sitting room they'd just vacated. No sign of her there, either.

A dressmaker's assistant attempted to sidle past him. "Begging your pardon," he said.

Servants knew the ins and outs of any establishment—better than their masters and mistresses most of the time.

Shy eyes lifted as far as his chin and stopped. A duke acknowledging her existence wouldn't have been an everyday occurrence. Gabriel supposed that would have to do. "Where can I find the Duchess of Acaster?"

The assistant hesitated so long that Gabriel thought he would have to repeat the question. Then a trepidatious finger pointed in the direction of a closed door. His feet were already on the move as he tossed, "Thank you," over his shoulder.

He supposed dukes didn't thank those of inferior consequence, but as was so often pointed out to him, he was young. Years stretched ahead for him to become a rude sot.

Without hesitation, he twisted the handle and pushed the door open. It was only when the sight before his eyes penetrated his brain that he understood he should've knocked first. There, across the room, wearing nothing but chemise, stays, and white stockings gartered above her knees, stood the duchess, back to him as she held up a garment for inspection.

Heat flushed through Gabriel. Never in his life had he been immobilized by the sight of a woman, but the sight of this half-clad woman stopped the functioning of every part of him—save one.

His cock, namely.

Until this moment, he'd understood the duchess to be a beauty—a renowned one, in fact. After all, he had eyes in his head. But this confirmation of it was nearly too much.

She cocked an ear to the side, but didn't turn. "You may set the riding habit on the chair, madame."

Sudden urgency flared through Gabriel. Standing here immobilized wasn't an option—neither was it an excuse.

In fact, he suspected the opposite. It might be possible he was leering at the duchess. More than behaving poorly, he might be actively in the wrong.

Before he could retreat, however, the duchess turned. Her amber eyes went wide, and her free hand flew to her mouth on a shocked gasp.

Gabriel stood, immobile. The back view of the duchess had only been prelude to this—the front view of her.

He'd understood her to be curvaceous, but, again, the reality —the *proof*—of her curves from deep décolletage to the sharp indent of her waist that gave way to the flare of her hips was almost too concrete to behold directly.

Then, too, were the protections and limitations of her clothing. Yes, she wore a chemise. But his gaze kept wanting to stray toward the shadows beneath gossamer muslin. The roses of her nipples. The dark triangle between her legs.

Then his gaze lifted and met hers. It seemed to be the impetus she needed to recover her speech. "Don't stand there," she hissed, careful her voice wouldn't carry. "Shut the door!"

And he did.

It was only when her eyebrows drew together in befuddlement that Gabriel realized he should've shut the door with him on the other side of it.

And now that they stood wordlessly staring at each other, his reason for returning eluded him. *Tongue-tied*, that was the word for him.

Not that he hadn't seen women in various states of dishabille. One couldn't run a gaming hell and not see women tumble headlong over the line of propriety on a regular basis—even when there was no brothel attached.

But *this* woman in a state of dishabille... *A body made for sin.*

He now understood the meaning of the phrase—and the pulsing viscerality of his reaction.

Carnality—the opposite of a mathematical mind.

Before him stood the very reason he avoided women—so he could avoid this reaction... this eruption of raw physical need.

Life was simpler without it.

"Are you lost, Your Grace?"

"No."

Again, time beat by in strained silence. Then he realized: She was waiting—for him to explain himself.

Right.

His mind began functioning again—as long as he kept his eyes trained north of her neck. "Are you trying to maneuver out of our deal?"

A line formed between her eyebrows. "Maneuver out of it?" A dismayed laugh escaped her. "Quite the opposite, I can assure you."

She'd spoken words—Gabriel understood this objectively. And though her eyes were compelling, his gaze kept wanting to drift toward other parts of her—the scantily clad parts.

"Would you like to dress before we continue this conversation?"

Honey amber eyes narrowed in assessment. "Am I making you uncomfortable?"

"Yes." Sometimes honesty truly was the best policy.

"*You* are the one who barged into my dressing room."

"I'm aware."

He grabbed the nearest garment and thrust it forward. She reached for it, and relief flooded Gabriel.

Except she didn't drape it over her body, but rather over the back of a chair, her eyes sparking with defiance.

Gabriel knew that look. He had three sisters, after all.

He wouldn't be getting his way.

Right.

In the level tone he used for business associates, he began. "Explain the presence of Mrs. Fairfax. If I'm not very mistaken, it's she who is seeing to my sisters' wardrobe. While *you*—" He swept his arm up and down, indicating the duchess's person. "While you are off seeing to yours." No mistaking the scorn in his voice.

The duchess canted her head. "You think I'm pawning your sisters off onto my cousin?"

"Well, aren't you?"

The duchess exhaled an irritated sigh. "Though she didn't marry a title, my cousin is one of the most respected women in society."

Gabriel felt his brow furrow. "And you?"

Had he been played false?

"Of course, I'm respected. I'm a duchess. But..."

Gabriel immediately intuited what that *but...* meant. "You

were married to a duke who commanded little respect beyond his title."

Her gaze shifted, and a light blush crept up her elegant throat. "Society likes my cousin, and it will only benefit your sisters to be closely associated with her."

"And doesn't society like you?"

She shrugged a vague shoulder.

The moment softened long enough for Gabriel to catch a glimpse of something new within the duchess. *Vulnerability.* He'd seen this duchess in many states—*imperious, desperate... half-clad*—but never vulnerable.

A knock sounded on the door. The duchess held a silencing finger to her mouth, imploring him with her eyes to keep quiet, as she swept around him and cracked the door a sliver wide enough to admit a few articles of clothing.

At the sight of them, Gabriel felt a strengthening of the resolve that had brought him into this room in the first place. He pointed at the garments held fast to her chest—*blessedly*—obscuring his view of her body. He ignored the pang of loss that tried to steal through him.

"Those," he said, pointing.

"*These?*"

"What are they?"

"Two riding habits."

Frustration, sudden and unexpected, growled through him. "Last night, you didn't have two farthings to rub together. Now, you're being fitted for new dresses? I'm beginning to altogether doubt the wisdom of my investment in you."

"*New* dresses?" Outrage bristled about her. "Are you referring to *these* dresses?"

She extended the dresses, offering a better view. Except in the process, she also offered a better view of herself.

And there it was, again—the flare of heat that shot straight through to his cock, which was perilously close to making a fool of him.

"Yes, I am referring to those dresses." Here was ground that didn't shake beneath his feet.

"They aren't new."

"I'm looking directly at them."

Her eyes flashed fire, even as a debate blazed within. At last, she said, "I haven't purchased a new dress in a decade. *These*, duke, are remade dresses. And before you mount your high horse, you need to understand something. I am a duchess, and as such, I must be dressed fashionably. But as you so helpfully pointed out, I haven't two farthings to rub together, so every year during the racing season, I have a few garments retrimmed. Appearances mean everything in our little, aristocratic world, as you're well aware. Now," she said, reaching for the door handle, "I'm sure you're a busy man and have a day to get on with."

She swung the door wide, her unspoken command clear.

He was to leave—*tout suite*.

The dressmaker's assistant happened by at that very moment. Her eyes went wide at the sight of duke and half-clad duchess before she scurried away on a suppressed *eek*.

"Is this modiste discreet?" Gabriel wondered if he would need to chase down the assistant and grease her palms with a few shillings.

"Has my little sartorial secret reached the ears of the gossip rags?"

She referred to the secret of a duchess having her clothes remade for ten years—a tidbit the *ton* would love nothing more than to dine on for a day or two.

Gabriel bowed his second farewell of the day, pivoted on his heel, and retraced his steps through the shop, avoiding the curious eyes of his sisters. He didn't want to explain his presence to them.

But mostly he didn't want to explain his presence to himself.

His boots hit the Bond Street cobbles with their usual resolute *click-clack*. In the time elapsed, rain had given way to crisp blue sky.

If only his mind were so easily cleared.

This bargain he'd struck with the duchess…

It was no straightforward business deal.

And not because she was different from his usual business partners.

It was him.

He was different with *her*.

He was the source of his own unsettled feeling.

For the first time in his life, he felt out of his depth.

For the first time in his life, he felt perilously close to tipping over into the unknown.

Powerless against its momentum.

CHAPTER NINE

EPSOM DOWNS, A WEEK LATER

*T*hough Gabriel heard it said that Derby Day was a spectacle beyond all others, nothing could have prepared him for its reality—and its noise... and its smells.

He glanced down at Mrs. Fairfax, whom he was escorting through the rowdy, jostling crowd. "You're certain this is a good way to introduce my sisters to society?"

Placid smile on her face, she patted his forearm.

He didn't doubt the woman's good intentions, but the Derby appeared to exist well wide of the rule of law—a sharper plying his three-card trick game over here and a thimblerig table set up over there, sights which were nothing to the crowds gathered around games of hazard and *rouge et noir*, lords and ladies weaving through the scrum on well-trained hacks, both a part of and above the fray, ever the privilege of aristocrats. Though situated on a stretch of land that appeared to stretch boundless for miles in every direction, the crowd intensified with each step they took toward the racecourse.

"Society possesses many facets, Your Grace." Mrs. Fairfax nearly had to shout to make herself heard. "Derby Day is but one of them."

A few feet ahead, Saskia and Viveca strolled arm in arm with the duchess. Grudgingly, he admitted she was a grounding presence for his sisters who had gone agog with wonderment and delight.

"All of London is here," continued Mrs. Fairfax, "and so, too, is all the *ton*. They will see your sisters on the arm of the Duchess of Acaster, and they will receive the message loud and clear. The new house of Acaster is to be accepted and embraced at the highest levels."

Gabriel had his doubts. "Surely, no one can see anyone in this mob." He wasn't one for crowds.

Mrs. Fairfax laughed. "Oh, society has eyes everywhere."

Once they'd squeezed through an exceptionally dense portion of the crowd and made their way to a clearing set aside for aristocratic attendees, Gabriel was able to hear the conversation flowing between the duchess and his sisters.

"The first Derby was run in seventeen-eighty as a colts and fillies race," she said, her voice infused with an authority Gabriel had only heard from her on the day they'd first met, in her stables.

"And the Oaks is the fillies race?" asked Viveca.

The duchess nodded. "It was established the year before. Legend has it the Derby came by its name on a coin toss."

Saskia snorted. "Seems fitting."

"The Earl of Derby and Sir Charles Bunbury tossed a coin to decide if the race should be called the Derby or the Bunbury." She spread her hands wide. "And the rest is history."

"The coin got it right, I think," said Viveca. "The Bunbury sounds very much like a tasty pastry."

The duchess smiled. "Although, Sir Charles might've had the last laugh as his colt, Diomed, won that first Derby. The Earl of Derby had to wait seven years for his Sir Peter Teazle to take it."

"That had to smart." Along with her penchant for questioning at every turn, Saskia was the most competitive sister, too.

What was becoming clear to Gabriel was that the duchess was winning his sisters over. He should've been glad, and he would've been, if not for…

The moment at the modiste's shop.

A moment that had lasted well beyond a moment.

A moment that had made matters awkward today when he and the duchess had first seen each other and avoided each other's eyes.

And when they'd all taken the same carriage together.

Still avoiding any point of direct contact.

Yet for all the avoidance, how supremely aware of her he was.

He'd never been as aware of another living being as he was of this woman.

He'd thought a week would be enough to calm the feeling she incited within him.

He'd been wrong.

All it had taken was one glimpse of her modestly clothed person today for him to see through layers of wool and muslin to her unclad person.

Even now, though his eyes most assiduously attempted to avoid her, she was strolling directly in front of him, not five feet away, and what were they to do but notice the feminine sway of her rounded hips—hips perfectly shaped for a man's hand.

At least, that was what his hands had begun to think.

They stopped on a short rise that offered a view of the racecourse.

Saskia held her hand to her forehead to better take in the lay of the Downs. "Do the horses start and finish in the same place? Because the course looks to be in the shape of a U."

"A very astute question," said the duchess, approvingly. "The racecourse is, in fact, in the shape of a U." She pointed toward a distant white post. "That's the start." She shifted the angle of her finger. "And the finish is there." Unable to help herself, she continued speaking. "The turf is fine as a Persian rug, and when the horses run, the grass releases a light scent of wild thyme and juniper. But for all those delights, Epsom is a bruising course. Though it's a flat, it's all up and down and sharp corners, the tightest being the Tattenham Corner half a mile before the finish. It's the length, too, that makes it a challenge. At a mile and a half, horses that ran well at the Two Thousand and One Thousand Guineas can struggle at the Derby. That's why it's so difficult for one horse to take the Triple Crown. Because the three legs of the season have different course lengths, with each leg longer than the previous one. For all the fun of Derby Day, the race itself is a stern challenge for inexperienced horses and a tough test of stamina, too."

As the duchess explained the ins and outs of the Derby, she did so with joy and excitement, her cheeks flushed and her eyes bright. This was her passion.

This duchess... She kept being not the duchess he'd dismissed as a shallow title huntress. Perhaps she wasn't one thing, but rather multifaceted. Like most people, he'd found over the years in dealing with those from all walks of life.

Or multifaceted like...

A diamond.

As she continued speaking, Gabriel nodded silent greetings toward more than a few patrons of The Archangel. *Lords.* Lords who now saw him as one of them, their nods said.

One such lord did more than nod. He joined their little grouping. A delighted smile spread across Mrs. Fairfax's face. "Lord Ormonde, how are you finding the day?"

Gabriel was tangentially acquainted with the Marquess of Ormonde, as the lord held a subscription to The Archangel and passed the odd evening there a few times a year.

"A perfect day for it." The marquess's longish hair glinted gold in the sun, his sky-blue eyes friendly.

From what Gabriel had gathered over time, everyone liked the Marquess of Ormonde, a man who would bear no small resemblance to a Viking raider of yore were it not for his general amiability.

The duchess, however, appeared to take a different view of the marquess. Her flushed cheeks suddenly blanched white, and she took a step back, as if poised to flee.

Gabriel felt his brow furrow. A history existed between duchess and marquess—one with which he wasn't acquainted.

One that made his back teeth grind together.

Ormonde shifted on his feet. It was clear the man had something to say to the duchess—and wasn't keen on the prospect. "I take it you've heard the news?"

It was a question—and it wasn't.

A flicker of curiosity flashed behind her eyes. She hadn't heard.

It was Mrs. Fairfax who asked, "What news?"

Ormonde drew in a deep breath. Clearly, he'd rather the earth swallow him whole than relate the news with which he'd arrived. "Rakesley is married."

A beat of silence ticked by. Then another. The duchess swallowed. "Oh?" she managed. Her chin notched higher. "To whom, may I ask?"

"To, *erm*, Gemma," said Ormonde. More news he didn't want to deliver.

The duchess's brow crinkled. "*Gemma?*"

"You've met."

Ormonde looked so uncomfortable, Gabriel's palms nearly perspired for him.

The duchess shook her head. "I'm not acquainted with a Gemma."

"She also went by Gem."

Realization dawned across the duchess's face. "*Gem?*" she gasped with utter disbelief.

Ormonde nodded.

"Rakesley married *Gem?*" The words seemed resistant to sinking into her brain.

"In Scotland a few days ago," supplied Ormonde. "I thought you should know as the news has started making the rounds of society."

The duchess squared her shoulders and gathered herself. "I appreciate your sensitivity, Ormonde."

The marquess offered a shallow bow of farewell, nodded at Gabriel, and pivoted on his heel.

The man wasn't gone five seconds before Gabriel turned to find a smile firmly affixed to the duchess's mouth.

He didn't like that smile.

Before he could ask what in the blazes that was about, she addressed his sisters, "This is important for you to learn. Always keep abreast of the latest gossip, because sometimes it's about you. Do you subscribe to the *London Diary?*"

Now Gabriel had yet another question—how had that gossip been about *her?*

"Of course not," scoffed Saskia.

"Well, see that you do," continued the duchess. "I predict you'll find yourself in there as soon as tomorrow."

Gabriel noticed subtle movement to his right. *The Earl of Wrexford.* The pleasant smile on the earl's face produced a frown on Gabriel's. "Wrexford," he said, no choice but to acknowledge the man.

"Acaster."

Though Wrexford was speaking to Gabriel, it clear he was attempting to insinuate himself into the group. Brotherly instinct forwarded itself. Here were two lovely young ladies and an imminently eligible young lord. He should stand back and let nature take its course. Which sister would the earl have his sights set on? Saskia? Or Viveca?

An instant later, Gabriel realized he'd gotten the angle wrong. The earl's gaze kept straying toward an altogether different lady.

The duchess.

Irritation prickled through him.

What was a green earl to a flesh-and-blood goddess?

Surely, she would take his measure with a single scathing glance and put him in his place.

However, when the earl asked, "Duchess, are you finding the day to your pleasure?" and she replied, "It would be difficult to dream up a better one," Gabriel saw he had it all wrong.

Again.

Irritation spiked into a feeling if more closely resembling anger.

Anger?

He wasn't a man disposed to anger. He'd always viewed it as a weakness. It made men act irrationally.

And Gabriel didn't have an irrational bone in his body.

He was a man of evenness and cool temper.

Everyone knew it.

A hand squeezed his arm. He glanced down to find Mrs. Fairfax smiling up at him. He'd forgotten her there. "Would you mind very much taking a turn with me about the grounds?"

"Of course," he said, determined to be agreeable—even if it was the last thing he wanted.

He wanted, in fact, to punch the Earl of Wrexford square in his aristocratic nose.

As he and Mrs. Fairfax separated from the group, Gabriel resisted the urge to glance over his shoulder. Wrexford needed an eye kept on him.

That last thought shook him out of this strange and shockingly bloodthirsty mood. The duchess wasn't actually his family —and she was certainly no young lady in need of protection.

Further, Wrexford was no scoundrel. A year below Gabriel through school, the earl had been nothing other than amiable, his mouth ever ready to smile at the slightest provocation.

The man was likeable.

Which made him no less irritating.

"Is the air of Surrey to your liking, Your Grace?" asked Mrs. Fairfax.

"I much prefer less noisy air," he said. "Less noisome, too."

A delighted laugh escaped her. "Derby Day is rather loud and smelly. But it's life lived to its fullest, too."

Gabriel supposed.

On a conversational tone, she continued, "The bargain you've struck with Celia is a good thing."

Gabriel suspected Mrs. Fairfax had pulled him away from the group to say exactly that. "We both benefit from our agreement."

"I happen to agree." They took a few more steps. "You don't much like Celia, do you?"

That was rather more bluntly put than he would've expected from the diminutive, agreeable woman. "I don't know your cousin with any sort of depth," he said diplomatically.

Unexpected hardness glinted within soft brown eyes. "That's right. You don't."

Gabriel had the distinct feeling he was about to be on the receiving end of a proper set down.

"You think her nothing more than a title huntress."

"Isn't she?"

"It was her father who was on the hunt for a title."

Gabriel snorted. "We no longer live in a feudal society where brides are bartered. Women have a choice about who they marry."

Mrs. Fairfax's brow lifted, as if this was news to her. "Do we?"

On this point, Gabriel was certain. "Yes."

She fully faced him. "So, you think a young lady of nineteen years has a choice when her father tells her she's to marry a seventy-five-year-old duke?"

"Of course, she does. She can say no."

"Then what?"

"Pardon?"

"Let's follow the path of your logic," said Mrs. Fairfax, patiently. Gabriel never could abide a patient tone of voice. "The young lady says *no* and stands her ground. Then what? When her father tells her he will cast her into the streets without a penny to her name, what is she to do? Can she plead her case in the courts? Will society take up her cause?" Though Mrs. Fairfax's tone remained friendly, her eyes were pointed as daggers. "She will not only be penniless, but friendless, too."

Gabriel felt strangely, yet appropriately, chastened.

In the distance, he caught sight of his sisters waving him over to their place at the railing. "I believe we're wanted," he said, relieved for an excuse to have this conversation at an end.

Mrs. Fairfax waved back. "I'll say one last thing on the subject of Celia. Why don't you get to know her before you judge her? That marriage was no easy thing to be endured." She fixed her attention on his sisters. "Ladies Saskia and Viveca are delightful. They will fare well in society, as they know their own minds and don't appear inclined toward silliness."

"Oh, they can be quite silly."

"Spoken like an older brother. But the silliness I speak of is the sort that gets a lovely young lady cast out. They are charming."

"Even Saskia?" Gabriel harbored doubts.

Mrs. Fairfax laughed. "Especially Saskia."

As they approached their group, Gabriel noted Wrexford yet hung about, gazing upon the duchess with such naked adoration that Gabriel felt embarrassed for him.

Which only reinforced his determination to keep his vow to avoid women until the age of thirty, if this was the sort of fool a woman turned a man into.

Meanwhile, Saskia, too, appeared enraptured by the duchess, albeit for different reasons. "Do you have a horse entered in the Derby?"

"I do." The light of competition entered the duchess's eyes. "*There*. Devil's Spawn."

"The fellow in the pink-and-white polka-dotted silks?" Viveca laughed, delighted by the irony.

"Horse names are rather colorful." The duchess began pointing out other horses. "There's Little Wicked in purple and black." Her brow crinkled. "I would've thought to see her entered in the Oaks for Ladies' Day, but really, that Mr. Deverill hasn't the faintest idea what he's doing with a racehorse of her caliber." She exhaled an annoyed sigh before getting herself back onto the original subject. "And that's Good Bottom beside her. Next, there's Squirrel. And Old Bugger is a particular favorite today, along with Ormonde's Filthy Habit." Her eyes narrowed. "Still, I think Devil's Spawn has an outside chance of winning it for me."

"*Us*," said Gabriel. All eyes swung toward him. "As partners, Devil's Spawn would win it for *us*."

Irritation flashed within the duchess's eyes. "Of course."

Viveca didn't notice the spark of tension in the air and asked, "If Devil's Spawn wins today, would you have two horses running in the Race of the Century?"

The duchess's smile returned—this one genuine. "Indeed, Lady Viveca. Which would better, my—" Her gaze flicked toward Gabriel. "*Our* odds of having a winner."

"And collecting the ten-thousand-pound purse," added Gabriel.

It hadn't escaped his notice that by both being an investor in the race and by running a horse or two, he would be a double winner.

In truth, his bargain with the duchess was no gamble.

It was business.

He couldn't lose.

"I believe the race is about to start." Mrs. Fairfax began leading Saskia and Viveca to the white railing running along the racecourse and waving at Wrexford to follow.

After a bit of shuffling about with other spectators, Gabriel found the duchess had made her way over as well.

Beside him—their bodies separated by inches.

Awareness streaked through him. He experienced a powerful urge to sidle left and touch her in some way. A light tap of shoulders... a brush of the back of his hand against hers...

Any part of her would do.

He wouldn't, of course.

Tension filled the air, as everyone waited for the starting gun to fire. Because of the U shape of the racecourse, their group's position at the finish line put them parallel with the start, though at a distance.

The duchess began rifling through her reticule. Her hand emerged with a compact pair of silver-and-pink enameled binoculars, which she held up to her eyes. Surprisingly, she began talking, more from nerves than a desire to keep him abreast of race developments, of course. "We'll be lucky to see them off with the first firing of the gun."

Gabriel squinted into the distance. "How do you mean?"

"False starts," she said. "The sport is rife with them."

A sudden puff of gray smoked the air, followed by the crack of a pistol. The horses jumped into motion, and the crowd went wild. The duchess held still, braced for a second firing of the gun to indicate a false start. When no such firing occurred, she shifted forward, one hand holding the binoculars, the other gripping the railing so tightly her knuckles went white.

Though the course was a flat, the first furlong of the race held an ascent, which served to string out the large scrum of horses and riders. Devil's Spawn—the only horse Gabriel knew on sight —wasn't leading the front grouping as they thundered up the rise, but he was tracking with them and holding his ground.

"Come on... come on... come on..." chanted the duchess.

Drawn in by the heat of competition, Gabriel pressed against the railing, his heart a hammer in his chest. After all, he did, indeed, have a horse in this race. "Come on," he found himself shouting, his voice one in a chorus of ten thousand.

Still, it didn't feel entirely futile. In fact, it felt mightily cleansing to give over to the collective emotion of the roaring thousands.

The horses shifted to take the first turn. The lead grouping that found Devil's Spawn tracking at the back made it round, but in the pack that followed, the legs of one horse became tangled with those of another and both crashed to the turf.

"That'll be Squirrel and Old Bugger out of it," muttered the duchess. She followed it up with another, "Come *on!*"

Next, the horses were making the second and sharpest turn at Tattenham Corner. Another horse and rider took a tumble. "That'll be Good Bottom," the duchess informed him. "And good riddance."

Horse racing was a cutthroat sport, there was no doubting it, and as the horses emerged from the corner and onto the final straight, Gabriel felt the bloodthirst flowing through his own veins, pinpricking his skin with perspiration. He hadn't been prepared for the sheer physicality of the sport—of horse, jockey, and spectator.

"They're entering the final straight. It's slightly downhill." The duchess continued her running commentary. "Now you're going to see what these horses can do."

The Thoroughbreds picked up speed, jockeys lying flat over their mounts, encouraging them to greater and greater speeds by word, crop, or spur—and any combination of the three. Devil's Spawn's jockey valiantly attempted to muscle into the lead pack, but couldn't seem to gain any ground on the lead three.

"Go around them, you fool," shouted the duchess.

Then Gabriel felt it—a light tangling of fingers, then a hand squeezing his. The duchess's hand. Gabriel doubted she had any awareness of the action, but the hand now clutching his was all he could think about. Amazing how one's existence could suddenly become centered within a stretch of skin that had heretofore been insignificant.

Instinctively, he turned his hand so he could squeeze back.

Now, they were holding hands.

As if Devil's Spawn's jockey heard the duchess's command, he angled his body subtly to the right, a signal the horse immediately understood as he shifted his trajectory to the outside. Given that the remaining quarter mile was a straight, the strategy held little risk, particularly when one was running fourth.

The duchess's grip turned to steel as the horses thundered toward them and the finish. At first, Gabriel was unable to believe his eyes, then he saw it was true—Devil's Spawn had drawn abreast of the third-place horse. The two lead horses ran a length ahead, neck and neck, and not ceding an inch of ground. They couldn't be caught as they raced across the finish line to a roar of cheers.

Then, a length behind, came Devil's Spawn, extending at just the right moment to capture third place.

The duchess threw ecstatic arms into the air. "And that's how we go!"

Before Gabriel knew what was happening, her arms around his neck as she bounced up and down with unfettered joy.

He felt a responding joy—how could he not?—though to a lesser degree.

Mostly what he felt was her body pressed against his.

A body he'd seen with far fewer layers of clothing.

Of their own accord, his arms wrapped around her.

Now, he not only knew the sight of her body, but the feel of it, too.

Lush... firm...

Precisely how he'd imagined.

Another sort of awareness stole through him, and his hands moved along her back. Her rapturous face lifted, her smile uncomplicated by anything other than pure happiness. "Third place," she exclaimed, thrilled and astonished.

For a wild instant, he thought she might kiss him.

And for a wilder instant, he thought he wouldn't mind it so much.

Then she blinked, and her smile changed. It grew considering as her gaze lowered to his mouth, then lifted again to meet his eyes. He saw within honey amber depths a responding awareness.

It would be nothing to angle his head and know the taste of her mouth.

Except it wouldn't be nothing.

It would instantly become everything.

CHAPTER TEN

*C*elia understood she should step away from the Duke of Acaster.

And she should most definitely untwine her arms from around his neck.

Both rational certainties.

Both certainties refused to take the next step into action.

It was simply that the duke was so solid and strong and *male* against her.

She'd never experienced such a masculine body along the full length of hers. She felt...

Feminine.

And all her arms wanted to do was tighten around his neck and bring his firm mouth to hers, to feel the scratch of his beard against her skin.

As his direct sea-blue eyes searched hers, he looked as if he might want the same.

Then something unknowable flashed behind his eyes, and all the muscles in his body went rigid. Suddenly, he was utterly himself again—a man who didn't bend... a man who didn't break.

Right.

Her arms loosened their hold around his neck, and she took that step back, disentangling herself from him, her fingers already trying to forget the silky slide of his hair, as she awkwardly avoided his gaze and accepted congratulations from all around.

In the commotion of the neck-and-neck finish, no one had noticed.

How long could've the hug lasted? The split of a second? And, really, what had she done? She'd hugged the nearest body.

She could've hugged anyone.

Except her body didn't feel the imprint of anyone.

It felt the imprint of *him*.

Carried away by the crowd, Celia found herself on the race-course, holding a large flower garland. As the owner of the third-place finisher, she was expected to partake in formalities and celebrations, which were a welcome rescue from whatever sort of moment she'd just experienced with the duke.

Yet in the little moments between placing the wreath around Devil's Spawn's neck and congratulating Ames on a brilliant ride and accepting the third-place finisher's purse, she caught her gaze drifting toward an unflinching pair of sea-blue eyes.

A warm shiver crawled through her, each and every time.

Eloise appeared at her side and threw her arms around Celia. "How does it feel to be the owner of the best horse racing stable in England?"

Celia hugged her cousin back, but over Eloise's shoulder, she locked eyes with Acaster. Within those cerulean depths, she found a question—the same as hers.

What had just happened between them?

"I, *erm*," she began, shouting into Eloise's ear to be heard over the din of the ecstatic crowd. "I must find the ladies' retiring room."

"Shall I walk with you?" asked Eloise.

Celia spotted Mr. Lancaster a few yards away and knew her cousin would want to spend time with him.

"Not at all. I won't be a moment."

As Celia began shoving her way through the crowd, it was all she could do not to glance in the duke's direction, like Lot's wife. Surely, she would turn into a pillar of salt, for that way lay temptation, untasted.

She made straight for the ladies' retiring room—*fled*, in reality.

Inside, she nodded toward a few ladies of passing acquaintance before slipping behind a privacy screen. She collapsed onto a velvet cushioned stool and exhaled the breath she'd been holding. She would try not to inhale too deeply, because, well, this was the ladies' retiring room on Derby Day and the bourdaloue didn't appear to have been emptied in hours.

Her blood still pumped hard in her veins from Devil's Spawn's third-place finish and the one-hundred-pound purse yet clutched in her hand.

Fifty pounds once the duke took his cut.

Still, she was satisfied. She needed every farthing she could muster.

But the third-place finish and the money weren't the true reasons her heart galloped in her chest.

The duke.

And that embrace.

No.

What she'd done was press the full length of her body against his—a body in its full masculine prime.

Though she was no prim young miss, she might never stop blushing. Not from having felt him, but rather from her reaction to him. A warm, liquid feeling that pooled deep inside her, that made her legs wobble and her mind race with wild imaginings.

It was all she could do even now not to run straight back and confirm the feel of him.

Temptation.

There it was—that word.

Except now it evoked the story of Eve. As if the duke were a delectable piece of fruit waiting to be…

Plucked.

Oh, this wouldn't do.

Because it wasn't only her reaction to him.

He'd reacted, too. Long masculine fingers trailing down the length of her spine, pressing into the small of her back, holding her fast against him. His mouth inches from hers.

Celia heard the door open and admit a group of ladies already in the middle of a conversation.

"They were seen by Lord and Lady Dalwinnie?"

"In Edinburgh."

"As husband and wife?" came a shocked voice.

And Celia knew.

They were speaking of Rakesley and his… *wife.*

"He introduced her as his duchess."

Scandalized gasps followed, and noxious odor notwithstanding, Celia would've gladly sunk into the bourdaloue, if it meant escape.

"Lady Gwyneth's sister witnessed it firsthand. She had to *curtsy* to a jockey!"

Actually, Celia had met the new duchess once—when the woman had been dressed as a jockey. Of course, the *lad's* feminine appearance had sparked suspicion within Celia, but she'd dismissed it as none of her concern. Little had she known that, in fact, it had been very much her concern. That Rakesley would run off with his jockey—his *jockey!*— and marry her.

And leave Celia in the lurch.

It wasn't that he'd treated Celia in an ungentlemanly manner or actually jilted her at the altar. No formal proposal or agreements had been in place—but she'd been *so* close to achieving a life of safety and security.

"Lady Gwyneth said they held hands throughout the entirety of their evening meal."

"So common."

"Standards are already lowering."

"Any word on how the Duchess of Acaster is taking it?"

The heat of humiliation spiked through Celia. Of course, London had known that a proposal of marriage from the Duke of Rakesley had been intended for the Duchess of Acaster.

She'd had practice warding off humiliation, having suffered myriad embarrassments at the hands of her late husband. But she'd thought she was finished with being humiliated.

It appeared not.

What sort of woman lost a man to his jockey?

Celia knew precisely what she needed to do. Rather than cower behind this screen, she must leave its protection and face the indignity awaiting her. She would have to endure society's gossipy glee sooner or later—better to have it done with.

Shoulders squared, she emerged. "How I'm taking what?"

All eyes swung her direction and went wide as saucers. Her eyes, however, dared them to speak another word about Rakesley.

A throat cleared. "How are you taking to the new Duke of Acaster and his sisters?"

Celia graced the room with her most brilliant smile. She'd struck a deal with Acaster, and here was an opportunity to fulfill its terms. "Ladies Saskia and Viveca are as delightful as they are lovely. They will be the lights of all social gatherings they are invited to attend and a credit to the family."

The eyes carefully watching Celia turned considering. "And the duke?" asked one intrepid lady.

Of course, they wanted to know about him.

"He will fill his role as duke capably, I believe."

There. She'd said all that would be expected of her.

But the eyes watching her weren't satisfied with the expected. If anything, they took a turn toward the avaricious.

"Yes, but..." began one lady.

"What *about* him," finished another.

The two ladies clearly spoke for all five.

Celia shrugged. "I don't know more than any of you."

That wasn't strictly true. She knew the scent of his starched shirt... the feel of his strong, solid, masculine body pressed against hers.

Knowledge she would keep to herself.

It was for her, alone.

"The Duke of Vice, they're calling him," said the one lady.

"Oh, I heard that one," said the other.

"If only," said a third lady, drawing knowing titters.

"What does that mean?" Unspoken knowledge lay between *if* and *only*, and Celia would have it.

"You must know he attended Eton and Cambridge on scholarship."

"Of course." Celia waited for the unspoken to reveal itself.

"My younger brother was in his year."

"Mine, too."

"*And?*" Impatience prickled through Celia.

"There were whisperings about Gabriel Siren."

"That'll be the Seventh Duke of Acaster to you," came a giggly impertinence.

Celia remained serious and intent on knowing what she didn't know—*yet*. "What sort of whisperings?"

The first lady's eyes glittered with gossip yet to be delivered. "He yet remains in possession of his flower."

Celia felt her brow gather. "Pardon?" Very little in that sentence made sense.

"You know," began the second lady on another giggle. "His virtue."

"*Virtue?*" Celia asked, flummoxed.

Which only incited more giggles.

"There are no virtuous men." It had to be said.

"At Eton, he never went carousing with the other boys," said one lady.

"That means nothing."

"The Archangel doesn't allow strumpets," said the other.

Celia shook her head, aghast. "How can you possibly know what you're saying?"

A lady who had just entered the room cut in, "Are you discussing Acaster?"

One of the ladies waggled her eyebrows suggestively.

"Ask any lady at the Derby today," the first lady.

"And what precisely am I to ask them?"

The second lady nodded as if her point had been proven. "He hasn't been with a single one."

"That doesn't tell you anything."

The ladies looked convinced to a one.

Celia spoke slowly, so they might understand. "Has it never occurred to you that there are other women in the world besides ladies?"

A beat of silence ticked by before a lady said, "Not any women that matter."

Celia wanted to throw frustrated hands into the air. Instead, she excused herself and slipped from the room. As she stalked blindly through the crowd, her mind raced. Thank goodness for her trusty smile. It could always be relied upon in times of need.

What if...

What if it was true?

What if... the new duke was a... virgin?

Surely, that couldn't be.

All one had to do was look at him, for starters. Women would be lining up at his door—ladies, too—to help him dispose of his *erm... flower.*

What utter silliness.

And yet...

His reaction to her state of dishabille at Madame Dubois's shop... It had puzzled her, but she hadn't been able to put a finger on why.

He hadn't reacted in a predictably male way.

He hadn't leered.

He hadn't apologized.

He'd panicked.

And here was the thing about this Duke of Acaster that she knew without a doubt: He was a man who prided himself on his even temperament and clear-headedness.

He didn't panic.

And yet...

He had.

At the sight of her in near undress.

She nearly gasped.

It was entirely possible that the Duke of Acaster was, indeed, still in possession of his *flower*.

Hysterical laughter wanted to bubble up at the very absurdity.

"*Your Grace?*" Celia heard behind her.

She turned to find Lady Tessa watching her expectantly, as if it hadn't been the first time she'd called out.

"Lady Tessa," she said. "I wasn't aware you were attending Derby Day. You could have ridden in the carriage with your family."

Lady Tessa gave a dismissive shrug. Even dressed much as she'd been at The Archangel—today her silk waistcoat was peacock blue—Lady Tessa could be characterized as nothing other than a formidable beauty—a statuesque woman with strawberry blonde tendrils that wanted to stray out from beneath functional wide-brimmed hat and into sunlight.

But it was the fierce intelligence that shone from her eyes that was most arresting. She was the eldest of the siblings once known as Siren, and her confident bearing stated as much. Celia couldn't help feeling the duke owed much of his gaming hell's success to this sister.

"I needed to be here by the crack of dawn to beat the crowd to the betting post," replied the lady.

"Did your favorite win?" Celia only asked to make small conversation.

"For me, the horses are incidental. I've never observed Derby Day in person."

"And has the day been to your satisfaction?"

"Actually, I—" Her attention caught on a figure in the near distance and all the color drained from her face.

Celia followed the direction of Lady Tessa's gaze, which was planted squarely on the Marquess of Ormonde. Her brow gathered. She wasn't especially keen to see him again after the news he'd delivered today.

She had no need of news ever again.

Still, her well-trained smile affixed itself to her mouth. "Lord Ormonde, it's so, *erm*, lovely to see you again... so soon." It was what one said, approximately. "May I introduce you to —"

"The marquess and I are, *erm*, acquainted," cut in Lady Tessa, visibly annoyed.

Ormonde offered no rejoinder, beyond a smile meant only for Lady Tessa. Then he bowed before pivoting and striding away.

"You know the marquess?" asked Celia, though the answer was only too apparent.

Lady Tessa looked decidedly—and uncharacteristically—cagey. "He's a member of The Archangel."

"So, *that* was about business?"

Of course, the question was impertinent, and Celia had no right to ask, but Lady Tessa was visibly rattled.

She nodded carefully, as if with great dread. "*That* was about a debt—a debt that must be paid."

Celia wasn't exactly sure what she'd just witnessed, but a

history existed between Lady Tessa and the Marquess of Ormonde.

And if she'd read the serious intention in the marquess's eyes correctly, a future, too.

Ormonde was a pleasant man, his looks the embodiment of good health and spirits, from his longish gold hair to blue eyes suggestive of open skies and his air of general amiability. And yet... Now she felt like she'd witnessed a different side of him.

One that wasn't intended for her to see—but very much for Lady Tessa.

"Your Grace," came a male voice to her right, and Celia remembered to affix the smile to her mouth before turning toward the Earl of Wrexford. "I've been looking for you everywhere."

"And yet, here I am," she said, weakly.

Lady Tessa took the opportunity to disappear into the crowd.

"I was wondering," began Wrexford, his cheeks twin blushes of radish red. "Well, I was wondering if you would, perhaps... someday... like to take the air with me?"

"*The air?*" Celia supposed she could've tried a little harder to keep the scorn from her voice.

"In Hyde Park." He'd taken the question as encouragement.

"The air of Hyde Park?"

"It's the best air in Town," he said, most earnest.

Celia wasn't sure an exchange could be more vacuous.

"In a fortnight, if that's agreeable to you," he continued. "I'll be staying in Surrey through the week on estate business."

"Your family seat is in Surrey?"

"Not five miles from Epsom." His blush, somehow, intensified. "You could visit sometime."

Finally, Celia saw what was happening here. This earl, who was not only younger than her, but also younger than Acaster, was asking to court her. She would let him down gently. "Oh, I'll need to consult my diary—"

The way his brown eyes were looking at her—so earnest, so hopeful.

"—but I'm sure it will be open."

A huge grin burst across his face, and Celia almost felt as if her assent had been worth it. Of course, she would send a note on the day and beg off—he really, truly, simply was too young for her—but now he looked like the happiest man on earth.

"Celia, there you are," came the voice she hadn't realized she'd been waiting for until this very moment.

She turned to find Eloise striding toward her, with Lady Saskia on one arm and Lady Viveca on the other.

She nodded at Wrexford. "Until then."

Understanding that he was dismissed, he offered a deep bow and ambled away, a lightness in his step.

Eloise didn't miss a beat. "The Ladies Saskia and Viveca are garnering a fair amount of attention of both the savory and unsavory variety."

"One gentleman asked if I would like to go behind the Royal Reform Club with him and pet his stallion," said Lady Viveca.

"*Stroke* was the word he used," said Lady Saskia.

"Yes, *stroke*," said Eloise with a message in her eyes for Celia only.

Right.

"Well," said Celia, "there will be no stroking of stallions today."

"Indeed," said Eloise. "Best we return to London."

Celia gave the crowd a quick scan. "And the duke? Will he be riding back with us?" she asked with utter indifference—if only.

"I've left him in the capable hands of Mr. Lancaster."

"Ah."

A feeling wended through Celia. It felt strangely akin to... disappointment.

Even so, as they made their way to the coach-and-four, she thought she caught a glimpse of a tall, broad-shouldered gentleman, his sun-streaked hair just meeting the collar of his coat.

Her heart drummed a few extra beats.

Acaster.

Or had the man been a figment of her imagination?

Which wasn't better.

In fact, it might be worse—for it meant she was making him appear where he wasn't.

That could have no good outcome.

CHAPTER ELEVEN

LONDON, A WEEK LATER

Celia was bored.

That was the short of it.

She didn't want to be in London.

That was the longer of it.

If only Lady Saskia and Lady Viveca's lessons in ladylike etiquette weren't so incredibly, dreadfully dull.

The thing was, Celia abhorred routine. While she could appreciate the structure it provided in a theoretical sense, the reality of it made her feel hemmed into a tight space. This was in large part why she disliked London and its social calendar. The instant she committed to a visit, she wanted to beg off—even if it had been her idea.

The routine they'd settled into these last few days was that Eloise would arrive at half eight in the morning to go over that day's schedule over breakfast tea. From there, it was a parade of masters, tutors, and former governesses. First of the day was the dancing master, who arrived with a pianist. That lasted an hour. Then they transitioned into the piano lesson. Fortunately, both ladies had received instruction in their younger years and were showing promise of having a few ready pieces they could play for a gathering.

Next, it was midday tea and on to language. Eloise had pushed French through, but with a concession to Lady Saskia—that it was alternated with Greek every other day. At one o'clock, the painting master arrived with his easel and watercolors. Neither sister showed much promise with a brush. Well, that wasn't strictly true. Lady Viveca simply refused to paint anything that was actually present in the room, much to the frustration of Master Fratelli.

Lady Viveca wasn't too bothered. "What I see in my mind is so much more interesting."

Then it was another hour with a former governess who was providing lessons in comportment. Even Celia took a few mental notes. Today's subject had been table settings.

Truly.

And, like a responsible chaperone, Celia sat through it all on the other side of the room, either gossiping with her cousin or reading or attending to correspondence. She'd even drifted into a nap on more than one occasion.

But a deal was a deal, and she was to see Acaster's sisters established in society.

And her stable was saved.

For now.

If only the dead boring succession of days hadn't begun to feel endless.

But the lessons were necessary, Celia grudgingly admitted. After the Derby, society had caught wind of the Duke of Acaster's lovely, surely-to-be-amply-dowried sisters, and though the season was almost over, the calling cards and invitations had begun to arrive *en masse*. A veritable avalanche of calling cards and invitations.

To keep the sisters from becoming a nine days' wonder, Celia and Eloise were being extremely selective about which invitations to reply with a *yes*. If society wanted to see more of the Duke of Acaster's sisters, they would have to attend their debut ball in three weeks. The invitations were going out tomorrow.

Now, it was gone midnight, and Celia couldn't sleep. She'd thought a glass of wine would help.

It hadn't.

And neither had the second one.

So, here she was, in what had become the dower wing of the St. James's Square mansion, alone. As her bedroom overlooked the square, she parted the curtain wide enough for a peek. The cobbles had gone quiet, no carriages having rattled across this last half hour.

And she would know.

She'd been keeping an eye out.

For the duke.

She suspected he didn't come home at night—which made sense for the owner of a gaming hell.

Still, he did pop into his sisters' lessons when he deigned to grace the house with his dukely presence. Celia made herself scarce during those visits on the pretext of allowing the siblings privacy.

But deep down she knew that wasn't the only—or even the main—reason for her absence.

Derby Day.

The mere combination of those two words stirred sensations inside Celia.

Uncomfortable, molten sensations.

She now knew too much about the duke.

She knew the feel of his body.

And she knew...

Oh... What was it precisely that she knew?

That he was a... *virgin?*

It wasn't merely that the duke might be a virgin. Rather, the conversation in the ladies' retiring room had laid open an idea Celia had avoided acknowledging to herself.

Without her permission, it cast Acaster in a sensual light.

She didn't want to think of him—or any other man—in a sensual light.

But now, her body couldn't stop.

Her body seemed to harbor the irritating notion that his body held promise.

Never in her life had her body harbored such a notion.

Her body's experience with another body was nothing she cared to dwell upon—*ever.*

Except her body had worked out that this body belonged to an altogether different man.

And that was a problem.

She attempted to make herself remember other aspects of the man. His arrogance... his condescension... his high handedness.

Where were the duke's lessons in comportment and dancing and French? Did this duke know a fish knife on sight? Sure, he'd gone to Eton and Cambridge, but Celia couldn't help suspecting this duke needed a lesson or two.

And, *really*, how had such a young man earned the right to be so assured and composed and commanding and capable?

She supposed it could be admitted that four-and-twenty wasn't all that young, but...

It wasn't thirty, either.

Her hand reached for the wine glass, which had gone dry. No great mystery there. She'd drunk it—along with the previous glass of wine. No matter. A dry glass was a predicament easily remedied by the half-full bottle of plonk near at hand. Mid-reach, however, an idea forwarded itself, and she froze.

The Archangel surely had wine—rivers of it.

Why should she sit here with her sad bottle of wine, bored and sleepless, while others were out drinking jolly wine and having the night of their lives?

A bold and reckless feeling had Celia on her feet and angling toward her wardrobe. She had just the dress for a little, wild night. Why should men be allowed all the fun, anyway?

She was the Dowager Duchess of Acaster, one of the most desirable women in London, and she'd spent the better part of an evening having the finer aspects of needlework explained to her by yet another former governess hired by Eloise.

Like a woman in her—*ugh*—dotage.

Celia held up the dress she'd been searching for. Oh, yes, that would do nicely. She may have spent ten years married to an aged lech, but she was nowhere near her dotage—and neither was she undesirable.

Tonight, this new Duke of Acaster, gaming hell owner, would see with his very own eyes that every man in The Archangel would give an eyetooth for five minutes with the woman he'd hugged on Derby Day.

And though Celia wasn't too clear on her motivations, she was determined to see him put that in his pipe and smoke it.

* * *

THE NIGHT WAS a usual one at The Archangel.

The clock chimed midnight, and Gabriel finished going over the night's expected take with Mr. Dupratt. Tessa had suddenly taken herself off on a holiday, leaving the running of the floor to him.

"With someone?" Gabriel had asked as a tease.

But his sister failed to see the humor. "What would make you think that?" she'd snapped.

And that had been the end of it.

Still, it was best he began involving Dupratt more closely in the day-to-day details of The Archangel, for Gabriel could see the writing on the wall. As a duke of the realm, myriad duties and responsibilities had begun pulling at him and requiring more and more of his time—journeys to various estates, rehabil-itating those estates or selling them off, and the accounting of the late duke's debts that continued to fly in from every direction.

Gabriel didn't have it in him to be the sort of duke who didn't take control of matters and see them through—which in this case was being a duke.

Which would become his life's work.

It only followed that he would have to give up the running of The Archangel—but not his investing. That was where his true passion lay, and besides, various investment ventures would align with him being a duke.

A stir on the other side of the room caught his ear. Not a clashing of voices, but rather a lifting of the collective energy, as if a surprise had walked through the front door. Gabriel looked up from the hazard notes and markers and saw that, indeed, a surprise had walked into The Archangel.

The duchess.

Celia, as he'd begun thinking of her for some unfathomable reason.

Actually, not unfathomable.

Quite fathomable, in fact.

When a man knew the feel of a woman's body, even through layers of wool and muslin, he tended to think of her in given name terms—and Gabriel didn't differ from other men in this regard, it seemed.

Sobering thought.

The Archangel's doorman, Ricard, caught Gabriel's eye. He wanted to know what to do with this woman who had invaded their masculine domain. Gabriel gave a curt nod, and Ricard stepped away from the duchess.

Along with every other man in the club, Gabriel's eyes couldn't help running over the length of her. It was the dress. The hue of blush pink. Nearly the color of her skin, but pinker. A pink that provoked ideas in a man's mind. It wasn't the color of her skin as it was now, but perhaps the color when she…

How was he planning to finish that sentence?

Then there were the curves beneath blush pink muslin, the thinness of the fabric suggesting transparency. Or was that an illusion? Or… wishful thinking?

She was mayhem in a pink dress.

Men would be falling over themselves to be near her, brawling over the right to please her.

She tended to have that effect.

And not only on other men.

Her gaze caught his, and he realized she'd been surveying the room for him. A smile tipped at the corner of her cherry-red mouth, glittered in her eyes, and the blood went light in Gabriel's veins. *Fizzy.* Blood as effervescent as champagne bubbles.

And all because she smiled at him with that bit of mischief in her eyes.

He should take himself away to his office and leave The Archangel to whatever mayhem was on her mind tonight.

But he couldn't.

Deliberately, he moved through the room—conversing with patrons, seeing to the needs of croupiers and card dealers, ensuring no shortages of spirits, addressing any conflicts that arose, be it personal or financial, and generally treating the night as if it were typical.

All the while holding half an eye on her.

As he moved, she moved, too, keeping to the opposite side of the room, flitting from table to table as if she were Duchess of The Archangel—tossing hazard dice here, playing a *rouge et noir* hand there, then a spin of the roulette wheel.

The Archangel had never seen such a lively night. Some of the gentlemen were perplexed and thoroughly unamused, and others were bewildered and generally confused, but most embraced the presence of a beautiful duchess out for a lively evening. Gabriel would have to slip some coin in more than a few directions to ensure this night didn't make the scandal sheets by morning.

All the while, her gaze kept periodically flicking toward him and meeting his, and he couldn't help feeling it was all a show...

For him.

Right.

Of their own volition, his feet cut right and clipped into a determined stride across the room. When he reached her a few seconds later, she was deeply interested in a game of Macao and decidedly presenting him her profile. Even as he felt himself glowering down at her and drawing an undue amount of amused attention from patrons, he couldn't stop himself.

"Ah, don't give her the boot," pleaded one recently anointed marquess.

"She's the best thing to happen to The Archangel in ages," came another plea.

The smile curling Celia's lips twitched with devilry. She was enjoying this.

Gabriel suspected *this* wasn't about the attention, but rather his reaction to it.

He cleared his throat. "Duchess."

Her attention to the game didn't waver, as if she hadn't heard him.

Impossible woman.

A few snickers sounded around the table.

They were putting on a show.

He should've sold tickets.

"*Duchess*," he said with more command in his voice.

Her head angled, and with a beatific smile, she met his gaze. "Oh, Duke, I didn't notice you standing there."

Didn't notice, his arse.

"I would like a word with you."

"Then I suggest you get in line," she said, unbothered.

No one could be unbothered like a duchess.

"In my office."

That got another cut of her eyes. No mistaking that glimmer of challenge. "Have you made yourself my headmaster?"

Stunned silence followed, then a beat later came the waggles of eyebrows and knowing smirks.

"Or would that be head boy?"

That brought out the guffaws and even a wolf whistle.

The jibe referred to his age, of course.

Celia had come here to perform, and she wasn't disappointing.

Gabriel held out a hand. "If you will come with me."

She could refuse, of course—and she looked as if she might.

Then she shrugged a shoulder and came to her feet. She placed a silk gloved hand on his forearm. "Lead away, Duke."

CHAPTER TWELVE

$\mathcal{G}$abriel did precisely that—lead the duchess through the club and up the stairs.

With all eyes upon them, it felt closer to a parade.

Yet all the while his mind remained centered in one place—the patch of forearm where her slender hand rested.

It wasn't a saucy or salacious touch.

But it was *her* touch.

Her warmth penetrating superfine and linen.

After the events of Derby Day—well, the one event that kept haunting his dreams—he'd vowed never to touch her again.

In a technical sense, he wasn't touching her. She was touching him.

But it was semantics.

She was pressed against him—*again*.

They crossed the threshold to his office, and as he shut the door, her hand fell away. Of course, it did. She couldn't go on touching him.

He wished his forearm didn't feel the ache of loss.

She ambled over to a bookcase and began perusing titles, her fingers moving lightly along leather spines.

He stepped directly to his desk and cocked a hip on the edge. Though he was interested in knowing if she enjoyed reading, he wouldn't ask. It wasn't what he needed to know. What he needed to know was... "Are you foxed?"

With great care, she slid the book she'd been considering back into its place and turned. "I've had two glasses of wine. I'd call that a seeing-life-more-clearly-and-honestly amount."

She began moving down the wall of shelves. At the end, she opened a door and poked her head inside. "Is that where you live?"

"My private quarters," he said. "If it gets too late, I stay over."

Celia closed the door and pressed her back against it, watching him as if studying him—as if there was something she wanted to say, but wasn't sure how.

Gabriel found himself tensing with anticipation. He very much wanted to hear what this woman had to say. Gone was the good-time duchess, and in her place was a woman far more alluring. He saw why she was the most beautiful woman in London. But it wasn't her perfection that made it so.

It was the small imperfections. The front tooth that slightly overlapped the one beside it, giving her smile a subtly lopsided quality. A dimple in one cheek and not the other. Imperfect qualities that combined to make her looks more singular and arresting. Hers was a face that stuck in the mind long after she herself had gone.

Her head canted. "Every man in that room downstairs wants me."

The blood rushed hot in his veins. "I've no doubt of it."

"Except you."

He kept his mouth shut. He avoided lying when he could.

"At the Derby..." Her teeth worried her bottom lip for a quick instant. "I heard the most extraordinary rumor about the new Duke of Acaster."

Gabriel crossed his arms over his chest. "There's always gossip."

"Don't you want to know it?"

He shrugged, indifferent to any tattle about him.

Again, her teeth nibbled her bottom lip. "It was in regard to your flower."

Gabriel felt his brow lift. "My... *flower?*"

He was genuinely flummoxed. Until...

Her gaze fell and drifted down his chest and didn't stop until it reached a point below the waistband of his trousers.

Where it remained for three full seconds.

An eternity.

Long enough to give what lay behind thin superfine ideas.

Her luminous amber gaze lifted. "Your *flower.*"

A laugh, both bemused and aghast, burst from Gabriel. "I can't say I've ever heard it described in such a euphemistic light."

Celia pushed off the door, flustered. "Not the... oh... *thing...* itself. What you, *erm,* do with it."

And here Gabriel had been living his life thinking himself unshockable.

The duchess opened her mouth to continue, and he braced himself. It seemed she wasn't finished shocking him. "Or, more specifically, what you *don't* do with it."

And there it was—the most shocking revelation.

He, of course, wasn't shocked by the fact of his, *erm,* flower, but rather that it had become public knowledge.

"Are you expecting me to deny it?"

Her eyebrows lifted, and she blinked. Now, he'd shocked her. "You don't?"

"I don't see any reason to."

"Why is that?"

"Because it's true."

Her mouth fell open before she snapped it shut. Then she opened it again. "You *are* a virgin."

Gabriel held his silence. Should he be taking offense?

"How can that be?"

"I'm sure I don't need to explain the mechanics to you."

A blush crept up her décolletage and the exposed column of her throat. "Not how, but *how*?"

"This subject is no longer up for discussion."

"But... but..." she sputtered. "Look at you."

After she'd pushed off the door, she'd begun stepping incrementally forward. Likely, she hadn't noticed.

Gabriel had.

With her every step closer to him, his control slipped another notch.

"You must have women crawling all over you."

Now, she was not three feet away.

"You would have to beat them off with a stick, especially now you're a duke."

Two feet.

"You haven't a chance of keeping them away."

One foot.

Twelve easily bridgeable inches was all that separated his body from hers.

And the look in her eyes said she knew it.

She reached out, fingers hovering a nervous hairsbreadth from his jaw, a war waging within her eyes.

Gabriel waited—all the while, his control slipping.

Soft fingertips touched his cheek.

Still, he didn't move.

The hint of a smile played about her mouth.

She swayed forward, and her other hand planted itself on his thigh as she lifted onto the tips of her toes and shifted, her body perilously close to stretching up the length of his. Every cell in his body sprang to attention at the remembered feel of her lush curves against him.

She angled forward, and still he remained unmoving, her

mouth so close to his he could feel the whisper of her breath across his lips.

"What would it take to make you…"

And still he didn't touch her.

Instead, his hands remained at his sides, gripping the edge of the desk with such force the wood might splinter into dust.

Then she shifted farther and all space between them disappeared and her mouth pressed against his.

Soft… lush… sweet… slick…

An elemental spark flared to life inside Gabriel, and his hands could no longer remain chastely at his sides. Fingers that held a slight tremor found her waist, one hand brushing across the deep curve, the other trailing up her spine, as he breathed her in—*jasmine… bergamot… Celia…*

Celia's lush curves pressed against his body… Celia's mouth against his… Celia in his arms.

Though he had not the advantage of experience, his body followed carnal drive, the hand against the small of her back applying pressure until she was fast against him, the other hand tangling through the silky chignon at the nape of her neck, deepening the kiss.

He hadn't expected this.

That his senses would become overwhelmed with her.

That *this* would be all that mattered in the world.

This oneness.

This.

Instinct took over, and his hands tightened around her waist as he stood and, in a swift efficient turn, had their positions reversed so it was now her perched on the edge of the desk and him standing between her legs, hiking her skirts above her knees.

What was he doing?

He didn't take time to think.

Thought was unnecessary to the moment—only *feel*.

He had all the time in the world to think later.

Now, he had Celia.

Celia, exhaling sighs of pleasure into his mouth, honey amber eyes half-lidded with desire for... *him.*

Why would he stop to think? Not with her thighs in his hands, the creamy expanse of skin bare above her garters, all the way to her...

His cock throbbed its demand. He knew exactly what waited above the hiked hem of her skirts... *Her cunny.* And the cock that throbbed inside his trousers wanted nothing more than to break free and bury itself deep inside her. A feeling borne of need and gravitational pull—no experience necessary.

His gaze tore itself away and met her eyes. Within those depths shone the same need.

One hand clutched around his neck, her other hand trailed down his stubbled cheek... his neck slicked with perspiration... his chest... *lower...* The breath caught in his lungs. His every cell strained toward the inevitable destination of her fingers as they hesitated above the waistband of his trousers.

He only just stopped himself from howling with frustration and desperate need. It was possible he would dissolve into an unsated mound of lust if her fingers didn't continue their downward trajectory.

"What would it take to make you lose all control?" soft lips whispered against his mouth.

"You don't know?" scraped across his throat.

He felt her smile.

The fact was he'd lost all control—was in the very act of doing so.

And that was enough.

Enough to bring him back into himself and take a large step backward, breaking apart from her, his untouched cock throbbing its protest in his trousers, even as the duchess cried out, voicing her own frustration.

Panting, they stared at each other.

Movement caught his eye as she squeezed her legs together, but not before he grabbed a parting glimpse of a shadow. It could've been naught more than that. Or... it could've been her quim—pink and slick and ready.

For him.

For the hard cock throbbing inside his trousers.

Oh, he wanted to know the feel of that slick, pink, *ready* cunny wrapped around him.

He would be lost forever, he understood in a flash.

He would be lost to lust.

He would be lost to her.

"This should've never happened," he said, taking another step back. "You'll regret it on the morrow."

Celia touched fingertips to still-swollen lips. Lost in her own thoughts, she didn't seem to have heard him. "That cannot have been your first kiss."

Her words were met with silence.

Kiss?

Was that what they were calling what just happened?

A... *kiss?*

"Am I your first kiss?"

How to answer that question? For the answer lay between *no* and *yes*. "I've been kissed."

Her eyes narrowed. "Family doesn't count."

Right.

"I'll send for Ricard to see you out through the back entrance."

He didn't want her getting distracted downstairs and setting tongues wagging any more than she already had—and he didn't trust himself to escort her himself.

He didn't trust himself not to get her alone—any dark corner would do—and finish what they'd started.

He needed her gone so his brain could start functioning again.

He jerked the door open to send for Ricard, but found Dupratt standing there, his fist poised to knock. "Ah, Dupratt," said Gabriel with a rush of relief, "will you escort Her Grace to her carriage?" He turned to Celia. "It's been a..."

He became suddenly distracted by the tousled sight of her bodice gone askew and her mouth looking delectably kiss crushed.

That mouth was all but begging to be kissed again.

"*Pleasure?*" she finished for him.

Not the word he'd been searching for.

But, of course, what other word sufficed?

She swept around him and out of the room, leaving him and the conundrum of this night—of *himself*—in her wake.

The conundrum lay in the idea of beginnings and endings.

The kiss felt like a start.

And every start had a finish.

So, the question wasn't what had they done.

Rather, it was what had they started?

And what had they yet to finish?

For of that Gabriel was certain.

He and Celia had only begun.

And they were far from finished.

CHAPTER THIRTEEN

ASHCOTE HALL, FIVE DAYS LATER

*S*he'd run.

It wasn't something Celia was proud of.

But it was exactly what she'd done.

She'd kissed the duke...

Fled his club...

And hadn't stopped until she reached Ashcote Hall.

Undoubtedly, she was in breach of their bargain—but needs must when the Devil drives.

Yet standing here in Ashcote's stables after a long, satisfying afternoon of watching Ames train and take Light Skirt through her paces, she harbored not a single regret.

"Isn't that right, my girl?" she said to the filly, who whickered softly while a lad groomed her.

Celia offered a chunk of carrot, which the filly took gently off her palm, as she stroked the velvety nose and allowed the warm, calm feeling inspired by her horses to flow through her. Here, the world was put to rights.

"Your Grace."

Her head groom, Mr. Haig, strode down the center aisle. Thirty or so years her senior, there was nothing the Scotsman didn't know about horses. Without preamble, he extended a letter. "The advertisement in the horse rags is getting traction."

Celia scanned the letter from the Earl of Coningsby, and a feeling of excitement stirred within her. "Coningsby has a serious interest in improving his stock."

"Aye."

"He's known to be a good owner, too." That was important.

"And ye noted his specifications?"

"He wants a foal from *King Arthur* and *Silky Sadie*."

"Aye."

"Which means he wants to mix the Godolphin and Darley lines." Celia folded the letter.

"A way of getting a bit of both Matchem and Eclipse into his stables."

As all English Thoroughbreds descended from three stallions—the Darley Arabian, the Byerley Turk, and the Godolphin Arabian—breeders were able to trace most characteristics ranging from temperament to speed to the relation of withers to quarters through breeding stock records and descendants. Breeding was so precise that it had almost become whittled down to a science. That *King Arthur* and *Silky Sadie* were descended from two of the last century's great Thoroughbred winners—Matchem and Eclipse—made them a much-desired sire and mare pairing.

"Write Coningsby back," Celia instructed. "Tell him that good faith money is required. Fifty pounds should do it. If he's serious, he won't flinch."

Haig nodded and, not one to mince words, set about his task.

For the first time since she'd decided to use her stables as a stud, Celia allowed a glimmer of hope to find purchase. Perhaps...

Perhaps she could make a success of it.

And if she could manage that, perhaps she might not need a

husband to provide for her at the end of her three-year bargain with Acaster.

Perhaps she could be an independent woman of means.

The instant she allowed herself to think it, she shied away from the idea. It was too bright to behold directly. Who was she to think she could successfully undertake such an enterprise when the reality was she'd never succeeded at anything in her life?

For now, she had a glimmer to cling to.

It was enough.

And she supposed she had the duke to thank.

Oh, the duke...

She'd avoided thinking about him these last five days.

And here she was—thinking about the duke.

A throat cleared behind her. Celia turned to find a scullery maid standing with her hands clasped before her, eyes demurely cast to her feet.

"Yes?" Celia asked, mildly, so as not to frighten the girl off. Duchesses were, apparently, fearsome creatures.

"Cook says to tell ye the evenin' meal is ready." Then the girl bobbed a curtsy and was off on legs like springs.

Celia only noticed now that the sky was graying with encroaching dusk. Though early for the evening meal by London standards, she tended to lose all track of time out here.

Wasn't it wonderful?

A faraway smile on her mouth, her feet turned right toward the cottage, instead of left toward the manor house.

Upon arriving with the dawn five days ago, her first order of business had been to move her belongings from Ashcote's manor house and into the estate's small thatched-roof cottage, claiming it as her dower house.

If a house could have a personality, the cottage would be characterized as bright and cheery with the sun shining through its mullioned windows and birds trilling in surrounding trees.

Besides, it was impossible for her to stay in the manor house.

Not with the chance of the duke occupying it any time the fancy struck.

In fact, that was one of the reasons she'd had to leave London.

Because he occupied it—not only the St. James's Square mansion, but *London*.

Town simply wasn't big enough for both of them.

Nay, that wasn't precisely true.

London wasn't big enough for her desire.

Not after that kiss.

Celia had kissed men.

Or, more accurately, she'd had kisses bestowed upon her by men. A young man at a ball once, with his inexperienced, slobbery mouth. An old man—her dead husband, in fact—with his thin, dry lips the consistency of parchment paper. Kisses she'd had to endure either from embarrassment or obligation.

But never a kiss like the one she'd experienced five nights ago.

A kiss freely given.

A kiss that sparked places inside her alight.

Places she'd been given to understand were missing from her.

Places that, even at this very moment, felt very much alive.

Desire, sparked alive.

And she'd learned something more.

Though she'd attempted, again and again, to put the duke in his place by using his age as a weapon, she had a fact to face.

He wasn't a lad, was he?

The duke was very much a man.

Young, yes, but assured and capable.

As Celia entered the cottage, she tossed her hat onto a footstool and called out to Mrs. Davies. "I'll pop upstairs for a quick freshen up." She took the stairs at a quick trot, her stomach giving an impatient rumble. The evening meal had filled the cottage with its delicious scent. "I need to get the smell of horse off me."

The truth was she preferred it out here to the manor house. This cottage held no bad memories attached to it—only good ones to be made.

She liked the way that idea made her feel. Optimistic thinking was a habit she might be able to take to.

In the bedroom, she was careful not to close the door all the way. If she did, she would have to call for a servant to open it from the corridor side. A man was coming to fix the lock on the morrow.

With the efficiency of a duchess accustomed to dressing herself, she shed the drab workaday woolen dress she wore for days spent in the stables and slipped into the gown Mrs. Davies had laid out for her.

The housekeeper wasn't best pleased that Celia had insisted on decamping to the cottage. It wasn't fitting for the station of duchess—Mrs. Davies's words. But these last five days, Celia had been able to draw a proper breath in a way she hadn't in a decade.

And that settled it.

She'd stayed.

Dressed for the evening meal, she caught an upward drift of voices from the ground floor and hesitated at the landing at the top of the stairs. One feminine voice. *Mrs. Davies.* The other masculine... with the consistency of crushed velvet... An assured voice...

Celia's heart threatened to stop in her chest.

His voice.

Here.

On light cat feet, she descended the steps, her ears attuned to what snippets of conversation she might catch.

"May I take your coat and hat, Your Grace?" said Mrs. Davies, as if he'd been expected.

"I don't think I'll be—"

"Yes, Mrs. Davies," said Celia from her place midway way down the staircase. "Thank you."

Both sets of eyes swung toward her.

Hardly breaking eye contact with Celia, the duke handed over his coat and hat to the housekeeper.

"And, Mrs. Davies," said Celia, "please set an additional place at the table for the duke."

* * *

GABRIEL HADN'T INTENDED to stay.

But it had been five days since, well, since *that* night.

Mrs. Fairfax had assured him all was well, that the duchess couldn't be expected to stay away from her stables for weeks on end.

He'd tried to listen. He had. But he'd needed to see for himself.

To see with his own eyes that all was well with Celia.

Of course, he wasn't here to see her for any other reason.

Then he'd arrived at Ashcote Hall and been told the duchess wasn't there.

"What do you mean she isn't here?" he'd demanded, myriad scenarios running through his mind. Had she met with misfortune on the road? Highwaymen? Had she been kidnapped?

"Of course she's here," he said, needing it to be true. No duchesses would be lost on his watch.

The butler, however, remained unruffled. "She's moved to the dower cottage."

Gabriel's brow furrowed. "Why would she—"

But he knew.

First, as the dowager duchess, it was her right.

Though that wasn't the real reason.

The real reason shone in her eyes now.

And neither of them needed to speak it aloud.

The kiss.

Mrs. Davies left the room with his coat and hat, and Celia finished descending the stairs. She was a vision in ivory muslin. He'd seen her in finer dress, but this was how he liked her best— her beauty unadorned.

"If you will follow me."

She didn't break step as she passed, leading him into a small, unassuming dining room.

Before he could pull her chair out for her, she raised a staying hand. "There is no need to stand on formality here."

Gabriel understood what she was actually saying.

He wasn't to come within five feet of her.

Whether it was because she didn't trust him or herself, he didn't know.

Still, he complied with her wishes and took the seat opposite hers. Though warm, flickering candlelight imbued the room with an intimate feel, he couldn't feel at ease. The duchess wasn't pleased with him. Displeasure showed in the intangibles. The brisk snap of her napkin before she laid it on her lap. Her avoidance of his eyes as she concentrated on her first course—a cold soup of some sort.

In truth, he wasn't able to taste it.

What the duchess was telling him without actually telling him was that while she was obliged to dine with him, she was under no obligation to converse.

Which left Gabriel little choice but to watch her eat from beneath hooded eyes. The taking of a meal had never been a sensual process for him. He thought of food as a necessity, some foods being better than others, but not much beyond that. But the woman seated across from him appeared to hold a different view of a meal beyond mere sustenance.

His eyes found themselves following each spoonful of soup to her mouth. The parting of cherry lips... the insertion of the spoon... the slide of the spoon out... the flick of tongue to catch an unruly morsel…

His mouth went dry, and his body went hot—heat racing through his veins, setting fire to nerve endings, centering in one place.

His cock.

Which had gone hard as stone.

Watching this woman savor a meal incited sensations within him he hadn't known were possible. Certainly, he'd experienced a hard cock. Every morning at waking, in fact.

But this hard cock held a demand.

And a plea.

To be satisfied.

By her.

Her cherry lips, more specifically.

Right.

He couldn't go on like this, staring at her like a lecher.

His cock couldn't take it.

He cleared his throat with more force than necessary, and she lifted her questioning gaze.

He was the one who had tracked her down, those luminous, amber eyes said, so out with it.

What was in his mind, he couldn't speak. So, he settled for… "Aren't you supposed to be in London with my sisters?"

Even as he asked the question, he felt a fool.

The duchess set her spoon down, carefully dabbed her mouth, and a smile condescended to curve about her lips. "Your sisters are thriving. Your Grace—"

"*Gabriel*," he said without thinking. "I want you to call me Gabriel."

Irritation flashed behind her eyes, and he couldn't help feeling a mild sense of triumph. She'd wanted to place distance between them with that superior *Your Grace*, and he wasn't allowing her.

"*Gabriel*," she said, deliberately drawing out each syllable. "All is proceeding according to our plan and agreement. My stables needed me, which is also part of our agreement."

She had him there, and the look in her eyes said she knew it.

Which left him with the other matter that had been nagging at him since Derby Day. Something he had no right to inquire about, but since he was here and they'd already strayed beyond the bounds of what was proper and improper...

"Do you have a history with the Duke of Rakesley?"

There it was.

The question he had no right to ask.

But the idea had become intolerable.

Her soup spoon stopped halfway to her mouth. "Not precisely."

"Then *imprecisely*?"

She exhaled a deep sigh. "If you must know, I was under the impression that Rakesley and I had an understanding, but—" She shook her head and shrugged a shoulder, as if that said everything.

It said nothing.

"*But?*"

"*But* he ran off with his jockey."

"That's rather... bold."

Even for a duke.

"And married her."

"*Her?*"

"His jockey was... *is*... a woman."

"Ah." That made moderately more sense. "*Gemma*."

Celia nodded.

"And you were heartbroken, I suppose." He tried to speak the words in an offhand manner, but feared they rather revealed the opposite.

"Hardly," she scoffed. "It would have been a marriage of mutual understanding."

"An understanding of...?" He wasn't following.

"We both love our stables," she said, her voice tight.

And Gabriel understood. "It was Rakesley who was supposed to save your stables."

She nodded and took a sip of wine.

"And, instead, you got me."

She blinked and met his gaze. "Something like that."

Gabriel should leave it.

He knew he should leave it, but... "Here's what I don't understand."

Wariness shimmered about her. "Yes?"

"Why seek out another marriage if your first was so terrible?"

Her eyebrows gathered, very like a storm cloud.

"I mean," he continued, unable to interpret her sudden shift of mood, "you have all the elements at Ashcote to run a successful stud and racing operation."

"I have the horses, yes, but I never had the blunt until..." Her lips pressed into a firm line.

He knew how the sentence ended. "Until me."

It was simply the truth.

However, the storm on her face abated not one bit. "What do you know about my *terrible* marriage?"

Blast. He'd put his foot in it.

"Was it my cousin?" she pressed.

Gabriel chose his words carefully. "Mrs. Fairfax merely related it was your father who arranged your marriage with the late duke, leaving you no choice in the matter. The rest was implied."

That marriage was no easy thing to be endured.

Those had been Mrs. Fairfax's exact words.

Unconscionable.

Another word used by Mrs. Fairfax.

"Were you—" Dread of the answer filled him. "Were you mistreated?"

The answer shone plain in Celia's eyes. "Sometimes," she

began, as if measuring the weight of words yet unspoken, "there would be bruises."

Gabriel's hands reflexively clenched into fists. Hands that had never once clenched into fists in all his life.

"Abrasions, too," she continued. "On my wrists." She swallowed. "On my neck."

Shock traced through Gabriel. "I've heard of such proclivities."

Eyes that had seen too much of the unsavory side of life met his. "A wide chasm exists between proclivities and crime." She didn't speak the words in anger, but rather as clarification. "The word *consent* is the only one that can bridge it."

And the duke hadn't received hers.

"Could you have gone to the authorities?"

Her eyebrows crinkled together. "Who holds authority over a duke? You would know the answer to that question by now."

No one.

"Ten years can feel longer than a lifetime and more akin to an eternity. I found solace in one place."

"Your horses."

She exhaled, like she'd been holding her breath, and reached for her wine. "If you don't mind, I'd rather not spend the rest of the evening poring over my failures."

Gabriel would allow her to change the subject if she liked, but he couldn't let her words stand unchallenged. "None of your past was *your* failure. It was the failure of those who were supposed to have protected you. Your youth and joy were stolen from you."

"That's not the way society sees it," she said, trying for dismissive.

The echo of past pain in her eyes told a different story.

"It's the way *I* see it."

CHAPTER FOURTEEN

$\mathcal{C}$elia's throat went tight with emotion she couldn't name.

It's the way I see it.

Gabriel's eyes, so sincere and serious... they saw *her*.

She must change the subject.

She must.

It was possible she was beginning to like this duke.

"How did you come to be a gaming hell owner?" Men usually liked to talk about themselves. "After all, you're a—" Sudden hesitation stopped the words in her mouth. "*Upright* man."

Good. She'd almost called him a good man.

But she couldn't go so far as that.

She wasn't entirely convinced there were any good men.

His mouth twitched, as if he might smile. Smiles were few and far between with this serious man. The twitching ceased, and the smile didn't materialize—and Celia found herself staring at his mouth.

She'd kissed that mouth.

With all the passion she had in her.

And she found she wanted to kiss it again.

It had been his first kiss.

But it had been her first *real* kiss.

And she wanted a second one.

Desperately.

His throat cleared, startling her gaze up. She found a question in his eyes—one she didn't want to answer.

"I had a family to support, didn't I," he said, matter of fact.

"Pardon?" *A family to support?* "Is there something I don't know about you?"

This time a smile did break through. A reserved one. But a smile, nonetheless. She didn't mind that it was at her expense. It wasn't a mean smile.

In fact, she understood something fundamental about this serious and sincere man.

He didn't have a mean bone in his body.

It might be his most attractive quality—which was saying something.

"My father died when I was eight years old."

"Oh."

He'd said *I* had a family to support. Celia almost didn't want to ask the next question... "And your mother?"

"She perished from a swift-moving fever six months later. Saskia and Viveca also caught it, but they barely had symptoms." He stared into the untouched glass of wine before him. "Even before Mum passed, we'd run through most of Papa's savings, and the bills were beginning to go unpaid."

That didn't square with the little she knew of his past. "How was it you received a scholarship to attend Eton College?"

"A stroke of conscience." Eyes the clarity of sea-blue glass lifted and met hers. "My father was a barrister's clerk in Gray's Inn and was struck down by a dray horse while attending their business. Mr. Ainsworth, the head of chambers, felt badly about the family's turn of events and arranged for me to have a scholarship to his *alma mater*, Eton College.

Her eyebrows lifted. "You went to boarding school at age eight?"

"Nine," he said. "And stayed until I graduated at sixteen."

"You must've been incredibly lonely."

Opaque emotion flickered behind his eyes. "I missed my sister Tessa terribly, as she's only a year older than me. It should've been her who went, in truth. She has an even better head for numbers than me."

"It must've been hard on you both."

A faraway laugh escaped him. "She demanded that I write her twice a week and pass along everything we learned in maths. When I came home during holidays, we spent most of the time going over lessons. Though young, she was determined to hold the family together in London during my education years. Miraculously, she succeeded."

"And I would wager you never shed a single one of the tears that clogged your throat as you lay in bed at night."

Celia knew loneliness—and she knew something of this man and perhaps the boy he'd been.

"I can tell you, in case you hadn't discerned this for yourself," he said. "The dark alleyways and snickets of the East End have nothing on Eton, its hallowed halls filled with gangs of mother-less lordlings thrown together to fend for themselves. One doesn't show weakness—or one is cut down."

From what Celia had observed of the adult versions of those lordlings, she would posit not much changed as they aged.

"Then everything flipped around."

"How so?"

"One day I was a nobody scholarship student, and the next my aptitude for numbers revealed itself. I'd always known it was there, of course, but word started getting around and, like that, those standoffish lordlings started calling me *old chap* and *chum*."

"They wanted you to revise for them."

He nodded. "But I didn't care about becoming *chums* or advancing myself socially. I cared about one thing."

"Your sisters."

"And their ability to have a roof above their heads and food on their table." He shrugged. "So, a fee was charged."

"How gauche of you," Celia said with no small amount of irony.

In truth, she was impressed.

By the enterprising boy he was.

By the man he was today.

This man was a force.

Strangely, she felt slightly envious of his sisters—their great good luck to be under his care. Celia had never been cared for in such a way—by such a man.

He spread his hands wide. "And my reputation grew, as did my business interests."

"You *are* a good man, aren't you?" Celia asked without thinking.

His head cocked. "Does that come as such a surprise?"

Celia went hot with immediate embarrassment. How to answer such a question?

Yes.

That had been her instinctive response.

But in his case, it didn't feel right—or true.

She had a business arrangement with this man—which was all that would ever exist between them.

Then why did it feel like it wanted to be more?

Right.

She pushed to a stand, her chair a loud scrape against pine floorboards with the suddenness of the movement. "I believe that's the evening meal at an end."

* * *

RATHER THAN REMOVE himself to the manor house like Celia was so clearly suggesting, Gabriel settled back in his chair and observed.

Her flushed cheeks.

Her skittish eyes.

Her need to be busy and out of this room.

She wished to be well shot of him.

Why?

The meal had been civil, and the conversation, too. In fact, their most civil conversation to date.

And yet she appeared more than a little unnerved.

He wished she would sit down.

Instead, the woman began stacking dishes.

"Don't you have servants for that?"

She kept adding to the pile until a wobbly, clanking heap of china from plates to saucers to teacups perched atop her extended arms. It would surely topple over any second now. Obviously, the duchess was new to clearing a table.

Gabriel couldn't help himself. He stood and only just caught a teacup on its descent to the floor. "Here," he said, commandeering the top half of the dishes.

"You don't have to..." The protest died away. How could one argue against the pragmatism of his assistance?

"After you," he said.

She hesitated. She didn't want him to follow her into the kitchen, that much was clear. But she couldn't very well refuse his help, either. Not only was he offering help, but he was the duke—and one didn't refuse the duke.

Gabriel could see how one could become accustomed to always having one's way—and how it would inevitably corrupt.

He followed her through the cottage until they reached the end of a dark, narrow corridor that opened into the kitchen, the room empty of all servants.

"You can still live like a duchess, you know."

He had to say it.

She stopped before a wide basin with about six inches of standing water. Carefully, she set her dishes down and stepped aside, indicating he do the same. "After Edwin died, I started living less like a duchess and more like me, I guess. I prefer to clean up after myself and keep my own hours." She shrugged. "Besides, I don't like imposing on people."

"It's literally their job to serve you."

"Not after dinner is served."

And that was the matter settled.

With every conversation and passing day, this duchess proved to be an altogether different duchess than the one he'd expected.

The next instant, she was sweeping around him and tossing over her shoulder, "You can find your way out."

And she was gone.

But Gabriel's feet didn't point toward the door that would lead him outside and to the manor house. Instead, they pointed toward the corridor she'd disappeared down—and he was following in her wake of jasmine and bergamot and up the stairs she'd ascended. Light glowed an orange rectangle around a door barely cracked open.

Her door—her *bedroom* door.

He shouldn't go where his feet now pointed.

He should point them in the opposite direction.

And yet he couldn't.

Step by foolish step, he moved toward her door... pushing it open...

Across the room lit by a single candle, she stood before her dressing table. The mirror was angled away, so she didn't see him in its reflection. She wasn't in the state of undress in which he'd found her at the modiste's, but rather she'd begun removing pins from her hair.

Gabriel stood, transfixed.

Pin by pin, the thick, twisted cable of hair at the nape of her neck loosened, until the final pin was pulled and the sable mass spilled like a silken waterfall to the small of her back.

Somehow, though she was fully clothed, this view felt more intimate than having seen her in chemise and stays.

And the longer he stood here without revealing his presence, the more wrong it felt.

When she reached for the buttons at the side of her gown, he knew he could wait no longer. He cleared his throat.

On a gasp, she startled around. Then wide amber eyes registered his presence, and she gasped again, her cheeks flushed crimson, her eyes bright, and her hair a wild tumble over her shoulders.

He'd seen beautiful women.

He'd been attracted to beautiful women.

He'd been stirred by them and even had them invade his dreams.

But never had he beheld a beautiful woman like *this*—in utter disarray.

But there she stood.

And here he stood, captivated.

He opened his mouth to speak, but the words refused to flow.

"Have you lost your sense of direction?"

"Pardon?"

"On your way out of my cottage."

Ah. Well… "As a matter of fact," he began, but she shushed him. Presumably so he wouldn't wake the servants.

So, he took the only logical action and stepped fully inside the bedroom and pushed the door shut behind him. As the latch clicked, she rushed forward with a futile, "No!" as she tried to catch the door before it closed.

Now, she was staring up at him with a thunderstorm on her face.

"I can assure you that you're safe with me." He couldn't help feeling slightly offended by her reaction.

She heaved a deep, resigned sigh. "We're stuck here until morning."

Gabriel's eyebrows dug trenches into his forehead. "Of course, we're not."

He reached for the handle and pulled. The door remained resolutely in place. He jiggled the handle. It didn't budge. He placed his free hand on top of the other and pulled harder, putting all his weight into it.

Nothing.

He glanced over his shoulder and found Celia with arms crossed, watching him make a fool of himself. "There's a latch on the outside of the door that catches and locks when the door is fully closed."

"On the *outside* of the door?" That made no sense.

"The work of a former Duke of Acaster." Celia's jaw clenched and released. "As to why he had it installed that way, it couldn't have been anything good."

Gabriel didn't understand what was happening here. He understood a faulty lock, but not the situation itself. "Ring the bell and send for a servant."

"No."

"*No?*"

"I won't disturb my staff at night."

"Surely, there are exceptions to be made," he said, trying for logic.

She shook her head.

He pointed across the room. "I could climb down from that window. It can't be more than twenty feet," he said with all sincerity. He'd never climbed out of a window in his life, but he supposed there was a first time for everything.

Eyebrows crinkled, she stared at him. Then it happened—a sudden chirrup of laughter burst from her. "You would rather jump out a window than be alone with me?"

Gabriel felt the tips of his ears heat. "That isn't quite true."

Or at all true.

Her head canted. "Then what is it?"

"The gentlemanly thing, I would've thought."

"Ah," she got out. Her laughter hadn't finished with her.

"*Ah*, what?" He was growing seriously irritated, even as the certainty set in that he would not like what he was about to hear.

"No one has told you the secret about being a gentleman."

"I know more than a few of their secrets, I can assure you," he said, purposefully misconstruing her words.

Her hair atumble about her shoulders, she took a step, as if to let him in on the secret. He doubted she realized she'd moved closer. "Once a gentleman, never a gentleman."

"Pardon?"

She lifted her hands as if helpless to the facts. "A gentleman is under no obligation to behave like a gentleman—or *be* one, for that matter."

Another laugh escaped her, this one hard as steel. A laugh that had been forged through fire. A laugh at complete odds with the lush and inviting appearance of her.

The laughter finally echoed away, and it was only them staring into each other's eyes. "You don't have a high opinion of men, do you?"

If she'd been inclined to laugh again, the impulse fell away with her smile. Unexpected vulnerability shone within the luminous depths of her eyes. "Perhaps I'm a dried-up, embittered harridan, and my opinion matters not in the least."

"You're none of those things."

Gabriel wasn't sure of the factual truth of his words, but he felt them to be true—which was an altogether novel experience for him. In his day-to-day dealings, he put his trust in the concrete—facts and numbers. Faith didn't factor in. He had no need for faith. But here he was, putting faith in a woman—heeding intuition and knowing in his gut that feeling to be true.

In her life, this duchess had played many roles for many

people, but, here, the two of them alone in her bedroom, she could be...

Herself.

Only a few feet separated them. If he chose, he could reach out and twine his fingers through her hair and know its silken feel.

In fact, he might've been on the verge of such an action, when her cherry lips parted and she said, "You can sleep on the floor."

Intention fell from his hand.

What would it take to make you lose all control?

Increasingly less and less.

CHAPTER FIFTEEN

*H*e'd been about to touch her.

Celia's skin had gone alight with the certainty.

She'd no choice but to put a stop to it.

She took two necessary steps backward, returned to her dressing table, and began busying herself with... nothing of import. Moving a brush from one side of the table to the other. Gathering hair pins into a tidy pile. It was the appearance of industry.

She couldn't let another touch happen—*not again.*

For she couldn't be held responsible for what would follow.

"If you open the bottom drawer of the wardrobe," she called over her shoulder, "you'll find a blanket."

Behind her, heavy footsteps crossed the room and a drawer opened and closed, followed by a soft shushing sound as heavy wool dropped to the floor.

"And I'll need you to turn around while I, *erm*..." It would sound suggestive any way she said it. "Disrobe."

More shuffling of feet. "My back is to you."

As Celia freed gown buttons and let the garment fall to her feet, she didn't need to check that he was keeping his word.

Somehow, in these last few weeks, this duke had become a man she could trust.

The very thought had the nerves jangling through her veins.

For in trusting him, she found she could trust herself less.

It was the way she reacted to him. Take now, for instance. She'd wanted with all her being to kiss him again.

With a few tugs of the ties, her stays came loose. She folded the garment and set it on a stool. Stockings discarded and tucked away, she pulled on her dressing robe over her chemise. When she turned, she found he, too, had made himself more comfortable, having shed his coat, waistcoat, cravat, and boots.

"I hope you don't mind," he said, with a return to formality.

"Not at all," she replied, equally formal, recognizing that formality was their best hope for the long night to come.

Here they were.

Two people locked in a room.

A *bedroom*.

A single candle lit, its flickering light warm and inviting.

Two people who knew intimacies about one another.

Two people who might like each other.

Two people who had kissed.

Two people who wanted to do it again.

Her gaze fell to the open V of his shirt. A fuzz of light hair... the shadowy hint of muscles. And lower... his shirt tucked into the waistband of his trousers, no hint of excess around his middle. Of course, there wouldn't be. And lower still, well... *thighs*.

In an attempt to shake all thoughts of his thighs away, she again busied herself, this time grabbing the candlestick and crossing the room to her...

Oh.

Bed.

She carefully set it on the nightstand and considered the bed before her.

She was supposed to lay there and… *sleep?*

With him but a few feet away on the floor?

She swiveled around. She couldn't look at the bed.

Of course, that left her looking at him.

Which was worse.

He'd taken a seat in an armchair, legs sprawled before him to accommodate his…

Thighs.

Thighs that would surely haunt her dreams.

Before she could ask, he said, "This will do for me."

Formal. Honorable. Trustworthy.

She was coming to appreciate all those qualities about this man, she was. But…

Her body found itself wishing he'd be a little less so of each.

One thing she knew for certain, however. There was no way she was sleeping in her bed with him sitting in this chair and his shirt revealing that V of lightly fuzzed chest, legs in a lazy sprawl, looking for all the world like a man waiting to be ravished.

Looking as if he hadn't the faintest idea.

Oh, how was she to survive this night?

She lowered onto the matching armchair adjacent to his.

That was a start.

After avoiding his steady gaze for as long as she could, she glanced up and realized she yet had a question for this man.

A question she shouldn't ask.

A question she had no right to ask.

A question she couldn't not ask.

The night was to be a long one, and she needed to know. "About your sisters," she began, tentative, "and your support of them these last several years."

What was she thinking? She most definitely couldn't ask the question.

"Yes?"

She had his full, fixed attention.

"Is that why—" She swallowed. "Is that why you abstain—"

No, that wasn't the correct way to ask.

"Why you're a—"

That wasn't either.

Oh, she couldn't ask, after all.

"A virgin?" he finished for her, unflinching blue eyes searching hers.

She nodded for the knot in her throat.

He continued, unbothered. "I couldn't risk the family I already have by starting a new one."

Celia saw his reasoning, but... "It's so logical." Another thought occurred to her. "And you're a duke now. The only risk you'll have for the rest of your life is what you introduce into it." She should stop here. Enough said. But... she couldn't. "Don't you ever just want to—" She searched for the correct word. "Let feeling take you where it will?"

Unreadable emotion passed behind his eyes. Like her, he appeared on the edge of saying something he shouldn't.

How she wished he would.

"You and I are alike, you know," emerged from his throat on a crushed velvet rumble.

Surprise lit through her. "We are?"

He gave a slow nod. "Your passion goes into your stables. Mine into my investments."

When he stated it like that...

Sudden clarity struck Celia.

All that passion...

None of it going into another person.

And she knew.

Only with this man could she experience it.

From the beginning, she'd seen him as temptation.

But he was more than temptation.

He was passion personified.

Her passion personified.

On legs that trembled not from hesitancy but from anticipation, she stood.

He settled back in his chair and observed. *Assessing... wary.* He had every reason to be, she supposed.

She took a step that halved the short distance between them.

"I want you."

"You shouldn't."

"You want me."

More impetuous words spoken. Another step taken.

His mouth twisted. "I shouldn't."

"Shouldn't you?"

She now stood above him. His head tipped back, so he could hold her gaze, his throat exposed. Without hesitation, she bent forward and trailed feathery fingers down the thick column, the heavy beat of his pulse visible, down the open V of his shirt, the soft hairs of his chest tickling fingertips, the muscles beneath, hard and unyielding... farther down to the waistband of his trousers. She didn't need to run fingertips over his engorged manhood to prove its existence. It was plain to see.

Yet her fingers hesitated. She wouldn't touch *him* without permission.

Her knee nudged his thighs open wide enough for her to step between and press her mouth to his ear. "All this pent-up passion and such an easy solution for it."

"Which is?"

"Pour it into each other."

If he said *no*, she would absolutely burst into flame.

The length of him—so hard and long and *ready*—pushing against the fabric of his trousers needed to be inside her.

Now.

"And then we'll be, *erm*, satisfied."

It was a lie.

Once she had this man, she would never be satisfied again.

"Because you're unsatisfied now?"

161

"Very."

"And you think I could satisfy you?"

"Yes." *Undoubtedly.* "We could satisfy each other." Uncertainty crept in. "Unless..."

He turned so his gaze held hers. *"Unless?"*

"Unless you think I'm the sort of woman who couldn't satisfy you?"

* * *

THE WOMAN WAS TRYING to kill him.

Instinctively, Gabriel covered her hand with his, and dragged it lower, holding her eyes and his breath as he pressed her palm onto his swollen length. "Does this answer your question?"

Slender fingers contracted around him through superfine, and Gabriel sucked in a sharp breath.

He was lost.

As if he'd ever stood a chance.

He reached up and cupped the back of her head, pulling her face toward his, her hair falling around them like a dense curtain, creating an intimate space of only they two. His mouth met hers.

Sweet.

As he remembered.

Deeply, irretrievably, he fell into the kiss, all his senses wrapped in this woman who was now perched on his lap, her knees straddling him, her fingers frantically working the buttons of his trousers.

Urgency had him tangling his tongue with hers, penetrating her mouth, a hand now cupping the heavy weight of her breast. Through the gossamer-thin chemise peeked hard, rosy nipples. He angled his head to suck one nub into his mouth and the final button of his falls slipped free. Trembly fingertips feathered across the bare skin of his swollen cock.

A pained groan escaped him, and he lifted his gaze. Eyes glazed with lust met his. "I want you inside me. But—"

"*But?*"

"But not if it isn't what you really want."

He didn't hesitate. "What more could a man want?"

Nothing had been more true in his life. His entire being felt purposed for this act—to join his body with hers.

He pushed her chemise to her hips, savoring their creamy feel, his gaze transfixed by every new inch of skin revealed.

This act was everything he'd never allowed himself to imagine.

And there it was—her quim, exposed to his gaze. A slick pink slit beneath sable curls.

His cock throbbed at the sight. What it lacked in experience, it made up for with instinct.

It knew it needed to be inside her.

"Celia," he growled... *pleaded.*

"You're so big," she said, as if in awe... as if in worship.

Worship... It played a role in this act.

One hand wrapped around his length, with her other hand she reached for his shoulder, and lifted to hover. His hands trailed beneath the gathered fabric of her chemise, her mouth humid and warm against the whorl of his ear, her ragged breath sending goosebumps across his skin.

Time stopped mattering as she positioned his length below her, the crown pressed against her slick cunny.

He would surely combust.

Slowly, deliberately, she lowered onto him, her sex impossibly tight around his length. A long moan poured from her parted mouth, and her head tipped back.

Pleasure pumped through him with every beat of his heart—rushing through veins to nerve endings lit alive. The pleasure of the physical—and a pleasure of another sort. Pleasure in the pleasure he was giving her, only confirming this was no mere physical act.

This act possessed layers—and however he might strive, he would never reach the center.

But he could try.

With the right person.

With *her*.

Her head arched back, as he pressed his mouth to her neck, tasting her, the heavy throb of her pulse beneath his tongue, *feeling* her... grasped in his hands... wrapped around his cock.

His cock... Somehow, it both ached and experienced the most exquisite pleasure imaginable.

And another feeling, too.

Urgency.

His hands tightened around her lush hips and with slow intention moved her up and then—*oh*—down on him.

Her breath caught, followed by a sharp cry.

Alarm screamed through him. "Have I hurt you?"

Her eyes opened and caught his.

"Never," she whispered. "My body and your body..." She swiveled her hips, grinding against him. "They were made for this. You're so big and hard and, *oh*, I need you to do it again."

Again, he brought her down on him, and again, she cried out and a feeling... a *drive*... came from nowhere and overtook him.

Though he'd never been with a woman, he knew this feeling. He had a hand, after all.

He wanted to stave it off, somehow.

But she looked so beautiful being ravished on his cock... and she *felt* so good being ravished on his cock... There was no escaping the inevitability relentlessly pursuing him.

"Are you about to spill?" she uttered.

"Aye," he exhaled into her neck.

The next moment, she lifted entirely off him and wrapped her hand around his throbbing length. All it took was a few tugs and his head was tipped back and he was shouting his release to the ceiling, literal stars bursting behind his eyes.

A few seconds or minutes or hours later, his lids slitted open to find her using her dressing gown to clean him up.

"Did you..." He couldn't finish the question.

She shook her head.

Embarrassment swept through him.

He had...

And she hadn't...

That wasn't right.

And she didn't seem the least upset about it—but rather... accepting.

That wasn't right, either.

In fact, it was intolerable.

He cupped her perfect, generous bottom in both hands and said, "Hold on," as he came to his feet and her legs wrapped around his waist, a laugh escaping her.

But he didn't laugh. He was determined to do something about this imbalance of orgasms.

It occurred to him that this particular tally sheet had never been balanced for her.

And he was the man to put it to rights.

He lowered her to the bed's cushy surface.

She propped herself onto her elbows and watched him lift his shirt over his head and fling it away. Then it was off with his trousers. Naked, he stood before her, his cock already at half-mast.

Her gaze lowered, and she bit her lower lip between her teeth.

Now, there was no half to it.

"Again?" She blinked in disbelief. "So soon?"

His gaze swept over her body, her curves, as she observed him with as hungry a look as woman ever gave man. Her legs were bent, but knocked at the knees, obscuring his view of her sweet cunny.

Guided by instinct, he took a leg in each hand and pressed them open, bussing a kiss to the creamy inner skin of this thigh, then the other. Her scent was no longer mere jasmine and bergamot, but *woman*, too. He followed instinct higher. He needed a taste of…

Her.

"What are you—"

He gave her slit a long, slow stroke, the skin delicate and slippery beneath his tongue, and stopped the question in her mouth.

What he was doing was self-evident.

His tongue was having its way with her.

He stayed away from cards, dice, and horses. Never drank more than a sip of whiskey for reasons of sociability. But this woman… He had no resistance to her. She'd slid into his veins, and now he would always be wanting.

Her arms stretched over her head, hands clasping the coverlet, back arched, legs splayed, as she strained toward his tongue.

"There is a place," she said, breathless. "Where I…"

He lifted his head and met her gaze. "Where you…?"

Her gaze shifted, suddenly shy. He waited. Her eyes met his again. "Where I touch myself."

And he'd thought his cock couldn't get any harder.

"Show me."

He had no qualms with being instructed. It was how one gained knowledge.

And how to bring this woman pleasure was a knowledge he couldn't live without.

He detected vulnerability within her eyes. To give another person this power over one's secrets—the power of pleasure— required trust.

One hand slid down her stomach, toward her *mons pubis* and lower. Her eyes glazed over as she found her pink cunny and began lightly rubbing herself. Gabriel watched, his mouth gone dry.

He angled forward, no longer content to sit by and spectate. He needed to put this newfound knowledge into practice. "May I?"

She swallowed and nodded.

He lifted her hand away and replaced her fingers with his tongue. There it was, he knew instinctually—*the place.* A firm little nub, easy to miss if one didn't know where to look.

Which he hadn't.

Until now.

He flicked the nub, and she gasped.

He did it again, and her fingers clawed through his hair.

This was why education mattered.

Instinctively, as his tongue worked her cunny, a finger slid lower and pressed inside her. On a cry, her head arched back, and she began to gasp and whimper and strain toward him. Not because she wasn't getting what she needed, but rather because she wanted... had to have... *more* of what he offered.

Her breath caught between an inhale and exhale, then a long, ragged moan poured from her throat and her sex pulsed against his tongue, around his finger. A mix of emotion streamed through Gabriel as he watched her climax—*triumph... desire... ache...*

Sated eyes met his across her enervated body. "That was..."

The sentence didn't need to be completed, for he felt it, too. No descriptor or adjective could come close to describing what *that was.*

"Gabriel," rasped across her throat.

He rose. Her eyes widened at the sight of his raging cock-stand. "Again?"

The question was spoken not with dread, but as if she couldn't quite believe her good luck.

"Again."

He took a creamy thigh in each hand and pulled her to the

edge of the bed. He held a hope that this time it would take longer than three strokes to achieve release.

His cock poised at her sex, he entered her in a slick, measured stroke. Every nerve ending in his body shot through with light as she stretched around him. He held still a moment. Long enough for her eyes to meet his, a question within.

By way of answer, he began to move, a thigh in each hand, with care not to hurt her for she was so very exquisitely *tight* around him.

And with care for himself that he not happen upon release too quickly.

This intimacy of two bodies joining… *Nay*, not simply bodies, but something more…

The something more he saw reflected in her eyes.

The something more he felt down to the marrow of his bones.

He slid a knee beneath her thigh and angled forward, so his mouth could touch her. One hand cupped beneath her bottom as he penetrated her, deep and hard… slow and relentless. His lips found the sensitive skin of her exposed throat, tasted the bead of sweat trickling down, then trailed lower to take a nipple between his teeth and flick his tongue across the tip.

"Oh, yes," she cried. "That feels… so… *good*."

Of their own volition, his hips moved with deeper intention, and she found the rhythm, her legs wrapped tight around his waist, receiving every inch of him, both of them gaining momentum, careening toward oblivion.

"Gabriel," she cried out and shattered beneath him, her quim pulsing its release around him. No longer could he hold on as he tumbled over the edge with her. Again, stars lit white behind his eyes—entire galaxies being formed—as he pulled from her at the very last moment to spill his seed onto the bed.

Sensations and emotions collided through him, ones new and unexpected as he collapsed to the side of her, both their bodies coated in a sheen of perspiration, their lungs grabbing air, their hearts heavily banging about their chests. He stretched out his arm and slid it beneath her head. Though the act was over, he still needed to be touching her. He wasn't ready to sever the connection, though he could feel its intensity fading as his breath grew regular and the beat of his heart slowed.

Just as he'd no experience with the act of sexual congress itself, he had no experience with this, either.

The after.

Their faces only inches from each other, she turned her head and met his eyes. He detected satiety within and more, too. A question... and a bit of confusion.

"That was a first," she said.

His eyebrows crinkled. "I thought you weren't a—"

"*Virgin?*" she finished for him. "I wasn't. But..." She worried her bottom lip. "That was the first time I felt pleasure in the act."

A feeling fired through Gabriel, unlike any he could've anticipated.

Protectiveness.

But that didn't account for this scorching emotion that had his hands wanting to clench into fists.

Ferocity.

That was new.

He wanted to punch a hole into something.

Instead, he gathered her closer.

Yet another feeling coursed through him. It, too, was new. A feeling he couldn't identify, but experienced, nonetheless.

As he drifted into the ether of sated sleep, he wondered if she felt it.

It shouldn't matter.

But it did.

CHAPTER SIXTEEN

NEXT DAY

*I*n the end, Gabriel had jumped out of the window.

At dawn, he'd begun banging on about servants and propriety.

Honestly, Celia hadn't heeded the specifics.

All she'd been able to hear was that he was leaving and she would be deprived of a fourth time with him.

Which she wanted... very much.

She'd never suffered an ache of the sort as when he'd left her bed.

He hadn't actually jumped out of the window. He'd climbed down rather more expertly than she'd expected. Once his feet were planted on the ground, he'd glanced up. Her throat had done a funny thing and tightened. It was the burning in his eyes —and a flash of something more, too.

Uncertainty.

The same one that had been burrowing into her as hazy dawn snuck up the horizon. Who knew what today held, that uncertainty said.

But they'd had the night.

It might have to be enough.

Enough?

Now, finishing an easy morning's ride on her favorite gray hunter Hyacinth, Celia considered the word—*enough*.

It suggested satiety.

After she'd somehow drifted off to sleep for another couple of hours, she'd awakened with an acute and ravenous hunger. She'd even requested a second scone and slice of bacon. Mrs. Davies had lifted an eyebrow, but had complied with her mistress's wishes.

Yet food wasn't all Celia's body hungered for—or even the main thing.

Him.

It wanted him with a raw ache. Three times hadn't been enough. Perhaps the fourth would've been...

That wouldn't have been enough, either.

Enough.

There was no *enough*.

Only an appetite whetted.

For here was the thing.

It hadn't been her first time coupling with a man.

It had been her first time coupling with a man she desired. No obligation or force—only inclination and absolute need for another person... a need she felt unreservedly helpless to.

In truth, the strength of this need frightened her no small bit.

So, after she'd finished stuffing herself with breakfast, she'd dressed and had Hyacinth saddled. She'd needed a ride, hoping time alone in dewy morning air on the back of a horse would give her mind a calm vista in which to clear itself.

But as she and Hyacinth passed through the stable yard gate, Celia felt no clearer on the subject than she had an hour ago. As if drawn by an internal lodestone, her eye happened upon a still figure across the cobbles, standing well away from the morning fray of lads and grooms hustling and bustling about on this or that duty.

Gabriel.

Shoulder propped against a window frame, arms crossed over his chest, gold-streaked hair tousled with the morning breeze, beard glinting a touch red in a shaft of sunlight.

He had a way about him.

One wanted to be worthy of such an intelligent and capable person—even when one knew she wasn't.

"Duke," she called out. She felt a smile lift about her mouth as their eyes held, secret knowledge passing between them.

"Duchess," he returned.

She allowed a lad to take Hyacinth's reins and lead them to the mounting block. As she rode sidesaddle, dismounting was a bit of a process. She had to unhook her right knee from the central pommel and slip her left foot from the slipper stirrup, then step onto the mounting block.

A hand appeared to assist her descent.

Not the stable lad's hand, but a hand she knew—*intimately.*

Or would it be fairer to say this hand knew *her... intimately.*

A shiver traced through her as long, capable fingers tightened and helped her down the three steps to the cobbles.

Though they stood in a stable yard of ten grooms and lads, a hunter, and two sixteen-hands Thoroughbreds being led to the paddock for their paces, she and Gabriel were alone.

Nerves jittered through her. For what she'd done with him last night—mere hours ago.

For what she wanted to do with him again.

"Was your morning—" She had no plan for the completion of the question. "*Good?*"

He nodded. "And yours?"

She nodded.

It seemed they'd run out of things to say.

Right.

"Are you out for a ride?" she asked. "It's a lovely morning for it."

He seemed to weigh his answer. At last, he said, "I don't ride."

Celia's brow gathered. "What do you mean you don't ride?"

He shrugged. "It was never a priority." A wry laugh escaped him. "Or an option."

Of course. He'd been a scholarship lad. He didn't ride.

"You cannot be a duke and not know how to ride." The words were out of her mouth before she could consider them.

He cocked his head, and a smile tipped about his mouth. "That's provably untrue," he said in the tone of voice he used when he was being completely reasonable. "I *am* a duke, and I *don't* know how to ride."

Celia let him finish, then said as reasonably, "Well, there are facts, and there are facts."

He didn't look convinced.

Too bad.

She would convince him. "You're going to learn how to ride today."

His eyebrows lifted toward the sky that was growing bluer by the minute. "I am?"

Celia didn't hesitate. She called out to the next groom who passed. "Leave Hyacinth saddled and bring out Bishop." At sixteen hands, the chestnut hunter would have no problem handling Gabriel's size.

"I suppose I should've asked if you wanted to ride," she said as if conciliatory. She wasn't. The man needed to know how to ride.

"I'm mostly indifferent to it."

"Oh, but you won't be, not once you get the knack of it," she said, unable to help herself. "The freedom will take hold of you. With a horse you can go places unreachable by carriage or foot. Just you and your mount."

Gabriel didn't look convinced, but he did look interested. "Horses truly are your passion."

Celia opened her mouth to say *yes*, but the word refused to cross her lips.

She might've found an additional passion.

But she couldn't say that.

Led by the groom, Bishop appeared at the entrance to the stable yard. Celia pointed. "There's your mount."

Gabriel's brow lifted as hunter and groom approached the mounting block. "He's quite the sizeable beast."

"He is," agreed Celia. "But he's also of a sweet-tempered and patient disposition."

"You're sure?" Gabriel's expression and tone said he yet harbored doubts.

"Absolutely," she said. "I know my horses."

Gabriel didn't hesitate. "I believe you."

A warm feeling stole through Celia. He trusted her judgment. It was the same when a stubborn horse eventually gave over and let her lead the way.

She dug a chunk of apple from her pocket and held it out. "First, you give your mount a treat."

Gabriel took the apple from her outstretched hand and turned toward Bishop. When he began to extend the treat between forefinger and thumb, Celia rushed to say, "Offer the apple on the flat of your palm."

Gabriel did as Celia instructed, and Bishop took the apple with gentle lips.

"Now," she said, "give the velvet of his nose a few strokes."

A smile tipped about Gabriel's mouth as he again followed instructions.

"When you're ready, Your Grace," said the groom, standing off to the side.

In unison, Celia and Gabriel said, "Thank you."

In unison, they smiled. "I suppose we're both *Your Graces*," said Celia.

She took the reins and dismissed the lad so he could continue with his morning duties. "It would be easiest if you mounted from the block, rather than the stirrup," she said. "It puts a good deal of strain on a horse's back to be repeatedly mounted from the ground." She continued without thinking, "Particularly as you're so big."

Her mouth snapped shut, and heat flared through her.

You're so big.

Words she'd spoken to this man—*last night*.

Words that had her gaze wanting to travel down his body—to confirm that he was, indeed, as big as she remembered.

Of course, she couldn't.

Instead, she kept her eyes, impossibly, trained on his.

* * *

GABRIEL UNDERSTOOD he had options here.

He could lift a cheeky eyebrow.

It was what most men would do in this situation.

Or like a gentleman—which apparently he wasn't required to be now that he was a duke—he could release her gaze.

Which was what he did.

He wasn't sure he would be able to drop the habit of being a gentleman.

Without another word, he ascended the mounting block and awkwardly swung his leg over Bishop's back. He exhaled a relieved laugh when the horse remained completely still. "That wasn't what I'd call smooth."

"To be expected the first time."

The first time.

And, again, there it was between them—*last night*.

The same knowledge shone in her eyes.

He wondered if she, like he, would never get over it.

If her body still felt like kindling aching to be lit into flame.

"Now," she began. He detected a slight wobble in the word. "Grab onto the pommel and hold tight while I lead you about the stable yard."

"I don't need to know anything else?"

Every muscle in his body flexed with tension. This lesson seemed... sudden.

She gave her head a dismissive shake. "I recommend not squeezing your knees too tight, as Bishop will take that as a signal to increase his speed."

"Reassuring."

A laugh escaped Celia. "Brace yourself. The first few steps will be jarring."

An understatement, Gabriel quickly found as every bone in his body rattled with each *clip-clop* of Bishop's hooves against unforgiving cobbles.

But he couldn't very well say *no*.

Not when it was Celia asking.

Nay.

She wasn't asking; she was commanding.

Well, he couldn't say *no* then, either.

She glanced over her shoulder, flashing him a hopeful expression. He tried to offer a confident smile, but suspected it emerged more of a grimace.

After several rounds of the stable yard, they finally stopped near the mounting block. Gabriel exhaled a slow sigh of relief. He would never make a horseman. It was a fact. At best, he could achieve basic competence.

And the joy she'd described with a glow bordering on the beatific?

Never.

Except she didn't lead him all the way back to the mounting block. Instead, she handed off the reins to a groom and stepped onto the mounting block herself, while her gray hunter was returned to her. "What are you doing?"

He had to ask, because he had his suspicions.

"We're going for a ride," she said, blithe.

"And you think I'm ready for that?"

Another question Gabriel had to ask.

"Oh, there's nothing to it. You appear to have grasped the basics. We'll take it slow as you need."

A little late for that. This *lesson* was proceeding at the speed of lightning.

Then the stable lad was handing the reins up to Gabriel—like he had the faintest idea what to do with them. He sat and watched, helpless, as Celia passed through the stable yard gate without a backward glance, like the queen of all she surveyed. Meanwhile, the stable lad glanced up with a cheeky smile, and Gabriel had only the split of a second to brace himself as the lad gave Bishop a light to slap on the hindquarters. The horse jolted into motion, nearly unseating Gabriel. Yet, somehow, he managed to stay on the horse's back.

Once through the gate, he called out, "Where are we going?"

"You'll see," drifted toward him. Then she directed her mount off the gravel road and onto a well-worn bridle path.

Gabriel could only offer a small prayer that his mount would follow, which the steady Bishop did—*blessedly*.

His gaze caught on the elegant line of Celia's back, her easy, natural sway with the gait of her horse. She wasn't inclined to talk, and he let it be. He was beginning to see her point of view as they ventured deeper into the woods, the high canopy providing sun-dappled shade... the only sounds the muted thud of horse hooves... wind soughing through the canopy green with summer leaves... birds trilling... the distant barking of a dog. *Nature.* It was easy to feel like one of God's chosen creatures out here.

He'd known he would find her in the stables this morning—and after last night, he hadn't been able to keep away.

To his credit, he had intended to try. He'd ventured into the study, intent on sorting through the late duke's papers—yet more unpaid bills, he quickly surmised—but for the first time in his life, his mind hadn't been able to concentrate on the numbers. Instead, it was memories of last night that stole into his brain and assailed him from every angle—*her feminine sigh in his ear... the humidity of her bare skin... the voluptuous weight of her breasts... the taste of her—*

There was no help for it.

He needed to leave Ashcote Hall.

But he hadn't.

Instead, he'd turned his feet toward the stables—where he'd known he would find her.

And now he was paying for his weakness.

Still, he supposed Bishop wasn't a bad sort—for a horse.

"Are you alright back there?" she called over her shoulder. She didn't seem all that concerned.

"I'm still in one piece, if that's what you're asking." He felt needled, unreasonably so. "Though not for my bones' lack of trying to rattle apart."

A laugh floated on the air. "Wait until you get up to a full gallop."

"That will not be happening," he said with certainty. "At least, not by choice." He was suddenly less certain of the supposedly good-natured Bishop.

Another laugh drifted in her wake.

"I'm glad my pain amuses you so."

Her laughter paused long enough for her to say, "Oh, it's not that. It's just refreshing that you're not the best at *everything* you put your hand to."

"Oh?" A question he shouldn't ask occurred to him. "And what, precisely, am I the best at?"

The question was met with hot silence. If they'd been facing one another, he suspected he would be presently watching a blush creeping up the column of her neck, pinking the tips of her ears. He supposed he could let her off the hook.

For now.

He wasn't finished proving to her exactly how capable he was. "Does Bishop race?"

Which would've been useful information to have *before* he'd mounted the beast.

This got another laugh, but this time she glanced over her shoulder. "No."

"What's his job, then?"

Even with his ignorance of horses, that was something he knew. All horses had work to do.

"Interesting way to put it." She slowed her mount so they could ride side by side.

If what Gabriel was doing could be called riding. More of a hanging-on-for-dear-life situation.

"Bishop and Hyacinth are hunters."

"So, not Thoroughbreds?"

"A Thoroughbred is a breed of horse, and a hunter is a type," she explained. "Both Bishop and Hyacinth have Thoroughbred blood flowing through their veins, but they aren't meant for racing."

Gabriel nodded, surprisingly interested in the subject. "So, what makes one decide a horse is a hunter?"

"A few physical qualities. Their legs aren't as long, which makes them better at venturing down steep hills and taking leaps at a gallop when there's a tree across the path. They also have good feet for a day following the hounds. As far as personality, they need to have good manners. In all, a hunter offers a comfortable ride."

"This is comfortable?"

Another smile burst from her. "Yes."

Gabriel had the distinct feeling she was teasing him—and he didn't mind a whit.

A secluded pond appeared a dozen yards off the path. "Shall we take a rest?" He tried not to sound too eager.

"Let's," she said, directing her mount.

Luckily, Bishop followed Celia and Hyacinth. He had little doubt the hunter was a fine horse, but Gabriel didn't know how to make him do anything.

Secluded and still, the pond was as picturesque a body of water as one was ever likely to encounter—willow trees elegantly draped over the surface, rushes swaying at the bank, and dragonflies whizzing through the air.

Gabriel swung one leg over the saddle and let gravity take him to the ground, relieved to feel *terra firma* beneath his feet again. He glanced over to find Celia still mounted. "Do you require assistance?"

She hesitated—after all, she was the accomplished horsewoman here—then nodded.

Leaving Bishop contentedly munching grass, Gabriel made his way to Celia. Dressed in a pale pink wool riding habit, she stared down at him from her perch, like a flamboyant bird from exotic locales.

"You'll need to come closer," she said.

At once, he saw the necessary logistics of the maneuver. Without a mounting block, close proximity would be required.

Perhaps this ride had been a good idea, after all.

Her scent of jasmine and bergamot mixed with horse as he reached up and took her waist in his hands. Though her hips were lush in proportion to her breasts, her waist naturally cinched in, so his hands could almost span it.

"I have you."

She nodded and shifted so she could plant her hands onto his shoulders, and she tipped forward. As he took the full weight of her, he held steady and she slid off her mount… and unhurriedly down the length of his body.

Feminine curves soft against him, he went hard.

Beneath layers of wool and muslin, he knew these curves—
intimately—their give and take... their taste...

It took a beat of time to register that her feet touched ground,
and yet, still, she pressed against him, her head angled back so
her honey amber gaze held his, her mouth parted a sliver... a
sliver wide enough for his tongue to slip inside and taste her
again...

CHAPTER SEVENTEEN

*F*or that was what Gabriel wanted with every fiber of his being.

To continue what he and Celia had begun last night.

What he was coming to understand about the physical act of coupling was that it was only the beginning. A gateway into something else… something *more*…

But the physical act itself…

He wanted more of that, too.

Much.

And though she looked as if she would be amenable to a kiss and possibly *more*, he took a step back, guided by an intuitive knowledge.

That was all he had.

For—*here… now… with her*—he was out of his depth.

Nothing that came before had prepared him for Celia.

She blinked and seemed to come to.

He took another step. This one felt more deliberate and awkward and necessary—a solidifying of intention.

He jutted his chin toward the pond. "Is this a place you visit often on your rides?"

She shook her head. "Not especially. Servants and a few locals use it as a swimming hole, I believe."

"Fairly perfect for it, I'd imagine."

"I'll have to take your word for that."

"What do you mean?" He'd detected a tone in her voice.

A nervous laugh escaped her. "I don't swim."

"*Don't?*" he asked. "Or *can't?*"

There was a distinction, and he would have it.

Hesitation lengthened into a long pause. "Can't," she admitted.

Gabriel's brow gathered. "No one taught you as a child?"

"It wasn't deemed a necessary part of my education." Her manner was offhand, but her mouth pulled tight. "I take it you learned at Eton?"

Gabriel opened his mouth to reply *yes*, then saw what she was doing. She was shifting the attention away from her. Well, he wasn't having it. "What *was* a necessary part of your education?" he pressed.

Even as the question emerged, he had a feeling he wouldn't like the answer.

Then she did something utterly unexpected. She canted her head to an angle that could only be described as saucy and smiled.

He'd seen this smile before.

At the Derby.

And he saw the smile for what it was—the smile she showed the world.

The presentation of this smile had been the necessary part of her education.

The tip of her tongue darted out and swiped across her bottom lip in a slow, deliberate glide.

Gabriel's mouth went dry.

When his gaze again lifted to meet hers, he saw knowledge there.

"*That,*" she said.

He'd reacted as predictably as any other man, the look in her eyes said.

Well, he was only a man.

But he understood something important about her. "You were raised to marry into the peerage."

"My father was… *is* a terribly wealthy man, and I was—" A laugh entirely without humor escaped her. "*Am* a beauty."

Her father… She wanted nothing to do with the man, even if it meant ruin. That said something about her.

Something Gabriel could only respect.

She didn't like to talk about this part of herself. He could see that. But it had defined the trajectory of her life.

"There are advantages to being a beauty, I would suppose."

Her eyebrows lifted, as if inviting him to go on.

"People smile at you," he said, reaching. Why had he said such a blasted stupid thing, anyway? "People make way for beautiful people."

"True, but…"

But…

She didn't have to complete her sentence aloud for them both to know.

But her beauty hadn't afforded her a pleasant life.

Rather the opposite, in fact.

Better to have been born with the sort of looks that didn't catch the eye. A happier life might've been sought and secured.

"Your beauty was used from the time you were a child?"

She gave a reluctant nod. "Beauty is a lot of things. People like to look at it. Surround themselves with it. People with the money and means enjoy procuring beauty for themselves."

"Like a possession." His brow furrowed. "You were taught to be a possession."

A concept troubling and completely foreign to him. In his household, a person's primary value was placed on their mind.

"I was."

And he understood... "You were taught to be an ornament."

Another nod.

Unaccountable anger surged through Gabriel.

"But, Gabriel," she said. Within her eyes shone not defeat or anger, but something else—*will*.

She'd endured.

"Beauty can be wielded," she continued. "It can afford one a measure of power if one becomes ensnared in a powerless situation."

"Like ten years in a terrible marriage."

The very idea made Gabriel's gut churn.

Her gaze turned assessing. "Surely, I'm not telling you anything you don't already know."

That caught him on the back foot. "How so?"

"Well, Duke, in case you haven't noticed, you're quite the beauty yourself."

Gabriel opened his mouth to reply, but words refused to form.

And the smile tipping about her mouth... Well, it was a smile of hers that he liked. Saucy and knowing, it was a smile that made him want to do nothing more than kiss those cherry lips.

On impulse, he shrugged off his coat and began working the buttons of his waistcoat.

Eyes wide with alarm, her smile slipped. "What are you doing?"

He tossed the waistcoat aside and grabbed his cravat. "Something that should've been done years ago."

When he began hopping on one foot to remove a boot, then the other, she laughed, both amused and befuddled. "And what is that?"

He untucked his shirt and pulled it over his head. Even as she gasped, her gaze swept over him, naked appreciation in her eyes. "I'm going to teach you how to swim."

She took a step backward, waving her hands before her. "Oh, no, no, no."

Down to naught but his trousers, his fingers hesitated at the falls. "Oh, yes."

She went as serious as he'd ever seen her. "No."

He slipped the buttons free. "Come with me, Celia."

* * *

THEN IT WAS the final button undone…

And Celia undone, too.

His falls dropped, and he flung his trousers away.

As he stood before her, a golden ray of sun shafted across his naked form… his—*oh*—manhood looked to be at half-mast.

Or was that its normal size?

Oh.

Heat suffused her.

It was possible he was no mere man. Didn't the Greeks have it that gods assumed human form when the whim caught them?

Was Gabriel a god come to life?

Adonis.

Then he turned and launched into the water in a smooth dive, Celia's parting view of his naked form a flash of taut white buttocks. Her breath caught and held until he surfaced, shaking his head, wet, tousled hair flung about him and dripping water.

And Celia ran out of *nos*.

Come with me, Celia.

It was a siren's call.

Gabriel Siren… *siren.*

"The water is perfect," he called out.

Even as she knew she shouldn't—that it was the worst idea in the world—trembly fingers found the buttons of her pelisse. As she tossed the garment aside, she hardly knew herself.

What was she doing? She wasn't the sort of woman who frolicked in ponds and had... *fun.*

And yet here she was, unbuttoning her dress, about to do exactly that—or something. Actually, she wasn't exactly sure what was about to happen.

It was as simple as it was he who asked, and she'd lost the ability around her third *no* to mean it.

All she wanted was to tell him yes, yes, and *yes.*

Stays lying in disarray in the grass, she was now down to chemise, stockings, and boots. The stockings and boots could go, but the chemise would stay. A woman must maintain a bit of mystery.

All the while, he swam. One arm slicing through the water like a blade, then the other. Over and over, like a machine, the movements perfectly calibrated and seemingly inevitable. And while she admired his skill in the water, it was also inevitable that she would admire the man—gold-streaked brown hair just touching his wide, muscled shoulders, water sluicing down his broad back in rivulets, narrowing to hips and waist, and that taut, white bottom of his...

Oh.

And she'd been worried that he would be watching her and leering?

Who was the lech here, anyway?

She stepped to the edge of the water, mud squishing through her bare toes, and realized he'd been keeping half an eye on her after all, for he stopped swimming and began treading water in the center of the pond.

"Ready for your lesson?"

Heaven help her, but a shiver of anticipation traced through her at the question, at the intent look in his eyes. All that intelligence and seriousness focused on her. "As I'll ever be, I suppose."

Truer—and breathier—words never spoken.

He began moving toward the shore—toward her. She braced herself. From the impending lesson or from him, she wasn't sure.

He only stopped when he could stand, the water hitting at his waist. Her gaze couldn't help roving over all that exposed, golden, muscled skin, the water dripping off him. Combined with the scruff of his beard and that look in his eyes... He was simply so masculine.

Which made her feel like the most feminine woman in the world.

Which drew her to him.

Which made her want to run very far away.

"You'll be able to stand here," he said.

She nodded and took a hesitant step forward. She'd never ventured into a pond, its beauty only to be admired from afar. The water wasn't as cold as she would've supposed, but then it was summer.

Her heart racing at a ridiculous pace, she took one step, then another, water reaching ankles... knees... thighs... bottom... waist... then below her breasts, which had become amusingly buoyant.

A smile curved his mouth. "Take my hand."

She reached out on a nervous laugh and strong, masculine fingers wrapped around hers.

"You can trust me."

The words were out of her mouth before she could consider them. "I know."

He tugged her gently forward and placed his other hand in the middle of her back. "Now, you're going to float."

"I am?" She doubted that very much. Although, if the buoyancy of her breasts was any indicator, she just might.

"You are." He was clearly determined. "Tip your torso backward and allow your legs to rise toward the surface."

"You're sure?"

"I am."

Her feet remained planted in their patch of mud. "Are humans meant to swim?" She yet harbored doubts.

"Humans are meant to do anything we set our minds to."

The way he spoke those words—so certain. She envied his certainty. The vagaries of life had never once stood in his way.

If Gabriel was determined she was to float, she would float.

And because he thought she could, perhaps she could.

So, heart racing in her throat, she let the moment take her and tipped backward and allowed her feet to lift off the silty pond bed, his palm flat and steadying on her back.

And... she was floating.

A confounded laugh bubbled up from her belly. "I'm floating," she said with no small amount of wonder.

Light and buoyant, her body felt somehow free of itself, her view the endless blue sky above with its puffs of white clouds drifting across, framed by the canopy of silver birch and willow trees. Her hair floating free in the water, along with her chemise around her. Sound muffled to a quiet underwater roar, it was if by tipping backward, she'd tipped into another world, one that had been under her nose her entire life.

Her gaze shifted toward his above her. "What a gift you've given me." She meant the words to her very core.

He nodded.

He knew.

This man who she'd so easily dismissed because of his age knew so much of life.

More than her in many ways.

His mouth moved, but she couldn't make out his words. She lifted an ear. "What was that?"

"You're floating on your own now."

And she realized it was true. His hand had fallen away... She was floating—on her own.

Twin surges of joy and fear flooded through her, causing her to wobble. Then her legs were kicking out to compensate, causing her to teeter the other way, then she was under, sudden panic spiking through her until...

Her feet touched silty bottom.

A sure hand pulled her to the surface. No longer weightless, she was a sputtering mess as she rubbed the water out of her eyes, heavy clumps of hair stuck to her face.

Then she heard it—a snort.

Her eyes flew open. There was Gabriel, biting back laughter. *Indignant*, that was how she should feel, but it was funny and there was her laughter joining his, irrepressible. This feeling of joy as weightless within her as the water had been around her. His arms, holding her steady, allowed her this freedom to laugh and be giddy.

Her arms twined around his neck and she pressed against him… their smiling faces inches from each other… their eyes locked. This feeling held no weight, yet it was visceral, too.

She lifted onto the tips of her toes, and her fingers wove through damp curls at the nape of his neck, pulling his head closer, the distance between their mouths closing…

And her lips were touching his, his beard a delicious scrape against her skin. A light kiss that lasted no longer than a second or two—but long enough to taste him and breathe him in.

Long enough to want more.

His head angled back, and questioning eyes met hers, black pupils pushing irises into thin blue rings. "If we have to stop, now is the time."

Alarm sheared through her. *Stop?* "And you think it's not already too late for that?"

"We could," he said, but she detected doubt in his eyes.

To prove her point, she unhooked one hand from around his neck and trailed it down his throat, chest, stomach, dipping below the water's surface, lower…

Ah, there it was. *His cock.* Thick and hard, throbbing with heat and need.

The very thought of his perfect cock—that it existed in the

world... for her—had her thighs squeezing together with utter ache.

"*I* could stop."

"But..." Her fingers slid along his velvety length. He sucked in a sharp breath. "But could I? For here is the thing, Duke. I need you... *this*—" One by one her fingers wrapped around him and squeezed. "Inside me."

"Need and want are two separate entities," he said, as if he were reading from a textbook. But it was his voice gone to gravel in his throat that gave him away.

Well, that and his rock-hard cock.

He was fighting for control, and it was a noble fight, but the fact was here they were—*naked... in a pond*—with only wild, reckless desire for company.

Celia didn't like control's chances.

And she wasn't about to make it any easier on him. "I want you, Duke. Really, I must have you."

On a low growl that took Celia by surprise, Gabriel tightened his hold, one hand squeezing her bottom as he pressed her against him, her sex dragging against his rigid length. Instinctively, her legs wrapped around his waist, laying her slit bare against his manhood.

Oh, the carnal, male feel of him.

"Remove your chemise."

It wasn't a request, but a demand. One that sent a delicious spike of desire through her.

"There will be nothing between us."

Though he spoke of clothing, it felt like he was speaking of more.

As he held her steady against him, she managed to shimmy clingy, wet muslin over her head and fling it toward the shore where it caught on a willow branch.

Again, he growled. With one hand, he cupped a breast and brought the nipple to his mouth, his tongue teasing the tip as he sucked. Bright sensation shimmered through Celia as she arched back. "Oh, yes."

His mouth on her, she began sliding her quim against his long, hard length...

Oh, it was pleasure, but pleasure building—pleasure delayed.

Her arms tightened around his neck. He might suffocate in her bosom, but she had the feeling he would die a happy man. Her legs around his waist loosened enough so she could reach between their bodies and take his massive girth in hand. Then she was guiding him to the entrance of her sex.

His head lifted as his hands grasped her bottom firmly. Then she was lowering onto him, one deliberate inch a time. As he filled her, it was as if lightning streaked through her veins, searing every nerve ending along the way.

It wasn't merely that he stretched and filled where there was a void.

It was a completion.

A completion that took pleasure beyond its bounds.

A notion that might frighten her at another moment—but not this one.

The defined muscles of his arms flexed and released as he began moving her on him, up and down, slowly, letting her adjust to his... *girth*. Her mouth found his neck, her teeth nipping lightly as he further impaled her. Apparently, there had been more of him to have.

"Oh," she cried out, swiveling her hips, finding a rhythm with him.

So slippery and weightless were their bodies against each other.

It felt magical—*oh... so... good...*

Of a sudden, they wobbled. Their gazes startled into focus. "My footing," he began just as it went completely, and they bobbed beneath the water. Scrambling up, they surfaced, sputtering and laughing.

"We need to take this to the shore," he said, ever the voice of reason.

Ever?

When had she come to know this about him and be so certain of its truth?

"Hold on tight," he said and began wading through the water toward the shore.

Their coupled selves bared to the elements felt slightly transgressive and strangely... *enlivening*. She'd never experienced the warming glow of sunlight on her bottom.

Her legs tight around his waist, he walked them to his discarded jacket. "I think we'll have to, *erm*," he began, and Celia took his meaning.

She unhooked her legs from around his waist and reluctantly slid off his hard length, her feet making contact with the ground. He lowered to a seat on the jacket, one hand propped behind him, his body open to her, again calling to mind a Greek god, while his other hand reached out. Her fingers twined through his and he tugged her so she had no choice but to bend at the waist and hover above him. She pressed her smiling mouth to his as the rest of her body followed, her legs straddling his thighs, her slit separated from *him* by mere inches, pulsing with utter ache. He took his shaft in hand, and she lowered onto him, inch by slow, deliberate inch, pulling a delicious groan from him.

Though the most animal of activities, coupling was also the most human. A blend of the two. A meeting of bodies...

A meeting of souls.

As their bodies and souls found a rhythm, a light breeze cooling the droplets of water streaming down their hot skin, sunlight falling in dappled shadows on them, Celia thought this must be a form of Elysium.

An earthly pleasure, but one bound up in the heavenly, too.

What had they been put on earth for, if not for this?

The same feeling from last time began to coil inside her. A

feeling of pleasure and promise—leaving one no choice but to strive toward it.

Her hips increased their rhythm, came down on him harder.

"Celia," he rasped into the curve of her neck, the rough velvet of his voice resonating through her. "*Yes*—like that," he added as she rode him.

That she was bringing him to the brink only brought her to the edge that much quicker.

Promise became certainty, and release was upon her, and she cried out, her sex somehow collapsing inward before expanding and bursting into ephemeral, golden sparks shooting through her veins. Hands clutched around her hips, he plunged and drove into her, relentless. Then he was shouting out in release, falling over the edge with her.

Body slick with water and perspiration, Celia floated in an ether of satiety. It was only him and her here. It was oblivion... It was wonder...

It was nothingness—and everything.

"*Celia*," she heard as if from a distance.

She resisted the intrusion. She never wanted this feeling to end. As long as her eyes remained closed, it wouldn't have to.

He kissed her neck. How she loved the scrape of his beard against her.

Love.

Her eyes flew open.

It was only the scrape of his beard she loved.

That was all it had to be.

"Celia," he muttered against her skin. "You feel it, too."

"Feel what?"

"The magic."

The way *magic* emerged, like it was composed of foreign elements, suggested he'd never spoken the word in his life.

Love... magic...

What were these words?

What had they to do with her?

Nothing.

They never had.

"I suppose we need to be getting back," she said, planting her palm against his shoulder. Even she could hear the lack of conviction in her voice.

"Must we?"

"Likely."

"*Must* I do anything?" A wicked smile tipped about his mouth. "I'm the duke."

A laugh burst from her. "You were absolutely born to be a duke."

"As was so recently discovered."

This got another laugh from her. "*Dukes.*"

"It's just that..." His hands tightened around her hips, fastening her down onto him, and she felt it—*him... impossibly...* growing thick inside her.

"But we..." she began, the protest instinctive.

A *bad* instinct, she decided.

His tongue trailed up her throat. "Might we need another time to reach satisfaction?"

Oh, the feel of him inside her—*hot... thick... hard*—*oh,* she needed it again.

And as he took her again, she couldn't help thinking she might never stop needing it—*this...* what he offered—his body... his cock... his passion...

Yet that wasn't all there was to him.

And she thought she might need those other parts of him, too.

Which wasn't at all the same as being able to have them as hers.

She suspected satisfaction would never be achieved.

Only this appetite forever whetted.

But for now, the magic.

Real life and that unsatisfied forever could wait.

CHAPTER EIGHTEEN

GREAT YARMOUTH RACECOURSE, NORFOLK, FOUR DAYS LATER

*G*abriel hadn't known it was possible to want someone as much as he wanted Celia.

Every hour... every minute... every second... of every day.

That was this wanting—so visceral, it pulled at the very fibers of his being.

Even now, with her arm threaded through his, as they strolled through the lightly populated crowd of fellow racegoers for a day's outing at Great Yarmouth Racecourse. It was the layers of clothing between them—and the fact that they were in a very public place—that he found intolerable after five days of clothing being no great obstacle.

But Celia had wanted to attend this racing meeting—*"The small local ones are more fun. You'll see"*—and, increasingly, it wasn't in Gabriel to deny her anything.

"Of course," she said around her bite of cinnamon bun, "Great Yarmouth does have a big race at the end of summer. Hordes attend, but not to see the three-year-olds, as the best of the threes are racing at Newmarket, Epsom, and Doncaster. Rather, they come for the two-year-old colts and fillies."

"Why is that?"

Though he was coming to know Celia in her various forms— duchess, adversary, partner... *lover*—he hadn't yet seen this version of her, loose and generous with her smile in a public setting.

"The two-year-olds who run best at Great Yarmouth this summer will go on to compete in the top races next summer. It's a sneak peek at next year's contenders."

"I suppose you'll have a colt or filly in that race?"

"Certainly." She flashed him a playful smile. "*We* shall."

Warmth stole through Gabriel.

We.

They were business partners; of course, it was *we*.

But a part of him wanted to interpret that *we* differently.

Increasingly, he wanted that *we* to be more.

The question he'd been tamping down the last few days worked its way to the tip of his tongue, demanding to be asked. But unlike those other days, today he was unable to resist its pull. "I have a question for you."

Best to begin casually.

"Yes?" With a carefree laugh, she clamped her hand onto her hat as the breeze threatened to take it. The sea was only a few miles to the east.

The answer he wanted to hear, but for the question yet unasked. He cleared his throat of nerves and plunged right in. "Do you ever plan to marry again?"

There.

That was the question asked.

Her breezy smile became an echo of itself as a shallow line formed between her eyebrows. "*Marry?*" she asked. "*Again?*"

He nodded, even as he wished with all his being that he could turn back the hand of time and leave the question unasked.

A complex tangle of emotions marched across her face. "If I had any choice in the matter, I would never be a wife again."

No.

Her answer was *no.*

A punch in the gut, that answer.

She wouldn't be his wife.

But he understood something: He didn't need her to be his wife.

He needed her to be his.

A vital distinction.

Gabriel noted a flake of bun on the corner of her mouth and instinctively flicked it away with his thumb. His gaze caught hers and held. How easily he fell into those honey amber depths. "Perhaps we've seen enough for today?"

The look in her eyes took his meaning.

They could leave.

In the carriage.

And they could do what he'd promised they would on their return journey to Ashcote—when it wouldn't matter if the duchess arrived in disarray and love-mussed.

The very thought had his cock half full.

A knowing smile flirted about her mouth and pushed the last remnants of his ill-advised question away. "We haven't even been here half an hour."

Was that all?

"*Duchess!*" came a feminine aristocratic voice.

Gabriel half turned to find a slight young woman approaching them. Her appearance rather nondescript, one might not pay her the faintest notice—until one met her eyes, which burned with unexpected fervency.

Celia stiffened at his side. She knew this woman—and was none too pleased to see her.

Discreetly, she untwined her arm from his and took a subtle step away.

Gabriel's brow furrowed. Who in the blazes was this woman, anyway?

"I thought it was you," said the young woman, lightly winded, as if she'd sprinted to catch them.

"Lady Beatrix." Celia spoke the greeting without an ounce of enthusiasm.

The lady's gaze flashed between Gabriel and Celia, as if she were writing notes in her mind to remember later.

"Are the two of you acquainted?" Only a thin veneer of civility coated Celia's question.

"Not formally." Lady Beatrix's eyes glinted with mischief. "But everyone knows of the new Duke of Acaster."

Gabriel offered a slight bow. "I'm afraid you have me at a disadvantage."

Lady Beatrix laughed as if she were enjoying herself.

She was the only one.

"You wouldn't know me, Your Grace," she said. "But I'm certain you must know my father—the Marquess of Lydon."

Ah. The Marquess of Lydon's wastrel proclivities were rivaled only by those of the late Sixth Duke of Acaster. The man held deep debt at every gaming hell in London—The Archangel included.

"Your Grace," said Celia, very properly, "may I introduce Lady Beatrix St. Vincent to you?"

"A pleasure." He spoke the words not because he meant them, but because they were what one said.

In truth, he'd only recently learned the meaning of the word *pleasure*, and it had nothing to do with Lady Beatrix, but rather the woman at his side who would no longer meet his eye.

The lady fixed her attention on Celia. "Do you have a horse in the running today?"

Though posed as an idle question, Gabriel didn't think it was. Lady Beatrix wasn't the sort of person to make empty queries.

Celia shook her head. "Simply enjoying a bit of Norfolk."

The trajectory of Lady Beatrix's gaze shifted and narrowed assessingly on Gabriel. "Ah, that's right. Ashcote Hall isn't too far from here. How does it feel to be in possession of one of the best racing stables in the country?"

"That's Cel—" He stopped before he spoke her given name in a public place. He had the feeling Lady Beatrix had heard it, anyway. "That's the duchess's enterprise."

Lady Beatrix canted her head in curiosity. "But is the rumor true?"

"What rumor?" asked Celia, quickly—too quickly.

Lady Beatrix's attention remained fixed on Gabriel. "The rumor that you're looking to sell Ashcote Hall and several other estates belonging to the late duke."

What was happening here? Though couched as conversation, this felt distinctly like an interrogation.

Before Gabriel could answer, Lady Beatrix continued. "Do you see Ashcote Hall as a conflict of interest?"

"Pardon?"

"You're one of the financiers of the Race of the Century, correct?"

"I am."

"And Ashcote has produced a qualifying horse for the Race of the Century with Light Skirt's win in the One Thousand Guineas. Some might see that as a conflict of interest."

"*Some* would be wrong." On this and all matters related to business, Gabriel was clear. Still, defensiveness prickled through him, and he didn't know precisely why. "Ashcote's stable of horses belongs to the duchess, not me. It's her capable hands that make it a success."

He owed Lady Beatrix St. Vincent no explanations. Yet he kept talking. It was the woman beside him that he owed something.

A defense.

When had anyone ever come to Celia's defense?

"I merely finance its operations for now. It's all down to her skill and talent that the stable is worth anything."

Lady Beatrix's brow lifted. "Is that so?"

Gabriel suspected he'd made a mistake.

"What do you mean by *for now*?"

Celia stepped forward. She was wearing the smile—the one Gabriel didn't like. "Lady Beatrix, it's been lovely to see you, but I've placed a wager on the next race, and I would like to watch."

Lady Beatrix's arch expression didn't shift a hair. "Of course."

She didn't believe Celia, but she could hardly say so.

Once they'd gotten well clear of Lady Beatrix, Celia said, "We should go."

Of course, Gabriel wanted to go. It had been his idea. But...

He didn't like Celia's rattled expression or the way she'd spoken the words. He didn't want to go because of fear or shame or second thoughts. He didn't want to flee.

The only reason for leaving that he would accept was that she couldn't abide not having her hands... or her mouth... or her quim... on him for a second longer.

"We should stay the course," he stated.

Wherever it led them, he kept to himself.

Not yet.

He didn't want to frighten her off.

But he would say it.

Soon.

He was determined.

Except didn't staying *this* course mean an altogether different and unexpected course for him?

For, increasingly, he was seeing the world in a way entirely novel to him.

Rationally, he understood they should heed her suggestion and, indeed, go. He should return to London and resume his real life. Except...

That life no longer existed.

The world as he knew it had changed, irrevocably.

And Celia was part of this new world—any way he could have her.

She stiffened at his side. Gabriel followed the direction of her gaze and caught sight of a couple approaching, their forms only vague from this distance. He glanced down to find her face drained of color.

An alarm bell clanged through him. "Who are they?" he demanded.

"The Duke and Duchess of Rakesley," she said under her breath.

Gabriel's brow gathered. "The duke who—"

"Yes," she said, cutting him off. "The duke who ran off with his jockey and married her."

Blast.

Gabriel watched with a feeling akin to horror as Celia's customary smile stretched across her face. "Isn't our world of the *haut ton* a small one?" she asked in a pleasant voice that made his back teeth grind together. "I suppose it was inevitable that we would meet. And, if we were to encounter them, better at a country racing meeting than before the prying eyes of society."

A defensive tension entered Gabriel's body.

It was ready.

For what, he wasn't precisely sure, but he was at the ready for whatever Celia needed of him.

Across the closing distance, he took measure of his adversary and his wife. The duchess was on the tall, lanky side for a woman with a riot of auburn curls that refused to be tamed by the loose chignon attempting to hold them. She was pretty, he supposed—a delicate beauty, some would say—but Gabriel was in no mood to think well of the woman who had done poorly by Celia. As for the duke, he was tall and dark of hair with a serious demeanor about him.

With a mild start of shock, Gabriel realized he hadn't met or even seen the duke, as the man had never been a habitué of The

Archangel. A benevolent Gabriel might think well of the duke for it—but Gabriel wasn't feeling charitable.

He caught the exact moment Rakesley and his duchess noticed Celia—and accepted they wouldn't be able to avoid greeting her.

They would meet and talk like the civilized lords and ladies they were.

Or something like that.

"Duke," said Celia through her smile that blazed bright enough to rival the sun.

No one else was smiling.

Rakesley gave a nod and a lackluster, "Duchess," before casting an assessing eye over Gabriel.

Gabriel willed his hands not to clench into fists.

"Duchess," said the Duchess of Rakesley, amicably. The duchess had warm eyes.

The duchess's warm eyes notwithstanding, Gabriel found himself wanting to square up to the duke and give the man a facer or challenge him to a duel—neither of which he'd ever felt compelled to do in his life. Really, though, it was as if the man was rubbing Celia's face in his wedded bliss.

"Rakesley," said Celia, as befitted her role in this impossible moment, "may I introduce the Duke of Acaster to you?"

The duke's eyebrows lifted with surprise, and the duchess's warm eyes turned assessing.

"Rakesley," said Gabriel, giving only as much as was required of him.

"Acaster," returned the duke with the same measure of generosity.

With a sudden flash of insight, Gabriel understood the source of his animosity toward Rakesley.

Standing before him was yet another man who had failed Celia.

Resolve strengthened to steel.

Never again.
Never again would she be failed by a man.
Not while he had breath in his body.

CHAPTER NINETEEN

*T*his day had been a mistake.

The certainty sank deep into Celia.

The Duke of Rakesley...

Here.

And he wasn't alone.

Of course, he wasn't.

His wife was by his side.

Stable lad... turned jockey... turned Duchess of Rakesley.

As it appeared no one else was going to hold up the polite end of conversation, she supposed it was up to her. "A beautiful day for the races."

There.

Polite conversation commenced.

Relief lit within the new Duchess of Rakesley's eyes. "Aye, it is. My brother is racing today on Dandy's Cravat for Lord Westcott."

Ah. Celia remembered the brother was a jockey, too. "What a talented family."

The duchess blinked. Celia supposed the words could've been taken as a jibe, but it wasn't intended so.

Even small conversation wasn't without its slings and arrows.

The nearest three-card sharper began barking enticements to try their luck at his table.

"Do you play the games?" asked the duchess.

Celia shook her head, even as she remembered her reckless night at The Archangel. "It's not a pleasure I partake of often."

"If she did," Gabriel cut in, staring at Rakesley, "she would win, of course."

An aghast moment crept past.

Celia bit her bottom lip, hard, but not out of distress.

Sudden, riotous laughter wanted to bubble up.

It was the way he'd spoken the words and the defensiveness of his manner, as if she could and would prevail victorious on any field of battle.

It was amusing—it was sweet.

She wanted to throw her arms around him and never let go.

And as silly as it was to feel this way, it made her feel valued— like she was important to someone.

A feeling she was unaccustomed to.

A feeling she could like.

Over these last five days, she and Gabriel had revealed new and unexpected sides of themselves to one another—and here was yet another one.

One that caused her insides to go light and tumble about.

She settled for a casual laugh, one that would break the tension. The dukes, however, continued evaluating one another like two cockerels in a hen yard, but the duchess smiled her appreciation. Former stable lad and jockey, this Duchess of Rakesley was a woman with a warm heart. That was apparent.

And Celia saw.

The love Rakesley and his duchess bore one another was so clear and bright, it could blind. They were utterly besotted with one another.

The marriage Celia had been willing to make with Rakesley—

one of convenience and mutual goals—would have been a pale shadow to the full-bodied love presently throwing itself in her face.

A chord of envy struck through her. She'd been so fixated on security for herself and her horses that she'd never once considered this—*love*—as a possibility for her future. She could choke on the feeling that she'd never had the luxury of experiencing.

"Do you have any horses in the running today?" asked Rakesley. "Maybe a two-year-old?"

He would ask that question. As his Somerton Manor and her Ashcote Hall were the two best horse racing stables in England, he would be keen to catch a glimpse of future competition.

"Not today," she said. "And you?"

He wasn't the only one keeping an eye out.

He shook his head.

"Celia wanted to show me what a small, local racing meeting was like," said Gabriel.

The words landed like a cannonball.

Nay. Not words in the plural sense—though their particular combination did imply a level of, *erm*, intimacy—but the one word.

Celia.

Gabriel had all but declared he and she were lovers.

Rakesley lifted an eyebrow, and the duchess's head canted. Neither had missed that *Celia*—and neither offered comment on it.

Celia flicked a quick glance toward Gabriel. If he knew what he'd done, he wasn't showing it.

Or was he?

He looked every inch the duke who would do as he pleased and damn anyone who dared question him.

So... was the *Celia* a misstep, or...

Was it a *claiming*?

The very idea... It shocked her to her toes.

It arrowed desire straight through her.

It made her want to hike up her skirts and start running and not stop until she reached the North Sea.

"I actually prefer these race venues," said Rakesley's wife, saving the moment. Bless the woman. "They're more fun."

Celia nodded with agreement and realized something. She would've liked this duchess under different circumstances. And perhaps she did under these, but she didn't see them becoming bosom friends. She simply wasn't strong enough to be in the presence of so much happiness.

Yet another failing of hers to add to the list of many.

"*Duchess!*" came a shout over the crowd.

The Duchess of Rakesley didn't turn—she wasn't yet accustomed to her new title—but Celia was and did. She blinked. The man waving and smiling as he approached was...

The Earl of Wrexford?

"What in the blazes is *he* doing here?" growled Gabriel.

Rakesley and his duchess seized the moment to excuse themselves, and Celia found herself wishing they would stay, much preferring the awkwardness with them to the awkwardness to come with Wrexford.

She risked a quick glance at Gabriel. His face had gone thunderous. "We leave," he ordered.

"Wrexford is not twenty feet away. We can't deliver the cut direct." Someone had to be the voice of reason. Surprisingly, it was her.

"Oh, I assure you, we can."

The statement emerged with such certainty that a laugh startled from Celia. "You cannot be serious."

"I can, and I am."

Gabriel may have only lately come by the title of duke, but he'd been one his entire life.

"Duchess," repeated Wrexford once he'd ventured within easy talking distance. Winded from his light sprint, the earl placed his hands on his knees for the duration of a few sharply drawn inhalations while he caught his breath.

Celia shot Gabriel an amused glance—which he didn't return.

The duke wasn't amused.

Celia took pity on Wrexford, who had gone his usual radish red from his exertions. "Are you out for a day at the races?" A benign enough question.

Wrexford opened his mouth to reply, but Gabriel beat him to it. "You're rather far from London." His eyes narrowed, as if he suspected the earl of foul play.

Which was silliness, except Wrexford's cheeks somehow went redder than radish. "Yes, well, *erm*, the duchess wasn't at Ashcote Hall when I called this morning." He turned toward Celia. "I was informed you were here for the day."

"Oh?" The question emerged rather more breathily than Celia would've liked. But... what did Gabriel suspect that she didn't?

Of course.

"Do you have a Thoroughbred stable, Lord Wrexford?"

"*Erm*, no," he said. A beat later, he added, "Not yet."

Ah... "So, you're thinking of starting a stable, and you saw my advertisement."

"*Erm*, yes."

Gabriel snorted.

Celia was growing seriously irritated with the duke. Here was potential business. As her partner, he of all people should understand. "At Ashcote stables, all three Thoroughbred sire lines are accounted for with our stallions. Our mares, too," she said, hoping to draw Wrexford into the conversation. His eyes, however, appeared to have glazed over, though his affable smile remained. She soldiered on. "So, it will come down to what physical and personality characteristics you wish to breed for."

Wrexford nodded, consideringly. "Ah, yes," he intoned, but said nothing more.

"Do you have some ideas?"

"Oh, do tell us," said Gabriel, sarcasm lacing every syllable.

Celia wanted nothing more than to deliver a swift kick to his shin.

Wrexford blinked, as if he'd only now registered the Duke of Acaster's presence. "*Erm…*" His smile went wobbly, and his eyes shifty.

The man looked as if he wanted the ground to swallow him whole, and Celia knew. He hadn't chased her down to discuss her stud operation. He'd sought her out for… *her.*

Annoyance prickled through her. *Men.* So predictable.

And Gabriel had seen it from the start.

Which only enhanced her annoyance, for Gabriel thought it his right to behave like a brute. He thought it was his right to…

Claim her.

And their five-day idyll at Ashcote was why.

Oh… no, no, no…

Wrexford gave his throat a deep and lengthy clearing. "Duchess." He looked as if sweat prickled his palms. "Would you care to… that is, if you'll be in Town… and, yes, if so, would you care to join me for an afternoon's ride on Rotten Row this Thursday?"

Celia caught herself before issuing an instinctive refusal, as both men willed an answer from her—one *no* and one *yes.* She bit back the *no.*

The last five days…

It might not be too late to rectify them.

At least, that was what her mind insisted.

But other parts of her felt less certain.

The other parts of her that would never get over the man at her side—and she understood something.

They would have to.

The last five days had been naught more than a dream.

And, now, she was awake; the dream was over.

The pang of loss strummed a chord through her.

A chord she'd experienced many times in her thirty years.

Before her stood reality personified in the eager form of the Earl of Wrexford.

She knew exactly what the moment demanded she say... "I would be most pleased to ride with you this Thursday."

Wrexford smiled as if he couldn't believe his good luck, the surprised *you would?* writ clear across his face.

Instead, it was Gabriel who spoke it. "You would?" he asked, flummoxed. "Won't you be at Ashcote Hall for the foreseeable future?"

"As a matter of fact," she began through her smile and the words that tasted like dust in her mouth, "I'm returning to London today."

"*Today?*"

"Yes, Your Grace."

A line formed between Gabriel's eyebrows, and his mouth clamped shut.

She had to keep talking. Only by speaking her intention aloud would she follow through with it, for she wanted nothing more than to return to Ashcote with Gabriel for the foreseeable future —for... *ever.*

No.

That was the dream.

This was reality.

She kept her gaze fixed on Wrexford. "Shall I plan to meet you at three of the clock on Thursday?"

"Indeed," said Wrexford. If he had a tail, it would've been wagging.

"Now," she said, all business, "if you gentlemen will excuse me, I shall be on my way."

With that, she pivoted and left the men in her dust—one smiling at his great good luck, the other glowering his great dukely displeasure.

In a matter of seconds, the earth at her back thudded with

determined footsteps. Which came as no surprise. When Gabriel drew abreast with her, she hissed, "Not here. In the carriage."

He didn't like it, but he agreed anyway.

Once seated opposite one another in the coach-and-four, he demanded, "What was that all about?"

"What do you mean?"

"Come now, Celia."

"Your sisters' debut ball is less than two weeks away." As excuses went, it was, at least, a truthful one.

"So?"

"It's time I return to London."

"You can't mean that."

"I do."

"But what of the last five days?"

And Celia spoke the three most difficult words of her life... "What of them?"

A series of emotions marched across Gabriel's face in quick succession. *Disbelief... anger... hurt...* It was the latter that penetrated Celia deepest.

He was young.

He lacked experience in matters of the opposite sex.

How had she allowed herself to forget?

She, however, was neither all that young nor inexperienced—which was rather the crux of the matter.

Gabriel deserved better than her.

He deserved the pure, full-bodied love they'd just witnessed between Rakesley and his new bride.

He deserved to experience that love with someone with a blameless past—not someone who dragged a trunk of damage and emotional trauma with her everywhere she went.

She reached over and turned the door latch, pushing the door open. "I shall be on my way if you don't mind, Your Grace."

Incredulous eyebrows lifted. "You intend to leave me here?"

She waved a hand, indicating the stables beyond. "Go buy yourself a horse," she said, unwavering. "You ride now."

He snorted. They both knew that for an exaggeration.

"Or buy a carriage," she said with studied indifference. "You're rich enough."

"But, Celia—" Exasperation wound through each syllable. "*This* is my carriage."

A fact, to be sure. Still… "I'm sure you won't mind lending it to a friend."

"Is that what we are? *Friends?*" he all but growled.

Unbidden, memory from this morning flashed across her mind.

He'd brought her tea in bed.

"Have you been talking to Eloise?" she'd asked.

He'd looked at her quizzically. "Since the Derby?"

"Oh, never mind."

Tea in bed… A gesture both small and grand.

One she couldn't think about now.

She lifted her chin an unflagging notch. "We're partners."

He held her gaze captive for an impossible trio of heartbeats, then he pushed off the leather squabs and out of the carriage, striding away without a backward glance.

Regret streamed through her—for what could have been.

No.

That way of thinking was a trap.

Of course, it never *could have been* with Gabriel.

With slow, determined purpose, a solution prickled through her and inveigled its way into her mind.

It was terribly, awfully, dreadfully simple.

She would find him a bride—one who was worthy of him.

And in doing so, place him firmly out of temptation's reach.

Of course, there was an additional measure of protection she could take. She could herself marry. Really…

She must marry.

If I had any choice in the matter, I would never be a wife again.

Those had been her exact words to him only an hour ago.

And she didn't have a choice, did she?

The reasons tumbled down on her like an avalanche—the foremost being that she'd never made a success of anything in her life. Her marriage... Her inability to bear a child... The Ashcote stud looked promising, but she would surely find a way to bollocks that up, too.

And then there was Gabriel.

She didn't see how she could be in business with him for the next three years and not want him every minute of every day... like she did at this very minute.

No.

She and Gabriel must marry—and not each other.

CHAPTER TWENTY

LONDON, THURSDAY

*T*he day hadn't dawned perfect—or anywhere near it.

In fact, London had been a gray soaked mess these last three days.

It seemed Celia had brought her mood with her from Norfolk.

However, amongst London's fashionable society, when an outing was to be had on Rotten Row, one didn't allow a little drizzly weather to stand in one's way, no matter how the jaunty ostrich feather in one's hat sagged in a limp, sodden clump. And, really, the colorful silks, sparkling jewels, and flashing smiles populating the Row were almost enough to make one forget that the sky above threatened to unleash yet another round of relentless rain.

Take the Ladies Saskia and Viveca riding in their brother's fashionable barouche with a pair of matched grays at the lead. Though a bit awe-struck by the promenade of dandies and ladies they'd only read about in gossip rags, their delight was evident in the vivacity of their smiles. Even Lady Saskia hadn't been able to suppress a giggle when a handsome young lord tipped his hat to her. It had never occurred to Celia until now that Lady Saskia might need a watchful eye kept on her.

Still, she experienced no small amount of relief that the sisters were warming to their new station in society. Acceptance would make life easier for them.

Of course, that was the lot of a woman, wasn't it?

Meekly accept what life threw your way, so it would go easier on you.

She squeezed her eyes shut against the memories such a thought conjured—of her marriage... of her marriage bed. Of what she'd had to accept—or life would go harder on her.

She attempted to shake the image away, but it was a stubborn image—of hands bound to bedposts, rope cutting into wrists, accepting and enduring—and the horror would steal upon her in unguarded moments. It took particular joy in snaking into her mind at times of happiness, as if she'd granted it permission.

She hadn't.

An intrusion was what it was.

And though she resented it with every fiber of her being, she was powerless against its will.

How she wished those memories and that past would finish with her, but she feared they never would.

A gust of wind swirled up the Row, promising the soggy afternoon would transform into a stormy night. Celia glanced over at Eloise, riding beside her and greeting all who passed with genuine pleasure. Instinctively, Celia stroked her hack Truffle's black mane, the soothing act pulling her away from the darkness that threatened to encroach.

She half turned toward Eloise. "I must thank you for letting me stay with you the last few nights."

Celia hadn't been able to return to the St. James's Square mansion and risk encountering... *him.*

"You are always welcome in my home."

"With the ball a little over a week away," continued Celia. "I think it would be best if I return to St. James's Square, so I can be near at hand."

"You're certain?" Eloise asked with concern, but Celia detected a relieved flicker in her cousin's eyes.

Celia nodded. "And I think Mr. Lancaster might not mind."

A light blush pinked Eloise's cheeks, but she didn't deny it.

Mr. Lancaster arrived at Eloise's Mayfair townhouse every evening at six sharp and shared the meal with them. Then, after brandies were consumed, he took himself away like a perfect gentleman.

It was time for Celia to leave, so Mr. Lancaster could stay.

Discreetly, she changed the subject. "You've done such a wonderful job with Lady Saskia and Lady Viveca these last few weeks. They are beautifully turned out in every way."

Eloise smiled with self-satisfaction, even as she demurred. "It's down to their own talents. They are a complementary pair of sisters. Where one has an interest, the other doesn't, and yet are bosom confidantes who are ever so harmonious. Life will proceed wonderfully for them."

"I think you're being too modest, cousin," said Celia. "Lady Saskia is smiling, and that's surely down to you. They must be making a good impression on the *ton* wherever they go."

"They are lovely, titled, and rich," said Eloise with a smile. "In combination, the three qualities go a long way toward popularity in our little world. Have you not noticed the correspondence basket overflowing with invitations and the bouquets of flowers strewn throughout the house?"

"I haven't stopped sneezing since my return to Town," quipped Celia.

A calculating look entered Eloise's eyes. "Come, cousin, let us ride toward the Serpentine. The young ladies will be safe without us."

"I should hope so," said Celia on another laugh. No fewer than three young gentlemen had sidled up to the barouche, all vying for the scantest second of the sisters' attention.

One hand loose around Truffle's reins and the other reaffixing her chapeau against the wind that was definitely picking up, Celia rode alongside Eloise.

A conversation was coming.

The minutes and seconds had only been ticking down until Eloise asked... "You were at Ashcote Hall for—*what?*—nearly a fortnight?"

Though the question made the attempt at nonchalance, Celia understood it for what it was. The thin edge of a crowbar meant to prise Celia open and extract information.

"Aye." She wasn't about to make it easy on Eloise.

"And the duke stayed at Ashcote the entire time?" Eloise wasn't beating about the bush.

"Not entirely."

It was the truth—or mostly. She *had* spent the first few nights alone.

Once they reached the Serpentine, they slowed their mounts to a stop at the riverbank. Eloise met Celia directly in the eye. "Whatever could the two of you have gotten up to with all that time... *alone?*"

"Between the household and stables, Ashcote has a staff of nearly thirty," returned Celia, willfully misconstruing her cousin's words—no matter how dead on the mark they were. "We were hardly *alone.*"

Eloise snorted.

"What, pray tell, are you insinuating, cousin?"

Eloise lifted an eyebrow. "*You* tell *me... cousin.*"

"You know I have my racing operation, and now with the stud beginning to gain traction, I'm quite occupied when I'm at Ashcote."

"Oh, yes, day and *night*, I'm sure." Eloise looked very much as if she was enjoying herself.

Celia decided to ignore the emphasis placed on *night*. "And Gabriel has much to occupy him, as well."

Eloise studied Celia with an expression that communicated pure, unadulterated triumph. *"Gabriel?"*

Oh, botheration.

With that *Gabriel*, Celia had given herself away. But when had there ever been any hiding from Eloise? If a truth was to be had, she would ferret it out.

What Celia needed to do was move this conversation along, for she could actually use her cousin's help. "Anyway, the duke is to marry."

Eloise's knowing smirk instantly transformed into an abundance of joy. "Celia!" she exclaimed. "Should I be offering you congratulations?"

Celia swallowed back a sudden surge of emotion. "The bride has yet to be found."

An instant frown tugged at the corners of Eloise's mouth. "Then how can you know such a thing?" Her mind working, luminous brown eyes narrowed. "Does the duke know about his plan to marry?"

Celia stared determinedly into the murky waters of the Serpentine. "That's entirely beside the point."

"Then what entirely *is* the point, Celia?"

Unable to meet her cousin's eye, she turned Truffle and gazed out at the park. Though a gray day, it was lovely here beside the Serpentine with verdant lawn stretching toward Rotten Row and parkland to the other side of the river. Not as untamed as what one enjoyed in the countryside, but a lovely respite from the London hustle and bustle, nonetheless.

Her eye caught upon a female figure seated on a bench. Even from this distance, the lady held a familiarity, though only her silhouette bent over a journal, her hand scribbling madly, was visible.

Lady Beatrix.

The woman seemed to be everywhere. Had it always been so? Or was it that Celia had never noticed? She couldn't help suspecting it was by the lady's design.

Celia jutted her chin. "What do you know about Lady Beatrix St. Vincent?"

Eloise gave an indifferent shrug. "She's the only child of the Marquess of Lydon."

Celia had known that much.

"I know little about her," continued Eloise. "She's bosom friends with Lady Artemis Keating, which you might've already known. I think she's mad about horse racing, for she's always at the courses. She could be as profligate a gambler as her father. They say that sort of thing gets in the blood in families."

Celia shook her head, definite. "I don't believe that sort of tattle. People make of themselves who they are." A belief Celia held to her core.

Besides, Lady Beatrix seemed like a different sort of person.

Really, she might be the perfect person...

The perfect *bride*.

Her mind went back to the racing meeting at Great Yarmouth. Lady Beatrix was an intelligent woman. Strong-willed, too, it would seem. Beyond the first flush of womanhood, she wasn't possessed of a flashy beauty, but rather a quiet sort of loveliness, if one looked closely.

And yet she remained unwed.

"Do you know why she hasn't married?"

"By her own preference? She is the daughter of a marquess, perhaps she decided connubial bliss wasn't worth losing her independence for."

"Perhaps," allowed Celia. Her mouth turned down in concentration as her mind whirred with possibility...

It could be worth a try.

Though a duke, Gabriel was also the owner of a gaming hell. He would need a less than conventional wife, and Lady Beatrix—

the daughter of a marquess and a woman who held no qualms with hying about the countryside by her lone self to every racing meeting on offer—was no conventional lady.

In fact, she might be the perfect lady.

Celia only realized her fingernails had dug red crescents into her palms.

Finding Gabriel a wife was the correct course.

Truly, it was.

Galloping movement caught the edge of her vision. *Wrexford*, his arm waving wildly, his broad smile visible from the moon as he charged toward her and Eloise.

"The earl certainly appears most, *erm...*" A bemused Eloise searched for a word. "*Eager.*"

"*Eager* surely must be his middle name."

Eloise's head canted. "He's rather like an overexcited puppy in man form."

For some inexplicable reason, Celia felt the compulsion to defend him. "I can think of worse qualities in a man."

Eloise set her wise gaze upon Celia. "Right you are, cousin."

Celia hadn't needed to say more to make her point heard. She'd experienced *worse qualities* in a man, and they both knew it.

"Now," said Eloise, pulling her reins and turning her mount. "I'll leave you to whatever it is you're doing with the earl."

"It's an innocent outing, cousin. That's all."

Eloise lifted a single eyebrow. "You might want to inform him."

If possible, Wrexford's smile had only increased in radiance.

And Eloise was off.

And Celia was left alone with her usual smile for company.

But not for long.

"Duchess," Wrexford called out, all—*eager*—smiles. "You came." He sounded equal parts surprised and delighted.

Celia found his palpable relief sweet. "I did." She searched her mind for something to say to this young earl to whom she had nothing to say. "Not the best weather for it."

English weather could always be relied upon in a conversational pinch.

He glanced up at the blanket of low-hanging clouds above their heads with complete surprise. "I hadn't noticed."

Of a sudden, Celia understood something about this young Earl of Wrexford. He wouldn't have noticed. A gray day would have no effect on him, for he always carried a bit of sunshine inside.

Celia couldn't help but warm to him. "Do you promenade on Rotten Row often?"

"I do try for three afternoons a week, but it can be difficult to manage what with all the other invitations and such." He spoke the words with utter, unironic seriousness.

Of course, socializing was the earl's occupation, and so it was for most of the *ton*—and all for the sole intention of showing off for one another in a variety of venues, be it Rotten Row or Almack's Assembly Rooms or a musicale or a ball. It was all the same.

And how exhaustingly dull it all was.

"What else occupies your time?" She sincerely wanted to know. She suspected a good half hour a day was spent on the intricate knot of his cravat.

"Oh, the usual pursuits," he said, breezy and unbothered.

Though Celia was disposed to like Wrexford on a certain level, he didn't seem to have much substance to him as he contentedly rode alongside her to the main straight of Rotten Row where they would be seen riding together—a sure signal to society that a potential courtship might be afoot.

As a widow, Celia's reputation was in no danger if nothing came of it—which, of course, it wouldn't. Wrexford's reputation, however, would only be enhanced as a young buck about Town to be seen with the widowed Duchess of Acaster, she understood with cold clarity. After all, this was her main value to the opposite sex.

Unbidden, a memory came to her…

Of riding alongside a different man…

Gabriel.

That ride hadn't been for show.

Those five days at Ashcote had been only for them.

Gabriel wasn't the sort of man interested in proving his status to society.

Suppressed ache crawled through her, settling as a heavy knot in the center of her chest.

She took one deep breath, then another, in an attempt to loosen it.

As ever, to no avail.

She set her attention on the man at her side—*Wrexford.*

He wasn't a bad sort.

Further, the possibility existed the earl himself might consider this outing as part of a courtship. She might not simply be the whim of a younger man or a feather in his cap, the earnestness of his eyes communicated.

She would have to tread carefully with him.

In the distance, a figure on horseback appeared on the path—a *familiar* figure.

Celia's heart leapt in her chest, even as she attempted to blink the apparition away.

Yet the figure remained—moved closer, in fact.

A light sheen of perspiration prickled across her body and the tips of her ears went hot. She wouldn't have thought to find this figure riding on Rotten Row in an eternity of years.

Gabriel.

As if her thoughts and aches had the power to conjure him.

Honestly, he was a terrible horseman. He could sit no way other than exceedingly unnaturally in the saddle.

A feeling expanded in her chest.

The very feeling she'd been tamping down since she'd lost sight of him at Great Yarmouth, now escaped its bonds.

Gabriel, with his instinctive dislike of riding, was choosing to ride a horse—*terribly*—a man accustomed to being the best at everything he set his mind to.

Yet he was here.

And Celia couldn't help thinking he was here for her.

Sudden emotion skittered through her, even as a delighted smile twitched about her mouth.

She caught herself immediately. Emotional smiles wouldn't do in her present circumstances.

So, she took the only logical course and tamped it down with a scowl.

CHAPTER TWENTY-ONE

*G*abriel felt like three kinds of fool.

Him... here... on Rotten Row... at a fashionable hour of day...

Yet he hadn't been able to stop himself.

Oh, that was a fair bit of self-deceit, now wasn't it?

In fact, *him... here... on Rotten Row... at a fashionable hour of day...* was a premeditated act.

With full knowledge of Celia's Thursday outing with Wrexford, Gabriel had secured riding lessons for himself these last three mornings. And they'd worked—somewhat. He still didn't like it, but he was, at least, competent enough to keep his seat and give the horse directions. The astonishing part was the horse obeyed.

Still, it had taken ages to travel from his mews to Hyde Park, as he'd made the horse walk the entire distance. No few draymen had vented their frustration at Gabriel's tortoise-like pace.

Ahead, Celia and Wrexford watched him approach. Wrexford looked his ever-same self, smiling and dreadfully cheery.

As for Celia... Well, she looked her ever-beautiful self in a dove gray riding habit trimmed with pale pink touches. Celia ever had a bit of pink on her person.

But as Gabriel neared them, enduring stares from other members of the *ton* who were only now catching their first sighting of the new Duke of Acaster, he noticed a shallow vertical line between Celia's eyebrows. She was wondering what in the blazes he was doing here... on a horse... on this day... at this precise time—the very day and time he'd heard her and Wrexford arrange.

Of course, Gabriel knew the reason he'd repeated to himself—that he was only here to see how Saskia and Viveca got on—wouldn't stand up beneath scrutiny.

Not even his own.

Not when he hadn't shown a lick of interest in bringing his sisters up to society snuff—his primary concern being the end, not the means.

"Acaster," Wrexford called out, his hale and hearty smile faltering not one bit. The man truly had an air of goodness about him.

It was too bad Gabriel couldn't stand the sight of him.

Celia, on the other hand, had dropped her smile. *Good.* If she wasn't going to give him her genuine smile—the one he'd pulled from her any number of occasions and variety of ways during their five-day idyll at Ashcote Hall—he'd rather suffer her annoyed frown. "Duke," was all she granted by way of greeting—even as he willed her with his unflinching gaze to grant him more.

"We're taking the afternoon air," volunteered Wrexford.

Gabriel tore his gaze from Celia's stubborn profile and fixed it on Wrexford, a poor substitute. "And how do you find the air?" he asked. "Breathable?" He'd always found the term *taking the air* silly.

Wrexford laughed, easily deflecting any hint of insult. "Eminently so."

"And what are *you* doing here, Your Grace?" There was no mistaking Celia's irritation. "It was my understanding you didn't care for riding."

"I'm coming around to caring for it." An outright lie, and they both knew it. "I'm coming around to caring for a lot of things."

Not a lie.

She blinked.

He'd caught her on the back foot.

Excellent.

"That's jolly good to hear, Acaster," exclaimed Wrexford. "After all, you're one of us now."

One of us.

Gabriel cared not for such nonsense, save in one way: Becoming *one of us* had led him to Celia.

Wrexford and everyone else could stuff the rest.

Gabriel, however, was only getting started with the earl. "At Great Yarmouth," he began, "you mentioned an interest in procuring a horse from the Ashcote stud."

Wrexford's gaze shifted, and he looked distinctly... squirmy. "*Erm*, yes," he said, "in a manner of speaking." The tips of the man's ears had gone bright red.

"Now that you've had a few days to contemplate it, have you decided which physical and personality characteristics you wish to breed for?" After a moment's flummoxed hesitation, Gabriel took pity on the man. "Four legs, I suppose."

A relieved laugh escaped Wrexford. "Most definitely four."

"And the color?"

"I hadn't—"

"Let me help you," said Gabriel. "The dominant colors for Thoroughbreds are bay, brown, black, chestnut, and gray."

Wrexford nodded with wobbly decision. "The last one." He offered Celia a tremulous smile. "Gray."

"Ah, but there you'll be out of luck at the Ashcote stables," said Gabriel, apologetically—and anything but.

"I will?"

"Indeed."

This was the other way Gabriel had filled his time these last three days: He'd been studying the history of the Thoroughbred and the breeding practices of a stud. It was actually fascinating—and it was clear Wrexford remained woefully ignorant of all things *horse*.

"The gray hue comes from the Alcock Arabian, and the Ashcote stable has none of that unique bloodline."

"Ah, of course, of course," said Wrexford, resembling a man treading water.

As for Celia, she observed the exchange quietly, her face giving none of her thoughts away, except for the slight purse of her mouth.

"Speaking of bloodline," Gabriel continued for some blasted reason.

He'd proven his point. Wrexford knew nothing about horses, and Gabriel had exposed him for a fraud. The man had been soundly conversationally defeated.

But for something inside Gabriel, it wasn't enough to defeat the man.

He must vanquish him.

"Do you know which sire line you would like your Thoroughbred to descend from?" A simple question... deceptively so.

"Well, with so many to choose from..." began Wrexford.

"There are three," stated Gabriel.

An uncomfortable beat of time ticked past.

"Right," said Wrexford, slowly.

"If you're interested in the oldest bloodline, then the Byerley Turk will be the tail male you're looking for."

Wrexford swallowed. "Right you are."

"If you're looking for the line that begat Flying Childers and Eclipse, then it'll be the Darley Arabian."

"Ah, yes." Wrexford nodded with some decisiveness. "Who wouldn't want progeny from those illustrious forbears?"

"Who, indeed? But as a sporting man, a sire line with a good story might grab your interest—which would be the Godolphin Arabian. Foaled in Yemen in seventeen twenty-four, he was sent to Tunis." Gabriel was beginning to sound like a history book come to life, but he couldn't help himself. "From there, he was given as a gift from the Bey to King Louis XV of France. Then his history becomes a little foggy. No one knows how he came into the possession of one Mr. Edward Coke of Derbyshire. Either he was sold, or more colorfully, found by Mr. Coke between the shafts of a water cart in Paris. Both tales are difficult to substantiate."

"*Right.*" For a moment, Wrexford appeared to be lost for any other words. "*Erm*, well, it all sounds good to me," he finished with his usual good nature.

A consideration had Gabriel's brow furrowing. Indeed, he was besting Wrexford for Celia to see, but...

Possibly, it was he who wasn't coming across to advantage.

The peeved crinkle of Celia's eyebrows told him as much.

Wrexford might be exposed for the vacuous twit he was, but —and the irony wasn't lost on Gabriel given the subject at hand— it could be he who appeared the horse's arse.

And yet, knowing this, he couldn't seem to stop... "Have you given thought to the mare line?"

"I haven't." The panic returned to Wrexford's eyes. "Should I?"

"It only matters if you require the foundation mares to have been Arabians. In which case, you'll want a horse from the Darley line and the decision is made for you."

"Well, there you have it." Wrexford's bright smile spoke of no small amount of relief. "That'll be the Thoroughbred for me."

"An interesting word—*Thoroughbred*," said Gabriel. "It was coined by Lord Bristol in seventeen-thirteen for horses that—"

"Your Grace," Celia cut in, both smoothly and abruptly.

Rather than having been impressed by all his recently acquired knowledge, Gabriel suspected she was rather... *not*.

"Might you wish to join your sisters for the remainder of their outing?" she continued. "I believe they would be most delighted to see you."

And that was the wind gone out of Gabriel's sails.

The implication was, of course, he was no source of great delight for present company.

Right.

There was nothing for it.

He'd been dismissed.

"Of course," he said, directing a curt tip of his hat toward Celia. He pivoted. "Wrexford."

The earl offered a sheepish, "Fare thee well, old chap," though he had nothing to apologize for, and the two were on their way.

Gabriel couldn't help gazing at their backs as they rode. Though seated side-saddle on her mount, Celia looked completely at ease, an elegance in the straights and curves of her body. So, too, did Wrexford appear in full control of his animal. Of course, he did. The man was an earl. He'd like as not learned to ride before he could walk.

And here was Gabriel, left alone with a mind that wanted to steam and stew. What a complete and utter fool he'd made of himself. Rather than making progress with Celia, he'd set himself back several paces.

"*Siren!*"

Gabriel turned and found a figure riding toward him. *Blake Deverill.* A man as out of place in society environs as he. But where Gabriel had his elevated status thrust upon him, Deverill was using every resource at his disposal to muscle his way in.

Gabriel didn't understand that particular drive in the man. Ambition, he understood. Deverill had made a success of his business. Beyond his wildest dreams, Gabriel would've reckoned. Yet he was trying to become part of the *haut ton*, a world that would never genuinely accept him—all because he had the wrong blood flowing through his veins and the wrong accent issuing from his mouth.

And Gabriel, as improbable as it was, had the right blood.

Yet he answered to the name *Siren*. It still felt like his real name.

Like the real him.

"Deverill," said Gabriel once they were within speaking distance—a distance bridged by Deverill, who appeared quite the accomplished horseman.

Did everyone in England know how to ride except him?

"Didn't suppose I'd find you here," said Deverill in his broad Yorkshire accent inflected with a bit of Irish. "Come to think of it, have I ever seen you outside The Archangel?"

"Doubtful."

"And now you're a duke and here on Rotten Row like any other fashionable dandy."

As if Gabriel hadn't already been uncomfortable in his seat, he squirmed. "Something like that."

Deverill glanced around and gave a low whistle. "Some heights we've ascended to, us two lads." His gaze narrowed. "Hard work for some, and an accident of birth for others." He shook his head in wonder. "And now you're one of them. Isn't that right, Acaster?"

The impulse to explain seized Gabriel, though he owed Deverill nothing. Mutual business interests bound them, that was all. "Being a duke is a sight more work than one might think, if one chooses to engage with it."

"Which most don't," scoffed Deverill. "You well know as much, given The Archangel's patrons."

Gabriel nodded his agreement.

A smile broadened across Deverill's face. "They call me Lord Devil."

With Deverill's black hair, piercing blue eyes, and intensity of purpose, they would. "They do like their nicknames."

A chuckle rumbled from Deverill. "They've taken to calling you the Duke of Vice."

"I hadn't heard that one."

"Well, they wouldn't say it to your face, would they?" His head cocked. "But you, Siren, you're still all business, correct?"

Though couched as light joshing, it was a dead-serious query from a business partner. Deverill was gaining a feel for the new Duke of Acaster.

Gabriel almost spoke a reflexive *of course*, and a few weeks ago, he would have, but now he couldn't. The last several days of his life hadn't been about business, at all. But rather about...

Celia.

Certainly, he'd conducted business—in between horse riding and Thoroughbred history lessons—but it hadn't been his reason for getting out of bed in the morning. The first thought on his mind when he woke was no longer numbers and how he would use the day to increase them in the form of pounds.

It was a different form that filled his mind.

Celia.

And none of this could be said to the man before him.

So, business it would have to be. Here, in such talk, they could sink into a conversation and speak as equals in a language they both understood.

"Are the engines ready for export?"

Deverill gave a firm nod. "They're being transported to the docks as we speak and will be off to France within the fortnight."

Deverill was an example of Gabriel's favorite sort of business venture. The vision to see a need in the market and the knowledge to meet it.

In Deverill's case, it was steam engines. For decades, the machines had only been of use in coal mines, because therein lay the fuel to power the massive beasts. But Deverill understood if steam engines could be made more efficient in their consumption of coal, they could be of use in myriad industries, because they wouldn't have to be near a coal mine to operate. So, he'd set to work on honing the engineering and securing the financing, which was where Gabriel entered the equation—and what a pretty penny his investment had begun to yield with no signs of stopping.

As a pair of riders approached—a lord and his fashionable lady—not with the intention to meet, but to pass, Gabriel and Deverill moved their mounts off the path. Gabriel recognized the lord as the Earl of Bridgewater, a man given to serious betting and gaming in every form gambling took, a pursuit which saw him inside The Archangel's four walls a few nights a week, in addition to his other gaming haunts strewn about Town.

The lady riding a proud white mount at his side would be his new countess. His *young* countess. His skin the permanent flushed red of a man given to drink and long past the prime of his youth, Gabriel would put the earl in his middle fifties. Given that his countess was a good thirty years younger, she would've been no older than five-and-twenty. Gabriel knew nothing about her, save what he could see with his own eyes now. With her sun-streaked hair, bright flashing eyes, and vivacious smile, she was a beauty—the sort an aging earl made his countess.

They didn't stop as they cantered past, the earl directing a nod toward Gabriel and the countess waving at a lady some twenty yards distant.

Gabriel glanced at Deverill, ready to resume their conversation, but the other man's demeanor had wholly altered as he stared at the backs of the earl and countess. Deverill ever held an edge to him. He wasn't a man one relaxed around, but now the edge appeared sharp as a razorblade—and his expression suggested a foul mood dark enough to rival the sky above.

Without another word, he tossed a grunt of farewell at Gabriel and galloped in the opposite direction.

A history existed between Deverill and Bridgewater, one Gabriel was content to leave them to. Although, he couldn't help wonder…

Perhaps it wasn't Bridgewater, at all.

Perhaps it was the countess.

It had to do with the suddenness and intensity of Deverill's foul mood.

For if recent history had taught Gabriel nothing else, it was that nothing could provoke a sudden and intense foul mood in a man like a woman.

Alone and unable to face an afternoon of further niceties, Gabriel gave his knees a light squeeze and directed his mount toward Park Lane. He would take himself home.

But not on horseback.

He slid from the mount and took reins in hand, leading the way on foot. If a few questioning glances and raised eyebrows flicked his way, he paid them no heed. He'd rather spend his afternoon with numbers. They were clear and predictable.

Very unlike his life since Celia came into it.

Celia…

Seeing her with Wrexford…

Gabriel couldn't fathom why she was allowing the flirtation.

Then, the dark sky that had been promising rain all day broke open and soaked Gabriel to the skin in five seconds.

And he felt it was only right.

CHAPTER TWENTY-TWO

*N*ight
Usually, Celia loved a rainy night.

But on this rainy night, her head refused to settle into sleep on her pillow, instead moving this way and that, failing to find a resting position that offered the oblivion of rain-soothed slumber.

Simply, her mind had been abuzz since her outing to Rotten Row.

Since seeing Gabriel, so gorgeous and awkward on his mount.

Her heart had possibly lifted in her chest.

She wanted him.

A wanting that pulled at her mind and body.

Why couldn't she want Wrexford?

He was an eminently better candidate for longing—and, possibly, she could have him if she made the slightest effort. After all, he was an earl, who would someday be a marquess. He had money and an interest in her stud operation.

Wrexford had potential.

He could be her answer to a secure future.

Finished wrestling with her pillow for comfort, Celia swept

the coverlet aside and swung her legs off the bed. Shrugging into a dressing robe over her sleeping chemise, she took herself to the library. When she'd shared this mansion with her late husband, it was the only room she'd known for certain she wouldn't find him. The servants always left a fire burning when she was in residence.

She'd never been much of a reader before her marriage, but she'd found solace in books during long, sleepless nights. She always selected a book at random. It was how she'd come to read a Greek play here and a treatise on capitalist economics there. She'd learned a bit about botany from Humboldt's compendium and a bit about Queen Elizabeth's England from Shakespeare's plays. She wasn't a bluestocking or especially erudite, but she enjoyed these late night forays into the library. It was the one thing she liked about London.

The mellow orange glow around the seams of the cracked door didn't alert her to another presence in the room. Rather, it was the large form seated at the imposing oak desk, concentrated upon a ledger, quill in hand.

Gabriel.

As it was wont to do, his youth struck her. *Four-and-twenty years.* A full six years younger than her. So young and yet...

Not.

Again, she felt that pull—*wanting.*

She shouldn't have returned to the St. James's Square mansion. Yes, she'd needed to leave Eloise's house before she overstayed her welcome, but she could've gone to a hotel. Mivart's would've been a perfectly suitable option.

Her safe return here had been sheer delusion... Delusion that she could be housed beneath the same roof as Gabriel.

She should run back to her bedroom before he sensed her presence, throw essentials into a valise, and flee this mansion.

She wasn't safe.

Not from her wanting.

And yet… she cleared her throat—and got his attention.

He twisted in the chair and met her gaze—as she'd known he would, leaving her feet no choice but to fully enter the room. "I see you discovered the library," she said, her mind desperately searching for something to say. The obvious would do in a pinch.

"It's the best room in the house."

He would see that.

She should find her way to the shelves, select a book at random, and flee without another word. In the short time they'd known each other, too much history had accumulated between them.

It doesn't have to be history, a shadowy voice insisted.

And it was that shadow part of herself that had her stepping deeper into the room and saying, "You seem to be hard at it."

"Bills for the ball." He held up a sheet of paper. "We're going to have twenty dozen pink roses and three flower bowers?"

Celia reached out and plucked the bill from his hand. She gave it a quick scan to verify everything was in order, then set it down, satisfied. She met his bemused gaze. "You're a duke, and a rich one while you're at it. There are expectations."

He rolled his eyes, unconvinced.

She tapped forefinger to solid oak. "The flowers will be nothing to the bill for champagne."

"I wait with bated breath."

A smile pulled at her mouth. It couldn't help itself. The man was so… *responsible*.

What a very attractive quality.

"It's possible you'll be the only financially solvent duke in the history of dukes."

He snorted.

The nearest open ledger caught her eye. Lots of numbers in vertical rows. She'd never seen Gabriel's handwriting before. Of course, his hand was neat and meticulous. "Is this from your business?"

He settled back in his chair. "The year-to-date ticket sales for the Race of the Century."

A question that had long been niggling at her presented itself. "How did you come to be involved in such a venture?"

He gave a light shrug. "The Duke of Richmond approached me with the idea."

"But—" Oh, how to say this without sounding superior. "You're not an especially horsey sort of person."

That pulled the hint of a smile. "My lack of horsiness notwithstanding, I do know something of numbers, which is why the partnership works. Richmond has all the connections for venue, vendors, and such, and I have the experience with finances and promotion." He tapped the ledger. "And I balance the books myself."

"You would never let another man balance your books, would you?"

"Never."

A slick of perspiration pinpricked Celia's skin. She wasn't sure they were talking about business dealings anymore. There seemed to be a conversation below this conversation—one that put a slight wobble in her knees.

She swallowed and attempted to pull herself out of this flight of fancy. "Don't you usually do this work at The Archangel?"

He gave a slow nod. "Yes, but…"

"But?"

"I've decided to separate myself from the club."

Unexpected, that answer. "Why? Because you're a duke now?"

"No and yes," he said after a long beat of time. "It's not *because* I'm a duke. It's because of all that comes with being a duke, particularly the Duke of Acaster. There's much work to be done to rehabilitate its lands and finances."

He appeared not intimidated by the prospect one bit. In fact, she rather thought it a task he would relish.

Which left Celia with a question she was afraid to ask—a question she *must* ask.

The idea of this question putting a definite wobble in her knees.

"Aren't you looking to sell every unentailed property belonging to the duchy?"

His gaze remained steady on hers. "I've decided on a different approach."

Celia's heart became a racehorse in her chest. Here was another question she must ask… "You won't be selling Ashcote?"

He shook his head. "After examining all the financials, I believe it will be running in the black in two years. Your enterprise is a good investment."

Celia took a moment to let those words settle in.

A good investment…

Her.

The idea defied belief.

No one had said as much or thought as much of her in all her life—including herself.

"You'll become the most powerful duke in the *ton*, if you're not careful."

This young man with his ambition, talent, and superior brain was absolutely destined to become the most powerful duke in England.

Give him ten years, and he would be a glory.

"For the duke you're set to become, you'll need a duchess, of course."

His head cocked, his gaze increasing with intensity. "Will I?"

She nodded, even as a hollow chasm opened inside her. "You'll need an heir."

"I don't care about heirs."

Celia wouldn't let it go—she couldn't. "What sort of bride are you looking for?"

He shoved to a stand—all six feet of him towering above her.

She had to tip her head back to hold his scorching gaze. "I don't want a bride," he said. "I want…"

The breath froze in Celia's chest. She might never draw breath again.

It was the two words he'd spoken.

I… want…

And the one he'd left unspoken.

The one that had her heart hammering in her chest.

The one every fiber in her being longed to hear.

You.

A word that was impossible.

"You're naïve, Duke."

She wielded the words like a weapon. Not against him—though he wouldn't know that—but against her own desire.

"*Naïve*," he repeated, and his eyes narrowed. "Is that yet another way of saying I'm young? I thought we'd put that subject to bed."

Quite literally, she wouldn't say.

Which only doubled her resolve not to cede an inch of ground. "If you think the *ton* will allow you to remain unmarried for long, you are in for a rude awakening."

"I cannot be forced to marry."

Where the conversational ground had been shaky beneath her feet only seconds ago, it grew firmer here. "But can't you?" she asked.

He remained silent. He was waiting for her to answer her own question.

"You're rich, handsome, titled, and honorable," she explained. "It's that last quality they'll use against you, if you don't find a bride yourself."

He lifted a skeptical eyebrow. "How can my honor possibly be used against me?"

Oh, this man had so much to learn… "You'll be caught in a compromising situation."

"Ah, but I won't."

He was just so naïvely certain.

"It will be painstakingly planned," she continued, as if he hadn't spoken. "You'll find yourself alone—somewhere private in a public place—and a perfectly lovely young lady will appear. She'll be lost and equal parts giggly and awed by your dukely presence. Perhaps her foot will catch on a root, and you'll gallantly catch her, so she doesn't fall. At that exact moment—with her in your arms—her mama will happen to be strolling past with a carefully selected witness, ideally a known gossip." Celia shrugged. "It's but one scenario, but a ball would be the likely setting."

Gabriel snorted. "Pure fantasy."

But Celia wasn't finished. "And that's how you'll find yourself engaged, for the young lady's mama and papa won't stand for their daughter being despoiled by the Duke of Vice, and if they have to suffer him becoming part of the family, so be it. They'll do so with forbearance, all the while secretly congratulating one another."

"You seem to know a lot about such happenings."

She gave a wry shrug. "*Such happenings* happen all the time, Your Grace. It isn't only your sisters who need to be prepared to enter the *ton*. You do, too. So, I'll say it again. You need a bride, duke."

While she was talking, she'd wandered over to stand before the hearth. Gabriel joined her at the other end, the mellow orange glow of the fireplace between them.

"So," she began with renewed purpose, "what sort of bride are you looking for?"

He propped a shoulder against the high mantle and crossed his arms over his chest. His eyes held a specific glint—one of... *challenge*. And something else, too—*determination*.

A wobble fluttered through her.

"Intelligent," he spoke, at last.

She nodded. "I would've expected that to be the first thing you said."

"Attractive."

She snorted. "Of course. You're a man."

"Talented."

"Plenty of talented women in the world."

"Knowledgeable about horses and racing."

Ah. Celia felt her mouth curve into a smile that held no small amount of triumph. At last, he'd played into her hands. "My thoughts exactly."

A line formed between his eyebrows. "They are?"

"I know of one such woman as you describe."

"You do?"

Celia spread her hands wide, like a magician on the verge of revealing her final, most spectacular trick of all. "You've perfectly described Lady Beatrix St. Vincent."

He blinked. "I have?"

"Indeed."

CHAPTER TWENTY-THREE

*T*en types of disbelief marched through Gabriel.
Indeed.

If that was the conclusion Celia had reached, he had his work cut out for him.

But when had he ever shied away from a test of will?

"Passionate."

He threw the word out like a challenge.

Her smile faltered. "In the initial generalities of early courtship, that might be difficult information to come by."

"Her attractiveness wouldn't simply be on the outside." He took a step forward. "She would be possessed of an interior beauty that she only lets the lucky few see, because it makes her too vulnerable to those who would fail her."

"Again," she began, her voice gone to a rasp in her throat, "I'm not sure how you could know that at first."

The woman was stubborn, that was a fact.

The time had arrived to erase all doubt of whom he spoke...
"With eyes the hue of sun shining through honey."

She blinked those honey amber eyes, her lips parted, her breath gone shallow.

So, this was what it was like to seduce a woman.

He could take to it.

He took another step closer—so close he could reach out and touch her.

Not yet.

"With sable hair that reaches the small of her back to brush the top of her lush, perfect bottom when her head arches in pleasure."

Celia swallowed. He would wager his every last farthing that her mouth had gone desperately dry.

"And when she cries out in ecstasy, there's a sound she makes, caught between a gasp and a whimper. It makes my cock hard just thinking about it."

"I... I... I'm not sure you should say that to a lady you're courting."

The fire crackled in the hearth. "Shouldn't I?"

He was now so close she had to angle her head back to meet his gaze, exposing the elegant length of her throat. It was all he could do not to press his mouth to that delicate flesh.

Not yet.

"That's a very specific list," she said in a near whisper, so entirely had her breath abandoned her.

"Really, I think there's but one woman who fits."

"Oh?"

Unable not to touch some part of her, he reached out and brushed the pad of his thumb along her parted lower lip. *Soft... plump... inviting...*

He angled his head and replaced thumb with mouth, the warm humidity of their breath mingling, his tongue sliding across that inviting lip. She released a sigh as she swayed forward, her arms reaching up, feminine fingers twining through the hair at the nape of his neck, sending goosebumps skittering across his skin. Pent-up desire carried the moment as his hand found the small of her back and pulled her to him, her body fast against his as he deepened the kiss into a carnal act, pivoting them so he had her pressed against the wall to the side of the hearth. His body up against hers, his hand slid lower, to her lush arse, tightening as he pulled her firmly against him.

One hand released its hold on his neck, and light fingers trailed along his stubbled cheek. She pulled back, enough to break the kiss, the pad of her thumb replacing her mouth as she slid it along his lower lip. Her other hand found his, slender fingers twining through his larger ones. Her gaze lifted. "Come with me." Then she slipped sideways along the wall and led him from the library.

At the threshold, he made to go left and met resistance. Her eyes caught his over her shoulder, and she gave her head a shake.

And he understood.

They wouldn't be going to his bedroom—the bedroom of the duke.

The bedroom that had once belonged to her late husband.

Instead, she pulled him in the opposite direction. Down one corridor, then another, his only point of contact with her was in the squeeze of their twined fingers, his entire being centered in the press of his palm against hers, her scent trailing in her wake. *Jasmine and bergamot.*

He breathed it in—breathing *her* in—and it occurred to him that she might simply want to continue their conversation some-where more private. He hadn't much experience in matters of intimacy between men and women, but surely his intentions had been as clear as the rigid outline of his cock in his trousers.

There could have been no mistaking them.

As she pulled him into her bedroom, he thought—*hoped*—there was no mistaking hers.

She released his hand and circled behind him to shut the door.

The key turned in the lock.

"Should I be worried?"

He hoped so.

"It depends."

"On?"

Wickedness in her eyes, she stepped toward him, stopping a hairsbreadth away, so they only just didn't touch.

Her head canted to a challenging angle, and her dark eyes held his. "On whether or not you wish to be ravished."

Her palms pressed flat against his chest, as if to push him away, then slid around his neck, the press of her curves soft and lush against him. She lifted onto the tips of her toes, and her mouth met his ear. "The choice is yours."

Gabriel remained very, very, *very* still, though his hands flexed with the need to tear off her robe and whatever other flimsy garment that lay beneath. His mouth needed to be on her skin.

But he sensed something vital.

Celia was in control.

She *needed* to be in control.

So, he stood and endured with hands empty, as she unknotted his cravat and flung it away, white silk fluttering to the floor. Then it was his coat sliding off his shoulders, nimble fingers making short work of the buttons of his waistcoat. It was tossed aside, too.

She leaned back and took in the sight of him, his shirt an open V, baring the dusting of hair and muscles of his chest.

Hunger.

That was what he saw in her eyes.

For him.

He wasn't sure how it was possible for his cock to go harder, but it did, her naked wanting of him an aphrodisiac like none other.

Again, her hands found his chest, the beat of his heart heavy beneath her palms. She shifted forward and pressed her mouth to him.

And, still, his hands remained empty of her.

He would only touch her when she allowed.

He closed his eyes and centered himself around sensation. The press of her full lips. The only sound in the room the ragged in and out of his breath. This intimacy between them, all-encompassing... all-consuming.

She could talk about brides and marriage and society expectations until she was blue in the face.

But she was the only woman for him.

It would ever be so.

Her hands trailed lower, and the breath froze in his lungs. She grabbed his shirt and began tugging, sliding it from the waistband of his trousers, bunching it up until he took the ends and slipped it over his head.

"Oh, Gabriel," she said, naked appreciation in her eyes. "You are magnificent."

He wasn't altogether immune to such flattery, he found.

Not when it came from her.

She lowered her gaze, its heat grazing across the outline of his manhood straining against his trousers, then lower to his feet. "I think you'll have to manage your boots."

As he began the inelegant business of removing his boots, she leaned against a bedpost, watching, a little smile curled about her mouth.

Once he'd finally completed the task without making too much of a fool of himself—an abundance of hopping about was involved in the removal of one's boots—she said, "Now, your trousers."

A note of shock traced through him. How long ago was it that he yet retained his, *erm... flower*? A fortnight ago?

How a man could change in a fortnight.

Except... was he changed?

Or was it possible he was—oh, to continue the dreadful flower metaphor—*blossoming*?

One button at a time, he released the falls, her gaze fast upon him. Then his trousers were dropping to the floor, and he stood before her naked and ready.

For her part, Celia looked as if she'd gone molten with lust against the bedpost, her gaze latched onto his cockstand, which was making no minor spectacle of itself.

Guided by instinct, Gabriel took himself in hand and gave his turgid length a long, slow stroke. She bit her bottom lip between her teeth. The house could catch fire, and she wouldn't notice.

But he quickly found he needed to be careful, because her eyes on him while he stroked himself urged him to increase his rhythm, which would only lead him to spending.

And he had other plans for his cock.

"Do you want this inside you?" The question emerged low and gravelly.

How was he speaking such words?

It was as if some of part of himself had been unleashed—a part this woman had only recently introduced him to.

Her knees squeezed together, and she swallowed.

"Do you *need* it inside you?"

"Oh, yes," she said, breathless, her voice in the middling space between a whisper and a plea.

He closed the distance between them, but stopped shy of her. "May I touch you?"

Her tongue swiped across her bottom lip, and she nodded.

With a few efficient flicks of fabric, he unknotted the tie of her sash, and the robe fell open, revealing a gossamer muslin chemise, dusky rose nipples puckered into hard buds beneath. Draped against the bedpost, she was all sensuous woman begging to be taken. Inch by inch, he gathered the chemise, exposing thighs... hips... *mons pubis*... and took her knee in hand, lifting, opening her to him.

He angled his head and stroked his tongue along her neck, tasting her salty skin. "Shall I ravish you, Duchess?"

Her head arched back in pleasure, offering him more access to her throat. "I'll expire of unrequited lust if you don't."

With his other hand, he found her quim. *Wet... hot... swollen... ready...*

For him.

Permission granted, he slid a finger along her slit, and a long moan poured from her.

Though his cock needed to be inside her, he liked pleasuring her this way, too. Pleasure, it seemed, was to be had in many forms—and he was only getting started.

But then, so was she.

Right.

He slid his finger into her, and she gasped, then swiveled her hips, her sex tight and wet around him, finding a rhythm, becoming wild against him. His hand tightened around her knee, as she strained against him. He used every ounce of willpower to keep his shaft carefully away.

Lust-glazed eyes slitted open. "I want you inside me when I release."

He didn't need to be told twice. He slipped his finger from her and shifted his hips forward, pressing his length against her slit, so slick and swollen with desire. He almost lost himself then and there.

"Remove your chemise," he said. Her robe had already fallen away.

Then the chemise was over her head and gone, leaving nothing but a slick of perspiration between them—his body pressed against hers... her nipples hard against his chest... the head of his cock poised to enter her.

With slow deliberation, he pressed inside her, inch by hard inch, taking the time to feel her around him. *So good.*

Her fingernails dug into his shoulders, making it obvious she wanted *more... faster.*

"Impatient, my love?"

My love.

He'd never called anyone *my love.*

Everything with Celia was a first.

How many more sides of himself would she introduce him to?

One thing he understood with certainty: He needed to take her slow—or he would immediately spill.

But slow didn't have to be frustrating.

Slow could be deliberate.

Much satisfaction could be derived from slow.

He didn't know it from experience, but from instinct.

So, he made himself go slow and deliberate as he moved in and out of her, allowing himself to truly *feel.*

There was the physical sensation of being inside her that, in truth, he was trying not to feel too much. But the joining of their sexes wasn't where physical sensation began and ended. The press of her mouth against his, soft and moist. Her breath humid and sweet. Her thigh creamy and smooth, thick and luscious, in the grip of his hand—the feel of that skin... the feel of her breath coming quick and ragged in his ear, tingling the fine hairs on his arms to a stand. Her hair silky against him as he kissed her neck, and all the while he was moving in and out of her, slowly, deliberately.

And here he arrived at that other—*deeper*—place... the place beyond the physical.

Intimacy.

Intimacy of the body... of the mind... of the soul.

He'd never believed in the soul.

Until now.

And now their souls were entwined.

He was hers—and she was his.

That was what he understood as sensation decided it had held out long enough. He began penetrating her harder, deeper, pushing her against the bedpost, the bed groaning with every thrust.

"Oh, yes, Gabriel," she moaned, her arms lifted above her head, her hands gripping the walnut post tight as he took her like an animal—there was no better description for it—driving into her, her heel digging into his arse.

How intimate and how animal was this act.

His tongue followed a bead of sweat that trailed down her neck—salty and *her*.

This woman was habit forming.

He was never letting her go.

Mouth parted, eyes drifted shut, she went deep inside herself in the way he'd come to recognize. She was close to climax—and he would drive her over that sweet edge.

His hands moved to her hips, gripping them, steadying her, as her movements became frenzied on him. "That's it, Celia," he muttered. "Use me for what you need."

Her head arched back, and an inhaled cry hitched in her throat as release teased her with its promise withheld, just out of reach until... until... she broke on him, her climax pulsing around his cock, her voice breaking free on a cry, sailing toward the ceiling, "*Gabriel.*"

The sound of his name on her cherry lips in the moment of climax...

It awakened a feeling inside him—territorial... ferocious...

Mine.

Only his name would ever pass those lips in this moment.

He could take no more as he drove into her. Then he was tumbling over the edge, shouting his release into the curve of her neck, the stars not simply bursting behind his eyes, but glittering through his veins.

By increments, his hips slowed before gradually stopping, spent, their bodies sticky with completion against each other, breath ragged, hearts racing in step.

He'd thought numbers were his whole life.

They made sense in his mind. He was able to order them and make them grow.

But now…

Celia was his life.

She… *they*… made sense.

And what was between them, it was growing, too.

He gathered her in his arms and lifted her onto the bed, following her there. Naked, they lay on their sides, facing one another, their eyes meeting in silence, but communicating so much.

Still, words needed to be spoken, too.

"I want to do that again."

A wondrous smile tipped about her mouth. "*Now?*"

"Well, I likely could." A laugh that sounded suspiciously care-free sprang up—another first. He'd never uttered a carefree laugh in his life. "But not at this moment."

Understanding lit within the amber of her eyes.

Good.

He reached out and twined a loose tendril through his fingers. He needed to be touching some part of her.

A shallow crinkle formed between her eyebrows.

Gabriel had learned to be wary of that crinkle.

She reached for the coverlet and dragged it up her body, over thighs, hips, and glorious breasts. He ached physically at the loss of the sight of them. Then she pushed up and sat against the headboard, hair tumbling about her in long sable waves, the shallow crinkle now a deep groove.

Reluctantly, Gabriel pushed to a seat and pulled a sheet over his lower half.

Celia had something to say to him.

Something he wouldn't want to hear.

It was there, in her eyes.

"That was some display of knowledge you performed for Wrexford and me this afternoon on Rotten Row." She spoke the words almost conversationally—except for the sharp edge running along their length. "You've certainly acquired a fair bit of knowledge about Thoroughbreds."

She wasn't offering him a compliment. In fact, she was no small amount miffed. "Knowledge is easily gained," he said with careful neutrality.

Her eyes sparked. "Wrexford didn't deserve such treatment."

After what they'd just done, they were discussing... *Wrexford*?

"Wrexford didn't deserve it?" scoffed Gabriel. "Wrexford isn't a child." He couldn't let it go. "Nor is he a puppy."

It had to be said.

"Still—"

Gabriel wasn't about to let her labor beneath delusions about Wrexford. "The earl is a nice chap, I'll grant you that, Celia, but you're forgetting one vital point about him."

A guarded quality entered her eyes. "And that is?"

"He's a *man*," Gabriel stated. "A man who wants of you what every man who meets you wants of you."

For an instant, her mouth fell agape. "I'm fairly certain I've been insulted."

"That's not all *you* are." He held her gaze steadily. "That's all those men are. They're too small-minded to see *you* for everything you are."

Her eyes narrowed. "And you do? You see me for everything I am?" There was no mistaking the scorn and disbelief in her voice.

"You know I do, Celia," he said with every bit of earnestness in his heart. "I not only see you. I understand you."

Emotion passed behind her eyes. Perhaps he detected vulnerability within. Hope held ready to flicker to life. For the continuation of this conversational tributary, she would need to be vulnerable—and he would, too.

He was ready.

Then she blinked, and it was gone, in its place an opacity that made her impossible to read. "You must understand," she began,

"I'm not the right bride for you, no matter how good *that*"—she pointed at the bedpost—"is between us."

Frustration licked through him, but he wouldn't allow it air to breathe and flame into life.

"I'm a widow," she continued, "and you're a—"

"I'm *what?*"

"You *were* a virgin."

"Meaning?"

"You're inexperienced with women," she said in that arch way of hers. A duchess condescending to the youth.

His back teeth ground together, and he kept silent frustration tamped down.

"How can you possibly know what sort of woman you want to spend the rest of your life with?"

Ah. At last, she'd revealed the flaw in her logic. "But weren't you just suggesting it was Lady Beatrix with whom I would meet my future wedded bliss? It can't be both ways."

Her mouth snapped shut, and her eyes blazed with irritation.

"I may be inexperienced in the ways of love, Celia, but even I know *that*"—now it was him pointing at the poor, beleaguered bedpost—"isn't merely *good* between us." He tempered his voice. "Even I know *that* can't be experienced with simply anyone."

He sensed a relenting in her eyes and understood here was his opportunity to plead his case.

"There's no law stating that a duke must take a wife," he said. "I don't have to marry."

If I had any choice, I would never be a wife again.

Those had been her words.

And he wanted her to see.

She didn't have to be a wife again.

They could be together in any way she wanted—as long as they were together.

His heart leading the way for the first time in his life, he said, "You don't have to marry, Celia. You have don't have to marry me, and you certainly don't have to marry Wrexford. You don't need him. You and I have our partnership." *And so much more,* he left unsaid.

But it was there, in the unspoken silence that drew long.

"For three years," she said, at last.

"Forever, if you like."

She shook her head. "No wife will tolerate me being in your life."

Wife? "Haven't you heard a word I've said?"

"You're young."

Again, she was attempting to dismiss him.

"Do not say that."

"But you are," she insisted. "You'll marry."

Though separated by only a few feet, it was as if a chasm had yawned open between them.

Even as anger flared inside him and demanded he battle this out, reason urged him to walk away—*for now.*

Sometimes, one had to walk away from a losing battle to win the war.

He slipped from the bed and jerked trousers up his legs, electing to carry the rest of his clothes.

All the while, she watched him.

He considered leaving in silence, but he had one more thing to say. Something she needed to understand. "Celia, this conversation isn't over."

Now, he could leave.

As he wended his way back to the library, determination solidified to steel inside him. He wasn't done pleading his case. Celia knew nothing about him if she thought he was the sort to give up easily.

He'd never backed down from fighting for what he wanted— and prevailing to get it.

He wanted her.

And he would have her.

CHAPTER TWENTY-FOUR

A WEEK LATER

*W*ith the clock a mere two ticks from striking midnight, the Duke of Acaster's ball was an unqualified success.

That was what all the chatter swirling about the ballroom was saying.

Celia could, at last, exhale the breath she'd been holding all evening.

The flow of guests clad in their finest silks and sparkliest jewels showed no signs of thinning, as the ballroom floor filled with countless couples dancing shoulder to shoulder, whirling laughter around and around to the *one-two-three* of the lively Weber waltz. Those not dancing, like Celia, conversed, sipped champagne on the periphery, and discreetly fanned themselves. The atmosphere had grown close and slightly sticky, a fact hardly noticed. Too good of a time was being had.

The ball would go until dawn or until the champagne ran dry —whichever eventuality arrived first.

No expense had been spared—and it showed. The bottomless champagne. The riots of roses. Even the mansion itself had undergone a renovation with those specializing in fabrics, upholstery, and carpentry taking over this last week and removing threadbare carpets, lumpy sofas, and musty curtains, replacing them with plush Aubusson rugs, cushioned silk settees, and curtains that didn't throw dust every time they were opened and closed.

This was a duke's mansion—and all the *ton* would know it.

While Celia had overseen the renovations during the day, she'd kept her vow to decamp to Mivart's Hotel—for her instincts had been correct.

She couldn't be trusted to be housed beneath the same roof as Gabriel.

She would keep happening upon him…

And ravishing him every time.

Her departure had worked. She hadn't seen him since, well, the last time she'd ravished him—or he'd ravished her.

It was always a mutual ravishing with them.

A distancing smile on her face, she nodded at a passing couple. In all her years as a duchess, she'd never once thrown a ball. Her wastrel lech of a husband hadn't the interest or, more pertinently, the blunt for such an undertaking.

A smiling Lady Saskia, then a laughing Lady Viveca, glided past in wide, looping whirls with their dancing partners. From the moment they'd been introduced alongside Gabriel and their older sister, Lady Tessa, the young men had practically formed a line to be introduced by Eloise. Their dance cards had been full within the quarter hour. The sisters would be icing their feet all day on the morrow, but this was the night—and the night was made for dancing.

Now, it was Eloise dancing past with her Mr. Lancaster. The man was so obviously besotted with Eloise. Celia couldn't help wondering if there would be marriage banns soon in her cousin's future.

Another couple caught Celia's eye—one she hadn't expected, though perhaps she should have.

Lady Tessa and the Marquess of Ormonde.

What a striking pair they made—both tall and attractive. Lady Tessa was even wearing a ballgown of pale blue silk that revealed her form to be quite feminine and voluptuous in a way that her usual attire of cravat and waistcoat did not.

Beyond Ormonde and Lady Tessa's striking good looks, however, it was their eyes one couldn't help noticing—how they were only for each other. Marquess and lady didn't dance like strangers, but rather like man and woman who knew each other... *well.*

Perhaps... *intimately.*

These days, it was easy for Celia to recognize such trivialities as soul-deep longing between two people.

Now that she'd been with Gabriel.

Gabriel.

She couldn't think of him without a corresponding ache in the center of her chest.

It wasn't until she'd been at it for a few minutes that she realized what she was doing. She was searching the room for him. She couldn't help herself. He'd made himself scarce immediately after introducing his sisters, and Celia hadn't caught sight of him since.

She did, after all, have good reason to speak with him tonight.

To thank him.

Reverently, her hand smoothed across the skirts of her silk ballgown the vibrant fuchsia of a hothouse orchid.

She simply couldn't stop touching this gown.

This morning, she'd awakened to a light *tap-tap-tap* on her hotel room door. A minute later, a line of maids were streaming into the room, delivering box after box with Madame Dubois's stamp emblazoned on top. Curiosity sparked within her, Celia began opening boxes. This square box containing satin slippers. That slender rectangular box housing white silk opera gloves. Yet another box filled with silk chemise, stays, and stockings. No expense had been spared.

But it was the final box that stole her breath away.

A ballgown.

And not any mere ballgown, but an exquisite garment in the first stare of fashion and of a bright pink that made her heart dance in her chest.

No note had accompanied the boxes, but she knew.

This gift could've only come from Gabriel.

In truth, she'd never worn a more beautiful gown, not even on her wedding day.

Unbidden, a memory stole in—of their five-day idyll at Ashcote... of Gabriel serving her tea in bed.

Though this dress was a grander gesture than tea in bed, it was no less personal.

She hadn't purchased a new dress in a decade.

He'd remembered.

Oh, how the memory of their last night continued to haunt her.

I'm a widow, and you're a... virgin.

His inexperience had been her justification for ending a relationship between them before it could find purchase and truly begin.

But the truer reason lay in what she hadn't said.

I'm a widow, and you...

Deserve better than me.

Those were the words she hadn't been able to bring herself to speak—though she felt their truth to the core of her being.

Gabriel deserved better than her.

She was a beautiful surface, and that was all. She wasn't actually worth anything. Her father and deceased husband had ground that lesson into her.

The degradation she'd endured at both men's hands would never touch Gabriel.

But the look in his eyes that night…

It was very possible he was in love with her—or thought himself so.

It was also very possible she was in love with him.

And knew herself so.

From the edge of her vision, Celia observed a lady sidle up to her right. *Lady Beatrix St. Vincent.* Though Celia paid little mind to the figures of other women—every woman had the right to privacy about her own person—she couldn't help noticing how very thin Lady Beatrix was. Her dress was far from the first stare of fashion—possibly from her come-out season several years ago —but it hung loosely on her, as if she'd shed several inches in the intervening years.

Though it was none of Celia's concern, she hoped all was well with the lady who, in all likelihood, wouldn't be marrying Gabriel.

Lady Beatrix nodded her greeting. "What do you know of *that* man?"

So much for small talk. Celia glanced around the crowd, which appeared to have doubled in density in the last five minutes. Eloise had insisted on inviting all the *ton*—and all the *ton* had accepted, heeding the call to enjoy a night of hospitality and dancing courtesy of the new Duke of Acaster.

"Which man?" There were just so many of them.

Lady Beatrix jutted her chin, and Celia followed the direction. *Ah.*

Mr. Blake Deverill.

Celia shrugged an indifferent shoulder. "Nothing, really."

Lady Beatrix nodded, as if Celia had confirmed something for her. "And yet he's here."

"I believe the duke has business dealings with him."

Lady Beatrix canted her head. "Don't you find it odd that a man none of us knew existed a year ago is suddenly everywhere?"

Celia's head canted at the same angle as Lady Beatrix's. Deverill wasn't short of stature, but neither was he the tallest man in the room. With his broad shoulders and muscles evident beneath his evening jacket, he was a man who held substance. And with his black hair and the bluest eyes Celia had ever seen, he was almost brutishly handsome, save for one defining feature —his mouth. With those full, pouty lips, the man had a pretty mouth.

Lord Devil.

Celia could see why he was called such. Deverill was a presence—and everyone who came into his orbit would have to reckon with him.

"He doesn't seem to be the sort of man who would be denied entry into any place he wanted to be."

"But that only further begs the question," insisted Lady Beatrix. "Why is he so hellbent on being in *these* rooms?"

Lady Beatrix wouldn't easily see the answer, for she'd been born to navigate these rooms. But Celia understood. She'd been sold to a lecherous old duke so her family could have a place in these rooms.

She could almost laugh at the irony. Her father couldn't abide the company of aristocrats and wouldn't have entered these rooms, even if Celia had invited him—which she hadn't.

But he *could*—and that was his point made.

Further, his future grandchildren would have the birthright.

Which, of course, hadn't come to fruition.

Simply, those born on the inside couldn't comprehend the desperation of those born on the outside. They sneered and lifted their noses at the grasping masses who tested Fate and strove.

Yet Lady Beatrix was doing neither. Instead, her curiosity was up.

Heaven help Lord Devil if Lady Beatrix had caught him in her sights.

Just above the fray of the crowd, Celia caught a glimpse of gold-streaked hair.

Gabriel.

Her feet began moving of their own volition. She still needed to thank him.

"Ah, I've found you, at last!"

At the sound of that voice, Celia's feet wanted to kick into a run. Instead, she willed them to a stop. Bright smile fastened onto her face, she turned. "Lord Wrexford, are you enjoying the delights of the duke's ball?"

It was the sort of question a good hostess would ask.

Wrexford beamed pure exhilaration. "My delight, dear duchess, has increased tenfold... a hundred fold!... now that you've graced me with your smile."

From anyone else, Celia would know those words for cheap flattery, but from Wrexford they emerged earnest, his brown eyes wide with sincerity.

"What a perfect... magical!... night you've created," he exclaimed. "Would you consent to the next dance with me?"

The string quartet struck up a lively waltz in that instant, and Celia saw she'd lost the option of polite refusal. She extended a white silk-gloved hand. "Of course."

As they began to move in the familiar *one-two-three* rhythm of the waltz—Wrexford was, *thankfully*, a more than competent dancing partner—he kept a running commentary of all Celia's attributes. "What a brilliant hostess you are," he'd said before they'd made their first turn about the floor. "And what a brilliant dancer, too. It's as if you walk on air."

Celia felt herself smile in a real sense as a stray thought wandered into her mind. Where had Lord Wrexford been a decade ago with all his fawning adoration? Father would've surely accepted an earl and future marquess for her hand.

Of course, at three-and-twenty today, Wrexford had still been a student at Eton College a decade ago.

Right.

And, yet, on he went. "You are surely an angel descended to earth," he rhapsodized. "You are perfection. Nay," he interrupted himself, "perfection itself would envy you."

Celia almost felt concern for him that he meant such words.

"Why..." His eyes were wide and wondrous upon her. "I think I'm quite in love with you."

If she'd been paying closer attention, Celia might have predicted the possibility of his proclamation. She tried to laugh and give him the chance to laugh his words off, too, but he'd gone absolutely serious.

"I think I can't live without you."

What was happening here?

"I think you'll find you can," she said lightly. *Would this waltz never end?* "You simply inhale one breath, then another."

A too-loud laugh escaped him. "What wit you possess!"

Vague unease expanded into genuine alarm. "Is all right with you, Lord Wrexford? Do you feel a fever coming on?"

His sincerity abated not a whit. "If I have a fever, dearest Celia —have I leave to call you by your given name?"

"If you must."

"And what a sense of propriety you possess." Another two turns of the dance. "*You* are my fever, Celia."

Oh, dear.

Somehow, she'd let matters get out of hand. But before she could formulate a plan for extricating herself from this situation that was quickly becoming wholly untenable, he pulled them to a stop...

In the middle of the dancing floor.

As several couples swerved to avoid crashing into them, Wrexford dropped to one knee.

Alarm erupted into a full-on clanging bell.

Inevitably, the gathered took notice, whispers sounding around the room, growing into a hive of buzzing.

Oh, there would be gossip… *much* gossip.

Violins slowed and straggled to a stop, and a ten-foot radius of space cleared around the Dowager Duchess of Acaster standing above a kneeling Earl of Wrexford.

All eyes were upon them, but it was one pair that mattered.

Gabriel.

Was he seeing this?

"Brilliant… beautiful… witty… proper…" began Wrexford, reciting all the adjectives he'd already used to describe her tonight. The man's moon-shaped face was positively glowing. "*Angel* descended to earth."

The tips of Celia's ears went very hot.

"I cannot live another day without you," he exclaimed from his place at her feet. "Will you…" He swallowed. "Will you consent to be my bride?"

Though Celia understood Wrexford had dropped to one knee with the sole intent of proposing marriage to her, the reality of the proposal took her completely by surprise.

Shocked her to her toes, in fact.

Yet through the fog of astonishment, an idea budded within her…

Here, in the form of one besotted earl, was the answer to her prayers. The mental calculation was performed in the split of a second.

If she accepted this marriage proposal, she would be secure.

Her horses would be safe.

And Gabriel would be free to forget about her.

Further, it wasn't as if Wrexford was drawing the short straw. She was precisely the sort of wife he wanted—one who would enhance his status in society. She'd been trained all her life to be precisely the sort of wife Wrexford wanted.

"Yes," she said.

A collective gasp sounded around the ballroom. Wrexford

may have gasped, too. No one had expected her to utter that word—not even Wrexford himself.

Then a cheer of congratulations sailed up to the frescoed ceiling and clapping commenced. Celia began moving as if through a cloud as Wrexford kissed her hand and they danced another waltz, this time alone on gleaming mahogany. Then the dance ended, and they were standing near the open double doors that led onto the terrace, a line having formed to offer them every happiness and all the other clichés one spoke to a newly affianced couple.

Was it possible?

Was she truly engaged to marry this man she hardly knew?

Somehow through the fog, she felt a light brush against the back of her hand. Likely a breeze catching the gossamer curtain.

Then she felt it again.

She glanced down and saw it wasn't the curtain at all.

Fingers reaching out from the terrace side of the curtain, knuckles discreetly grazing hers. Sensation rippled through her as long, masculine fingers attempted to twine through. She knew those fingers… *intimately.*

Gabriel.

She should resist.

She should stay right here like a good hostess and future countess and play the role she'd—*improbably*—accepted.

Yet…

It was Gabriel's fingers threading through hers, holding them fast from the other side of the curtain.

And when he tugged, all resistance fell away, and of course, she was making hasty excuses about seeing to the champagne—the only excuse she could think of that would grant immediate release—before slipping behind the curtain and onto to the moonlit terrace, her hand—*wrongly*—secure in *his.*

CHAPTER TWENTY-FIVE

*W*hat Gabriel was doing... It should've felt wrong. But it didn't.

Celia had made a very erroneous decision based on flawed logic, and someone needed to point it out to her.

He was that someone.

After that blasted proposal of marriage—and her improbable *yes*—he'd had to take himself immediately off to the terrace to cool his blood before he caused a scene. What sort of man had she turned him into, anyway?

He was a man who took care of his business behind the scenes; he didn't cause them.

So, he'd paced about the terrace for a good quarter of an hour before he'd noticed her... standing beside the open terrace doors... her silk-gloved hand, elegant and empty at her side.

Empty of his hand.

On impulse, he'd stepped close and reached out and touched her.

And now, it was still impulse guiding him as he held her hand fast in his, leading her down a set of stairs into the garden, muted strains of violin and cello following them as they entered the hedge maze he hadn't been aware of until this very night.

They came to the first turn. He went left and met resistance. He glanced over his shoulder.

"Follow me," she whispered. She would know the way, of course.

As she led him, he took in the back of her. Sable tresses, half up and half trailing down her back in artful waves, accentuating the narrow indent of her waist and flare of lush hips.

As for the dress... Vibrant pink setting off the ivory of her skin and the honey amber of her eyes, she was a goddess. It was little wonder Wrexford had been overcome.

But that was no excuse for Celia.

One final turn and they entered the center of the labyrinth. Curved stone benches formed a circle around a five-tiered fountain. On any other night, the tinkling flow of water might've been soothing.

Not on this night.

Gabriel willed his fingers to release Celia's. A stray thought wondered if he would ever touch her again, and anger sparked within him anew.

She kept walking, away from him, to the other side of the fountain, and he allowed her the distance. He needed it, too.

He cut straight to the point. "It occurs to me that a few errors of logic regarding your recent engagement need to be pointed out to you."

Her brow lifted. "Is that so?" she said, all haughty duchess. "Go on then."

And Gabriel understood. He would get nowhere by approaching this as a sermon. *The man who knows everything, knows nothing.* A favorite saying of his father's.

He needed to ask questions.

The first one was easy... "Why, Celia?"

The moment softened, and she inhaled a deep breath. "Wrexford has an easy and agreeable temperament."

Gabriel would allow it. Everyone knew this about the man. "Go on."

"And kind eyes."

He could see how this logic made perfect sense in her mind—which only exasperated the blazes out of him. "How many times do I have to say this, Celia? The man is not a puppy."

"My stables will be safe," she stated, unmoved.

"Your stables are already safe," he pointed out. "With me."

The moment stretched long, and Gabriel braced himself. There was yet more she would say.

"*I* will be safe."

The words hung on the night air, and before Gabriel could say what every cell in his body demanded he say, she continued. "I'll no longer always be teetering on the edge of disaster. No one else is exactly clamoring to take my hand in marriage."

The breath caught in Gabriel's lungs. The blood might've stopped in his veins. He couldn't have heard her correctly. "Pardon?"

"You heard me."

"You said you didn't want to marry again," he stated, clearly enunciating each word.

"I said I wouldn't marry again if I had the choice. I've never had the choice, though. It's the way the world is."

The axis of Gabriel's universe suddenly shifted. He'd had time, hadn't he? Time... for what?

He'd never qualified that in his mind.

Time to live outside the bounds of reality with Celia.

But that would never work, would it?

Not for Celia.

Not for a woman who had lived bad reality, and simply wanted peaceful, stable, good reality as the basis of her life.

A woman who deserved as much.

A woman who deserved better than uncertainty about her

future.

He needed to right this situation before it spiraled irredeemably out of control—for he saw now he'd gone about everything all wrong.

He began walking—toward her. An instinctive closing of the distance between them. She remained where she was, still and watchful.

The lively strains of a waltz drifted on midnight air.

"Dance with me," he said on impulse.

Any excuse to touch her, he suspected.

He wasn't above it, he knew.

A war shone in her eyes. She shouldn't dance with him, but neither should she be alone in the center of a labyrinth with him. That was what he saw in those honey amber depths.

Then he saw a shift.

Surrender.

She needed this, too.

Whatever *this* was.

He suspected she thought it was goodbye.

It wasn't.

They were still at the beginning.

He was determined it was so.

He reached for her hand, but rather than clasping it in his, he tugged the tips of her white silk glove, finger by finger, loosening it. Then his hand trailed up the elegant curve of her arm and began rolling the silk, exposing ivory flesh inch by inch, her head angled so her gaze remained fast on him, her breath held.

"Does Wrexford make the breath catch in your lungs?"

Even as the question emerged, he understood he had no right to ask it—but the desperation that spurred him on had no regard for right or wrong or the means to the end.

It only cared about the end—making Celia his.

Words weren't required, anyway, for they both knew the answer.

No.

First glove tossed aside, he started on the other one. When his fingertips touched the bare skin of her upper arm, it was all he could do not to shift forward and press his mouth to that exposed patch of skin. Instead, he began rolling, a wake of goosebumps lifting the fine hairs all the way down her arm.

"And does Wrexford cause goosebumps to race across your skin?" The spark of need inside Gabriel demanded he push her.

Another question they both knew the answer to. But he would ask…

And keep asking…

Until she found the nerve to ask these questions of herself.

Second glove discarded, he took her bare hand in his, their palms warm and so *alive* against each other. Her slender fingers lifted to rest lightly on his shoulder, so close that all he had to do was turn his head to press his mouth to the back of her hand.

So, he did… breathing her scent in the intimate press of his lips to her skin.

She exhaled a light sigh that his ears only just caught.

"Does Wrexford inspire sighs of longing and desire?" he muttered against her.

Again, she didn't answer.

His hand trailed down her spine, one vertebra at a time, until it settled on the small of her back, drawing her into his embrace. As their feet moved in a slow *one-two-three*, their bodies pressed together, they didn't dance to the rhythm set for them by stringed instruments, but to a timing of their own. She, too, must feel the rightness of them together.

Know it.

Down to the very cells that composed her being.

"When you're in Wrexford's arms," he rumbled into her ear, "do you feel *this*, Celia?"

* * *

YET ANOTHER OF Gabriel's questions that didn't require an answer.

It was plain.

No.

An interesting word—*feel*. One she'd avoided for years. It had been better *not* to feel.

Then Gabriel had entered her life and, now, *feel* was all she could do.

She should resist.

But the fact was she didn't want to resist.

His head angled, and she felt the delicious scrape of stubble before his tongue slid up her neck. "I've been wanting to do that all night," he rumbled into her ear.

She swayed into him. *More*, her body demanded, heedless of consequence.

Consequence could be sorted tomorrow.

For now, there was only desperation and need and *Gabriel*.

A moan escaped her parted mouth.

"Will Wrexford be able to make you moan like that?" Strong, masculine hands cupped her breasts as he bent his head and tested nipples through silk with his teeth, careful not to leave a damp spot. "Can Wrexford make your nipples hard as cherry pits?"

Celia felt the backs of her knees bump against something—a bench, she worked out—then she was lowering onto cool stone, perching on the edge, her legs spread and Gabriel on his knees, between. His gaze held hers captive, as he reached beneath her ballgown, his fingers trailing up her thighs. A shiver of desire traced through her, centered in her sex, which was throbbing... aching... The anticipation of his touch—*oh*—it was too much.

A light, masculine fingertip slid along her slit, grazing across flesh swollen with need and want. A mewl of frustration escaped her. It wasn't enough.

Not nearly.

Intense and serious, Gabriel watched her squirm beneath his touch. "Can Wrexford make you wet and ready?"

A smile that Celia hadn't yet seen from this man curved the corners of his mouth, lit within his eyes—a *wicked* smile.

Oh, that a bit of wickedness inside her didn't respond.

"Enough of Wrexford," she said. "This is about you and me."

Absolutely desperate, she closed the distance between their mouths and kissed him, tongues tangling as fierce desire broke free. Trembly fingers reached down and began working buttons of his falls.

And yet for all the ferocity of the moment, the tip of his finger only touched her lightly along her slit...

Not giving her what she wanted.

Yet.

She wrapped her arms around his neck and slid forward so her legs were around his waist. The crown of his cock poised at her sex, the moment suspended for a breath of time.

"*Celia.*"

Her name on his mouth was a plea and a promise.

If she allowed it, he would give her all of himself.

That was what she heard—what she wanted more than anything else the world could offer.

Gabriel... hers.

For this night.

A contraction of arms and legs... a shift of her hips... and she slid onto his thick, heavy length, the breath caught in her lungs as he impaled her. Compelled by competing forces of frustration and desperation and lust, her sex took him, only just, this coupling about pure need.

Oh, how good and right he felt inside her. As if her body were an aching void without him inside her.

It wasn't only Wrexford who couldn't make her feel like this—but no other man.

Only Gabriel.

Masterful and certain, he was a quick learner when it came to loving. Easily, he could become the most desired rake in London, if word ever got out about *this*.

How he could—*oh*—fuck.

For—*oh*—this was a fucking.

And—*oh*—how she wanted it.

All of it.

They were individuals, yet... they were one, even as they were broken down to singular elements. Elements colliding, but also... uniting.

Everywhere she touched him, she was memorizing him—the silken feel of his hair... the scratch of his beard... the width of his shoulders... the dense muscles of his arse... the velvet hardness of his manhood.

So, too, were there other touches. The inhaled scent of him, as if a bit of him had evaporated into her... suffusing through her lungs with every breath... through arteries and veins... and into a place intimate.

Her heart.

Long after the scent of him drifted off on the breeze and they were no longer joined, there in that secret, intimate space would he remain as one with her.

Only for her to know.

Her arms tightened around his neck, drawing her as close as one body could be to another, desperation driving her, body and soul, toward completion as he penetrated her— punishing her... pleasuring her.

"Gabriel," she whimpered.

Whimpered.

She'd whimpered.

And she would do it again.

He angled his head back, his mouth leaving a moist slick on her neck, and met her gaze. "Don't look away, Celia."

Within the command, she detected a plea.

He felt *it*, too—this connection… this intimacy…

With controlled intention, his hands tightened around her hips and he gave a hard, deep thrust, then another, and her entire being felt transported to another realm, the force of his gaze her only tether to earth.

Thoughts came to her—thoughts that refused to be held at bay—thoughts that held a wild edge to them.

How could she live without *this*—without this man?

As he penetrated her, over and over, his manhood steady and hard, her quim began its interior coil and her body became not her own. It belonged to this man—to what he could do to her… how only he could make her feel… the pleasure only he could bring. She was enslaved to it, utterly at his mercy.

So, she didn't look away from his eyes.

Though she wanted to.

Though she *needed* to.

For he was demanding an intimacy she needed to protect herself against…

If she was to walk away from him.

Then her body was tipping over the edge, into release, she was crying out, her voice mingling with the strains of violin and cello on the breeze. A few seconds later, his shout of release was joining hers, even as he pulled from her and spilled onto the grass. She understood its necessity, but felt the loss, nonetheless.

Unable to move, they panted into each other's necks, their hearts racing as one, the hot slick of sweat coating exposed skin cooling with midnight air.

It was Celia who drew back first.

She didn't want to meet his gaze—absolutely couldn't—but she felt its demand on her lowered lids and she had no choice. There was no hiding from Gabriel when his steady blue eyes were fixed and determined.

The complex march of emotions she met there didn't surprise her.

"I think..." she began and swallowed. "I think we should, *erm...*"

Oh, she couldn't complete a sentence.

"We should *what*, Celia?" His gaze searched hers, the question a dare, a note of anger embedded within.

"We should," she began with a little more determination, somehow pulling away from him, drawing her legs together, allowing gravity to take her dress to the ground as she stood and moved to the other side of the bench. "We should return to the ball."

He buttoned the falls of his trousers and lifted his gaze. "Is that what we should do? You're so adept at saying what we *should* do. Tell me, Celia, *should* we have done *that* just now?"

"*Erm*, no, but..."

"*But?*"

"But now we can walk away from one another."

"We can?" He made no attempt to mask his disbelief.

Somehow, she nodded, her gaze wanting nothing more than to slide away from the accusation she met within his.

"*Ah*," he said. "I see."

"You do?"

"So you can marry Wrexford, and I can marry Lady Beatrix, correct?"

"Actually," she began. "I've rethought my position."

"Oh?" he asked, the question a scoff.

"I don't think you should marry, yet."

"You don't?"

"You're too young."

A moment beat past in which he looked absolutely flummoxed. Then he barked an equally stunned laugh. "Wrexford is a year younger than me!"

Celia could see that he did rather have a point.

The next instant, all signs of levity fell away. "You must decline Wrexford's proposal."

"I've already accepted."

"And now you must tell him you were carried away by the moment and take it back." The intent within his eyes told her he wouldn't cede this ground easily.

Somehow, she found it within her to say, "I shall marry Wrexford."

She even said it without a wobble in her voice.

"For the sake of security?"

She gave a firm, most definite nod.

"Celia," he began, a too-patient tone in his voice, "you don't need a man or marriage for that. You can do it all on your own. You *are* doing it all on your own. Your stud will be a success."

A stunned scoff escaped her. "I've never made a success of anything in my life—"

"That's because you never had the opportunity." He spread his hands wide. "I believe in you."

Oh, how those words wanted to penetrate skin and bone and sink into her soul.

But she couldn't let them.

Gabriel might believe them to be true, but she knew them to be false.

"I'm releasing you from our arrangement."

She simply could not be in business with him.

What she and Gabriel had together was too tempting and too volatile. Frankly, it frightened her. How easily she would give up everything—her security, her reputation, her horses, her life—and take up with him in any way he asked.

"There's been a lot of talk about security, but something else has gone unmentioned."

"What is that?" No hiding the suspicion in her voice.

"What of your heart?"

"My *heart*?" she scoffed. "What has a heart to do with marriage? You're the one so bound by logic, surely you understand as much."

"I'm realizing allowances can be made."

"What allowances?"

"*Love*," he said. "I love you, Celia, and logic has nothing to do with it."

Even as her heart wanted leave to expand in her chest and bask in the warm glow of that word—*love*—she gathered her resolve and said, "Have I been insulted?"

He shook his head. "Don't do that, Celia. Hear me."

She did hear him, but it changed nothing. The time for the truth had arrived. She'd tried to avoid saying it, but Gabriel wasn't the sort of man one could avoid.

"You deserve better than me. I'm little more than a beautiful surface hiding damaged goods."

There.

The truth.

A deep groove dug into his forehead. *"Damaged goods? Better? I don't want better. I want you."*

"That isn't how it works."

"Wrexford cannot possibly make you happy, Celia."

"*Happy?*" She struggled to tamp down a sudden rush of tears. "I once had an unhappy marriage, Gabriel, but it taught me something. How to find small bits of happiness. A morning's ride. A day at the Derby. Wrexford has kind eyes."

Gabriel's jaw tensed and released, but he said nothing.

"Kindness can be enough."

"You would choose a bland, tepid life over the heat and passion between us?"

For Gabriel's own good… "Yes."

His head cocked, as if he were regarding a new species of creature. "You know what? I believe you. I wish you every joy of your bland, tepid future."

Before Celia could formulate a reply, he was gone.

And she was alone—with her bland, tepid future.

CHAPTER TWENTY-SIX

TWO WEEKS LATER

*H*ands in her lap, body subtly swaying with the jostle of the carriage, Celia watched the last remnants of London roll past and fall away as they entered the countryside.

She didn't have it in her to look directly at the man very properly seated on the bench opposite her.

Her fiancé's affable smile was quite enough from the periphery of her vision.

Her... *fiancé*.

Impossibly.

Yet Wrexford was.

The man with whom she would be spending the rest of her life.

And she felt not a single, solitary emotion about it.

He, on the other hand, appeared happy as a lark.

In fact, he had enough happiness inside him for the both of them.

She directed a smile toward her future husband. "Are you going to tell me where our outing is leading us today?"

He wagged a playfully chastising finger. "Now, you know it's a surprise, my bauble."

My bauble.

His new endearment for her.

She tried not to grind her back teeth together every time he said it.

Still, if that was to be the worst part of being married to this man, she could endure it.

She'd endured worse.

"Let's see," she said, trying for coquettish—almost succeeding. "We are now south of London..."

All verdant, rolling chalk downs and rich grasslands, it was beautiful country as they headed into Surrey, the air fresh and sun-drenched, after weeks spent in the fug of London.

She entertained a suspicion about this outing... "Are we by chance paying a visit to your family seat?"

Impossibly, Wrexford's smile grew brighter. She envisioned a great deal of smiling in her future.

She would endure.

"What intelligence you possess, my bauble," he said, shaking his head as if in wonder. "Imagine the intelligent children we shall bring into the world."

Celia's smile didn't slip a hair. *Children.* Of course, she wanted children. It was simply that she had difficulty imagining the physical act of attempting to make children with this man. It was a different man who sprang to her mind's eye when she considered the act.

A very different man.

And she didn't have to use her imagination.

She knew.

She gave herself a mental shake. Her mind's eye wasn't being helpful.

"But, first," said Wrexford, "we are to make a stop."

"Oh?"

Wrexford looked as if he might burst from holding the information inside. She glanced out the window and gazed upon familiar environs. "Is Epsom Downs our first destination?"

She hoped so. It had been too many weeks since she'd laid eyes on a racecourse.

Wrexford clasped his hands together in delight. "It's impossible for you to disappoint, isn't it?"

While Celia didn't mind being admired, the bar set by her future husband was remarkably low. She should be grateful.

She should.

"There aren't any races today, are there?" she asked.

"We're merely stopping to gauge the progress of an investment for Papa."

A note of foreboding traced through Celia. "An investment in a racehorse?"

"It happens the Duke of Richmond came to Papa with an opportunity, and Papa decided I could check in every so often."

"What sort of opportunity?" Foreboding turned to dread in her stomach. She knew of an investment opportunity involving Epsom Downs...

"Oh, to throw a few guineas into that Race of the Century venture with him and—"

"Gabriel," she finished for Wrexford and instantly realized her mistake. She couldn't go around calling Gabriel *Gabriel*. "*Erm*, Siren."

"The Duke of Acaster, my bauble," Wrexford corrected gently. "But I can see as you're family—"

"The duke is no family of mine," she cut in quickly and decisively.

"In a manner of speaking."

Celia held her tongue. *In* no *manner of speaking*, she wouldn't say.

"Anyway," continued Wrexford, "as Epsom has no permanent grandstand, Papa wants me to happen by and see how the temporary stands are coming along. Papa always says a man should know where his money is going."

Such statements only reinforced Celia's decision to marry the earl. She wanted a man who thought about money in that way. Of course, Wrexford wasn't the only man to think about money thusly...

Wrexford wasn't finished. "Five minutes should do it. Then we'll be on our way." He nodded generously. "*Then* we'll visit Mama and Papa."

Word of their only son's engagement to the Duchess of Acaster must've traveled to the family seat in Surrey with the speed of lightning, for the marquess and marchioness had arrived in London the very next afternoon following the ball. The marquess had looked Celia over like a prize heifer, grunted his approval, and taken himself off to his study. The marchioness had been a very nice woman, blandly approving of anyone loved by her son, and insisted Celia call her Mama.

In all, they were in-laws Celia could easily abide.

Across the footwell, Wrexford's eyes twinkled. They *twinkled.* "Mama would like to further discuss our nuptials. Only a week away."

Celia didn't need to be reminded.

Only a week away.

"And we'll be returned to London by nightfall?" she asked.

Doubtful. The midday sun was already directly overhead.

Wrexford gave an indifferent shrug. "I thought it would be lovely if we stayed the night."

Stay the night? "But I haven't brought a travel valise with me."

A smile that couldn't contain itself spread across Wrexford's face. "Or so you think."

"Oh?"

Celia instinctively knew she wouldn't like whatever he was about to say next.

"Your cousin provided me with the name of your modiste, *Madame Dubois.*"

He spoke the last in an exaggerated French accent meant to amuse. Celia mustered the shadow of a smile.

"Anyway," he continued, "I had her make a few items of clothing for you."

Celia felt her mouth go agape.

Wrexford, however, appeared immune to the distress that would've been evident to anyone else. "You'll have everything you need. You can't see Mama in the old clothes you go about wearing."

A sudden and hot blush of shame flared through Celia. She'd thought she'd had the *ton* fooled all these years by having her garments retrimmed? She should've known better. Society's critical eye missed nothing.

And yet...

When she'd received a ballgown from Gabriel, it had felt magical.

An entire new wardrobe from Wrexford felt very much the opposite.

A mutinous feeling stirred within her. "But I've made plans to return to Ashcote tomorrow. Mr. Haig is expecting me."

Wrexford waved her protest away with a flick of the wrist. "Such plans can be moved."

"I need to see to my horses," she pressed. "I must know that their training is proceeding according to schedule. And there's also the stud. I'm needed," she finished with stern finality.

The earl's head cocked. "But are you, in fact?"

"What do you mean?"

"Doesn't Mr. Haig run Ashcote's operation?"

"The stud was my idea."

His smile broadened. "Of course it was. As I keep saying, you're an intelligent woman."

Something about the way he said *woman...*

It sounded suspiciously like intelligent *for a* woman.

Which wasn't the same as being an intelligent woman—*at all.*

Her future husband needed to understand something. She looked him straight in the eye. "I am involved in every single decision regarding Ashcote's racing and stud."

That should settle it.

Wrexford reached across the footwell and patted her knee. "Of course you are."

Until this moment, Celia had only seen Wrexford as amiable and harmless. But now she detected something else in his smile—*condescension.*

He was *condescending* to her. Further...

Perhaps he had been all this time.

He's a man, *Celia. A man who wants of you what every man who meets you wants of you.*

And Celia saw.

It was true.

Every word Gabriel had spoken. No one knew men like other men, after all.

And she saw something more—her future.

My bauble.

Wrexford was young. She'd always viewed him so. But this young man would be her husband. He would be above her—and would see himself so.

That was marriage.

How could she have forgotten?

"Ah, here we are," exclaimed her future husband, unaware of the direction of his future bride's thoughts.

Epsom Downs had, indeed, rolled into view. Set like a jewel in the Surrey countryside, the course was a beauty. Celia much preferred it to Newmarket, which had grown increasingly centered on the brutish commerce of horse racing. Epsom yet retained an elegance.

The coach-and-four rolled to a stop, and like a courtier

worthy of the royal court, Wrexford hastily exited the carriage and extravagantly—that was the only word for the style of his assistance—handed Celia down onto the gravel drive.

"Wrexford," came a shout of greeting.

The Duke of Richmond approached, and Celia experienced no small amount of relief to no longer be the object—*bauble*—of her fiancé's attention for a while. As greetings were exchanged and the men began to discuss their business venture and provide updates on the progress of the temporary stands, a strange feeling crept through Celia.

Was this her future?

To simply be the woman?

For the last year—for better and worse—she'd been the mistress of her life. Now, she was ceding all that responsibility to Wrexford.

And so, too, was she ceding all her agency... her freedom.

A bland, tepid future.

But wasn't that what she wanted? Wasn't that the price for the security she so craved?

It was only when Richmond's gaze began casting about in every direction that she realized he was looking for someone.

A feeling snuck through her—a feeling she'd come to know well. *Anticipation.* For Richmond could only be seeking one man.

Which meant...

He was here.

Richmond's gaze landed on a cluster of two figures conversing in the distance—a man and a woman.

Celia's stomach fell to her feet, and her heart doubled its rate of beats.

Gabriel.

"We should go," she found herself hurrying to say. "We don't want to keep Mama waiting."

But her words landed on deaf ears.

"*Acaster,*" Richmond called out.

Gabriel's head whipped around, and Celia sensed when his gaze landed on her—though there was no possible way she could know that with certainty from this distance.

Still, she felt like a nerve ending exposed to the raw elements.

"Do you have a minute?" shouted Richmond.

Did she detect hesitation? Or was that in her imagination, too?

Then Gabriel was striding toward them, and Celia's entire being became wholly concentrated upon him, the voices of Richmond and her future husband sounding in her ears as if through a dense layer of cotton.

Gabriel.

Here, in verdant Surrey on a bright summer's day, he was beautiful.

She hadn't seen him since the night of the ball.

And if he was going to walk around looking impossibly beautiful and sun-kissed, it was for the best.

I love you, Celia.

Those had been among his last words to her.

The ones that dogged her steps during the day and haunted her dreams at night.

As they neared the group, Celia noticed Lady Tessa at his side, wearing her usual unusual attire of cravat, waistcoat, and skirts. All stern business was Lady Tessa.

A pang of envy sheared through Celia. Lady Tessa went her own way and determined the course of her life. To be such a woman had never been within Celia's reach. And yet...

You don't need a man or marriage... You can do it all on your own.

More of Gabriel's words.

And he'd believed them.

But she...

Couldn't.

Life had taught her differently.

And would life with Wrexford be such a sacrifice?

Beneath lowered lashes, she risked a glance at Gabriel as he stood conversing with the other men. Feet planted wide and arms crossed over his chest, he looked pugnacious and implacable.

Further, as the conversation progressed, his intense gaze fixed square upon her—as if he were looking directly into her soul.

"Why don't we ask the duchess?" he said, as if snatching the question from the clear blue sky, when really it must've been in response to something either Richmond or Wrexford said.

Since she'd been deemed unnecessary to the conversation by her future husband, she'd stopped paying attention. Otherwise, she might have opinions—and feel the need to voice them.

Feel the need to be more than a bauble.

"After all," Gabriel continued. Pugnacious was most definitely an accurate descriptor. "She is the leading expert on all matters horse racing."

All eyes shifted her direction, and stupidly she felt a blush rise. "Surely, you flatter me, Your Grace," she managed without meeting Gabriel's gaze.

"I don't flatter," he replied, so utterly, attractively serious.

She could sigh.

"I'm afraid my mind went wandering," she confessed without admitting the destination of its travels. "What is it you're discussing?"

"The timeline of the temporary stands."

"They look to be nearly completed." Her gaze settled on the turf itself. "Which is well and good, but if I may ask…"

Even as Gabriel's manner challenged and encouraged, Wrexford observed her like she was a pampered child who had been granted a seat at the adult's table for supper.

"Please," said Richmond, all magnanimous duke. Some men were born for the role.

"What about the turf?" Celia asked.

"We are taking the utmost care," returned Richmond.

"Your workers are likely destroying roots and creating divots," she warned. "If you keep allowing them to use the racing turf as a walkway, you will be endangering the lives of the horses."

Richmond's brow furrowed in sudden concentration. "*Blast,*" he uttered beneath his breath.

Gabriel watched the exchange, impossible to read, while his sister observed with the shadow of a smirk on her mouth.

As for Wrexford... "Now, my bauble, best leave it to the men. Richmond has all well in hand."

A spark flashed within Gabriel's sea-blue eyes. His head cocked. "*Bauble?*"

"It's..." Oh, that she possessed the strength to say what needed to be said with conviction... "It's my fiancé's endearment for me." Her smile beamed far and wide, all the way to the sun. "Charming, isn't it?"

Gabriel snorted. "That's one word for it."

He was clearly thinking of other words.

Words Celia wouldn't allow herself to think...

Couldn't allow herself to think.

For if she did, she might see this was all one big mistake.

And then where would she be?

Exactly where she'd started...

Nowhere.

Left with nothing.

CHAPTER TWENTY-SEVEN

*B*auble.

Wrexford called Celia his bauble, and here she stood—this talented, intelligent, glorious woman—content to be a husband's bauble.

Just as she'd been trained to be.

Gabriel found it impossible to reconcile the concept with the woman he knew.

He could hardly look at her.

He couldn't *not* look at her.

He wanted her, still.

And she couldn't *not* look at him, either. Not obviously, of course. But he caught furtive glances from beneath lowered lashes.

Richmond and Wrexford made to move the conversation along, but Gabriel couldn't leave it. "Wrexford."

The earl turned his affable smile onto Gabriel. "Yes, Your Grace?"

Since Gabriel's elevation to the status of duke, there were those who openly resented him, even as they spoke the niceties.

Wrexford wasn't one of them. When he said those words—*Your Grace*—it was without the faintest whiff of irony.

"How would you define the word *bauble*?"

Celia's gaze startled up. Gabriel knew because its heat was presently burning a hole into the side of his face. He cared not. He needed Wrexford's answer.

And so did she.

The earl gave a laugh that wobbled with uncertainty. "Doesn't everyone know what a bauble is?"

Gabriel nodded. The man made it almost too easy... "A bright, shiny object."

Wrexford exhaled a none-too-subtle sigh of relief. "And few shine as bright as Celia." He appeared rather pleased with himself.

Celia's smile had fallen by degrees and now formed into a small frown at the corners of her mouth. She knew what Gabriel was about—and she wasn't best pleased.

Too bad.

He wasn't finished.

"A trinket."

He was possibly going too far, but if *too far* was where he must venture, so be it. Celia would know these weren't his thoughts of her. But she needed to know they were her future husband's.

"An attractive plaything."

Wrexford looked as if the ground beneath his feet had gone shaky. "No one could doubt Celia's attractiveness."

Gabriel caught her gaze and held it. Her eyes blazed with suppressed fury, willing him to stop.

Well, he was no small bit furious with her, too.

He loathed to see potential wasted, and that was what she was doing—wasting herself on a man who could never possibly see or value her. The man thought her a trinket when, in fact, she was a diamond.

Damaged goods... You deserve better than me.

Those had been her words.

Words wrong at their very core.

Words that had her undervaluing and selling herself cheap.

"Sometimes," he began, "one thinks one holds a mere bauble in their hand, when in reality, it's a diamond."

Celia's gaze captive to his, the world fell away. It was only the two of them—and the words of truth he was speaking to her.

"A diamond should know she's a diamond, not a cheap imitation. A diamond should know her worth."

"That is quite accurate," chimed Wrexford—ever one to chime in. "Happened to Lord Billingsley on Bond Street. His eye caught a bit of sparkle on the cobbles, and he picked it up. A cheap paste bracelet. Turns out, though, it wasn't paste at all, but diamonds belonging to a visiting Russian princess. She gave him a kiss on the cheek for it, and I don't think Billingsley has washed that cheek since."

Gabriel lifted a brow toward Celia, as if to say, *Not only does the man call you bauble, but that's the sort of story you can look forward to all the rest of your days.*

Her jaw clenched and released.

She'd heard the words as if he'd spoken them aloud.

She lifted her hand and pressed it to her forehead. "Wrexford, I find that my head has taken an ache. It would be for the best to save the rest of our outing for another day when I can enjoy it."

Wrexford's brow creased with concern. Gabriel would give him that much. But he knew Celia's words for a complete fabrication.

"Are you certain, my bauble? Mama will be ever so disappointed."

"Quite."

And with that, Wrexford was leading Celia toward his crest-emblazoned coach-and-four. Once inside, she presented Gabriel with her profile and didn't turn her head once before the conveyance lurched into motion.

He almost regretted upsetting her.

Almost.

She'd needed to hear his words. After all, her wedding was in a week.

The carriage rounded a bend in the road and disappeared from view. It was only then that Gabriel realized he'd been watching the entire time. He turned to find Richmond conferring with a grounds man about the turf. Celia had been right to be worried, it appeared.

Then he felt eyes upon him.

Tessa.

His sister had caught every word and nuance between him and Celia—and understood.

Richmond spared him a quick glance. "I'm off to Town. Anything else today, Acaster?"

Gabriel almost replied *no*, but he did, in fact, have a question for the duke. "How has Wrexford become involved in our venture?"

Richmond gave a dismissive shrug. "His papa wanted to find something for the boy to do, so I cut him into my stake."

Thereby minimizing his own risk, Gabriel left unsaid. He had something else to say. "*Boy?* Wrexford's but a year younger than me."

"Well, some men are boys longer than others."

That was certainly one way of putting it.

And the matter settled, too, as Richmond delivered a curt nod and went on his way.

Leaving Gabriel alone with Tessa—and that knowing look in her eyes.

He didn't attempt to deny what she knew… "I possibly just made a fool of myself."

She gave a slow, considering nod. "Very possibly."

Sisters… They ever told one what one didn't want to hear.

"Have you considered courting the duchess yourself?"

Gabriel exhaled the sigh he'd been holding since the ball two weeks ago. "I mucked that up."

Actually, he still wasn't all that clear how. It didn't follow logic.

Of course, nothing with Celia did.

Tessa let the matter go. She had other concerns on her mind. "You don't have to sell me your stake in The Archangel."

Gabriel shook his head. On this, at least, he was clear. "I could never be halfway into anything." Like in love with Celia, for example. "Best I'm completely out. The Acaster duchy is in complete shambles. Its rehabilitation will take a lifetime."

"You could be a silent investor."

"I couldn't."

"No, I suppose not." She glanced around Epsom's grounds. "The Race of the Century is truly going to be the spectacle promised, isn't it?"

"Aye."

"You'll be going out of the game on top, that's for sure." But even as she said it, a worry shone in her eyes.

"What is it, Tessa?"

"I've picked up little whisperings."

"About the race?"

She nodded. "The Ring isn't taking nicely to you cutting them out of the betting post on race day."

"What do I care?"

Tessa was as serious as he'd ever seen her. "I don't think they can be ignored."

"Watch me."

"Blaze Jagger isn't to be underestimated. Someone must deal with him."

Tessa didn't make such statements idly. Not with that particular look in her eye.

"And are *you* that someone, sister?"

"Wheels are in motion."

Alarm pinged through Gabriel. "I don't like the sound of this, Tessa."

She snorted. "With all due respect, Gabriel, you are my younger brother—even if you are a duke now—and you don't have to like it. I don't need your permission to live my life as I see fit." A scoff escaped her. "I don't need anyone's permission. Besides, have you ever known me to take on something I can't handle?"

There was a first time for everything, but he refrained from pointing out as much. So, he changed the subject, for that topic was clearly closed. "And your holiday?"

Her straight eyebrows crinkled. "What *holiday*?"

"That was your word for it."

A blotch of crimson crept up her throat. In his entire life, he'd never seen his sister blush.

"It was, *erm*, less holiday than a debt I had to settle."

Gabriel's brow furrowed. "Why is this the first I'm hearing of a debt?"

"It wasn't a debt you could've handled for me."

"To whom are you beholden, sister?"

Tessa gave her head a little shake, as if to brush away the question.

"And the debt is paid?" he pressed.

"Yes."

That note of uncertainty... It was unlike her. Tessa navigated the world with a clarity of purpose that even Gabriel envied.

Her gaze sharpened. "And the wedding?"

That snapped Gabriel to. "*Wedding?*"

"Celia's wedding."

He grunted. He hadn't allowed himself to think about the wedding.

"Will you be attending?"

"Why would I?"

Tessa was looking at him as if he were the biggest dolt in England. He didn't like receiving that look from his older sister.

He liked even less that she was usually justified in giving it.

"*You* are the duke," she said, clearly enunciating each word. "*She* is the widow of the previous duke. The wedding will be taking place beneath your roof and—"

"And?"

"And didn't you notice the way she was looking at you?"

"Like she wanted to stab me in the gut with a rusty knife?"

Tessa snorted. "Well, there was that, and I wouldn't have blamed her."

Gabriel was ready to have done with this conversation. "Is there anything else?"

Tessa's head tipped subtly to the side, considering. "Since you met the duchess… *hmm*."

"*Hmm*, what?" His sister was beginning to fiddle on his last nerve.

"You've changed a bit, is all." Those enigmatic words spoken, she began walking. "Meet me at the carriage when you're ready to return to London."

Gabriel wanted to resist the observation, but it held the kernel of truth, and for better and sometimes worse, he never denied the truth. Since he'd met Celia, he *had* changed in myriad ways, but in one way that mattered most.

It was bound up in the idea of need.

For most of his life, he'd run from need. If there was a need, he would see it met and have it gone.

Need was weakness.

Then along came Celia.

She'd taught him need from every angle—need of the body… need of the soul…

And another sort of need—one deeper.

Need of the heart.

Celia wasn't a need to meet and have done with, for she was in his heart.

A truth arrived at too late.

She'd made up her mind.

And they would all just have to live with it, wouldn't they?

CHAPTER TWENTY-EIGHT

ONE WEEK LATER

"*Y*ou certainly look… modest."

Celia could see that Eloise had more to say on the matter of her bridal dress, but was determinedly keeping it to herself.

"Yes, well, Mama"—Wrexford had most earnestly insisted she call his mother Mama—"doesn't have a daughter and was most keen to be involved in the marriage preparations." She plucked at the white lace skirt. "I hadn't the heart to deny her."

Celia liked lace as much as the next woman, but the yards of it enshrouding her from head to toe—her face was the only lace-less part of her person—was a bit… much.

Eloise nodded in agreement. "Better to have an ug— *unusual* dress on your wedding day, and a happy Mama in your married life."

Celia's thoughts exactly.

But standing before the mirror, she wondered if her wedding dress had to be *this* aggressively modest.

Would aggressive modesty be expected for her married life, too?

Well, she would take it one day at a time, and today was her wedding day.

She tried not to glance at the far end of the room—at the pile of trunks stacked near the door. Those trunks contained everything that belonged to her outright in this world, aside from her horses. After today, she would never see the inside of this room again.

Familiar ache sheared through her. Not one borne of sentiment for all the years she'd called this room hers.

But for the man she'd called hers within it.

She took a seat at the dressing table, Eloise busily and unnecessarily fluffing pillows behind her.

Actually, Eloise had gone unusually quiet.

Celia didn't know what to make of a quiet Eloise.

She suspected a quiet Eloise was a disapproving Eloise.

"Which do you think?" Celia held up a triple strand of pearls with an amethyst clasp in one hand and a diamond necklace worked in a delicate floral motif in the other.

Eloise would have an opinion, and she would have to give it. It was her nature.

"The pearls." She was unable not to add, "Diamonds are too much for the day."

Celia clasped the pearls and stared at herself in the dressing-table mirror. Here she was about to marry Wrexford, clad head to toe in clothes and jewels from him. She looked like an exquisite confection in South Sea pearls and Brussels lace. She looked like a...

Bauble.

She'd fashioned a peace with it.

After all, her first marriage had been a cage of unyielding iron: The only way out had been death.

Wasn't a cage composed of lace, pearls, and diamonds much better?

But, suggested a little voice, *perhaps marriage doesn't have to be a cage at all.*

That little voice got tamped right down.

Little voices could have short memories.

She was doing what was best for everyone.

Eloise joined her at the dressing table, her face peeking over Celia's shoulder and meeting her eyes in the mirror. "You are a beautiful bride, cousin, and I wish you every happiness."

Celia tried to swallow back the sudden lump in her throat.

Happiness.

What a concept.

Eloise wrapped her arms around Celia and squeezed. "You know it's possible, don't you?"

Eloise had decided now was the time to speak.

Celia braced herself and asked, "What's possible?"

"To be happy in marriage."

A scorched feeling seared through Celia. *Anger.* The sort that wanted to cut and make another feel the pain. But as she opened her mouth, a sharp *no* screeched through her. Eloise didn't deserve such treatment.

So, she settled for reciting aloud the reasons she'd been repeating to herself, over and over, this last week. "I shall be secure. I shall be taken care of. My stable will be safe. I shall be treated with kindness and consideration, which is so much more than I ever received in my first marriage."

There.

Her reasons were indisputable.

Celia detected understanding and empathy in Eloise's eyes. But her cousin wasn't finished. "True. Marriage to Wrexford will offer more," she said gently. "But will it offer *enough*?"

And there it was.

The question spoken aloud that even Celia's little voice had been too afraid to ask.

Will it offer enough?

"You've been hurt, Celia, I know this," continued Eloise. "But life can be more than survival. You can have more than what you can hold onto with two hands."

Celia went stone still.

"You can have the life you want."

"I'm gaining that life," Celia spoke around the lump in her throat. "My horses—"

Eloise shook her head, cutting Celia off. "You're lying to me and everyone, and you don't even know it, because you're lying to yourself. What do *you* want?"

And like that, Celia's want would no longer be suppressed. It rose and expanded in her chest, making it difficult to draw breath.

Her want wasn't a *what*, but a *who*.

Gabriel.

An impossible want.

"Eloise," she began, pique competing with want, "why are you trying to ruin my life?"

A stunned laugh escaped her cousin. "Pardon?"

"I'm about to have everything I need for a secure future, and you are trying to sow discord into it. I can have a very pleasant life with Wrexford."

Eloise's brow furrowed, and annoyance flashed in her eyes. "What is Wrexford's given name?"

"Pardon?" What was her cousin on about?

"What is your soon-to-be husband's given name?" Eloise asked, slower this time.

"I, erm…" Celia's mind raced. He'd mentioned it once. *Gerald? Gerard? James? Jasper?*

Eloise's brow released. "Just as I thought. You don't know."

"I can hardly see how it matters." What was in a name, anyway?

"You're to marry the man in ten minutes," exclaimed Eloise. "And you don't know your future husband's given name."

"Every relationship is different, cousin."

Eloise snorted, and her gaze narrowed. "I need you to make something clear for me."

"What is that?"

"Why can't you marry the duke?"

Celia had never been punched in the gut, but she suspected this was what it felt like. "It's simple," she managed.

"*Simple?*"

"He's young."

The old excuse—a safe place to hide.

"As far as I can tell," said Eloise. The look in her eyes told Celia there would be no hiding today. "The duke is very much a man, and I think you know that better than most."

Celia didn't bother denying it. "Further, I'm sure you know he deserves much better than the likes of me."

She spoke the words in an off-hand manner, as if they could breeze through the air and float out the window. Instead, they landed with a heavy, sodden thud.

A shift occurred in Eloise's eyes that looked suspiciously close to smugness, as if these were the words her cousin had been hunting for all along—words that had been skillfully flushed out into the open and cornered.

Now they would have to be dealt with.

"You think yourself unworthy of him."

Celia didn't think it.

She knew it.

"Gabriel has a purity to him."

Eloise's smug smile slipped, and her brow gathered with distress. "Do you think yourself impure, Celia?"

She attempted to shrug the question away, but Eloise's unflinching gaze wasn't having it. "I *am* impure."

"Because you were a dutiful daughter who did as her father told her? Because you were an obedient wife who suffered the attentions of a lecherous and criminal husband? Those men foisted their impurity onto you."

"That's beside the point." Celia was certain on this matter. "The fact remains I'm a damaged bit of goods, and Gabriel deserves better."

"Does he see you that way?"

No.

Celia knew it instinctively.

Still... "That doesn't change the fact of it. I'm not worthy of him."

"*Not worthy?*" Eloise exhaled a gust of frustration. "Aren't you worthy of happiness? Haven't you earned it? What about what *you* deserve, Celia?"

This hard and unforgiving angle that she viewed herself from...

Gabriel didn't see her from that perspective.

All along, he'd seen a Celia different from the one she saw. He saw a woman capable of taking care of herself and her stable—of making a success of herself.

You can do it all on your own... You are doing it all on your own.

And he saw her as the woman for him.

The time had arrived.

Not for her to forgive herself for past transgressions. Eloise was right. She'd done nothing wrong.

The time had arrived for her to feel compassion for her past self who had been mistreated and wronged... who hadn't had a choice.

Which left her with her present self—who did have a choice.

Who could choose happiness.

Who could choose Gabriel.

It wasn't enough to have *more.*

Not when Gabriel was offering her *everything.*

She could have kindness and consideration and Gabriel...

"I can't marry Wrexford," fell from her mouth.

Eloise exhaled another sigh—this one of relief. "It's about bloody time you came to your senses."

Celia shot to her feet. "I must tell him."

"I believe he's already in the chapel."

Celia nearly groaned. To jilt a man was one matter... But to jilt him at the altar was an altogether different one.

But her only chance was at stake.

She must.

Then she was hugging a teary-eyed Eloise—and fighting her own onslaught of tears—before hiking up her skirts and scrambling into a run. Down one corridor, then another. Down one staircase, then another.

Within the minute, she arrived at the threshold of the chapel, a small room with soaring neo-Gothic arches and a light-filled rose window above the altar. The pews remained mostly empty, save for the few invited guests. Wrexford's solemn-eyed parents sat to one side, and the Ladies Saskia and Viveca to the other. The latter tossed a giggly glance over her shoulder and nudged her sister. At the end of the aisle stood the bishop and...

Wrexford.

Celia almost felt like she would have to go through with this wedding after all.

Almost.

Skirts still in hand, she made her way up the short aisle—not like an eager bride, but rather like a woman on a mission. Mama's eyebrows almost lifted off her forehead, and the pent-up giggle escaped Lady Viveca.

Celia reached the end of the aisle, and just as she swiveled toward Wrexford, a figure passing the open doorway caught the edge of her vision. In the split of the second before she looked, she knew—*Gabriel.*

Like a magnet drawn to a lodestone, her gaze caught his. A slow heartbeat crawled past, time gone immaterial. Then it snapped to as suddenly when he didn't break stride and disappeared out of sight.

A questioning, "Celia?" sounded at her side.

She turned to find Wrexford watching her, a quizzical expression on his face.

Right.

She couldn't simply hitch up her skirts and bolt after Gabriel.

Not yet, anyway.

She had a bit of business to finish first.

"Wrexford, there is something I must say to you." She inhaled as deeply as her shallow breath would allow. "I can't possibly marry—"

He reached out and took her hand, cutting her off with a few firm pats. "Can we share a private word?"

A private word?

Of course, a private word was much better than jilting him in front of everyone.

She allowed herself to be led into an empty room off the side of the chapel. As she opened her mouth to finish her jilting of him, Wrexford held up a hand, again staying the words in her mouth. "Your Grace, you know in what high esteem I regard you."

Your Grace... He was no longer calling her *bauble*.

She reclaimed her hand and took a step back, giving him a nod in response.

He gave his throat a loud clearing, as if he were about to perform a Shakespeare monologue for a crowd of five hundred. "We feel—"

"*We?*" Celia interrupted.

"Mama and I," he clarified. "We feel it would be best if this marriage doesn't proceed."

Celia's breath caught. "Oh?"

"It may be that my proposal was made in the heat of a hasty

moment. Mama thinks you the sort of woman who, *erm*, provokes men into making such declarations."

Though Wrexford's words were the answer to her prayers, Celia couldn't help feeling a bit stung. Still... "To be clear, you're calling off the wedding."

This needed to be clear.

"I am."

"*You* are jilting *me?*"

A sheepish blush pinked Wrexford's cheeks. "I would prefer we not use that word."

A chirrup of laughter bubbled up, which she attempted to suppress, truly she did. Except it wouldn't be contained and spilled over until she was nearly hiccupping with laughter that felt less inspired by hilarity, than genuine, soul-deep relief. "*You,*" she said between gasps for air, "are... jilting... *me.*"

Wrexford's brow creased with distress. "Are you in good health, Your Grace?"

She waved the question away and attempted to compose herself, but not before another hiccup of laughter escaped her. A shadow of mild offense clouded his features. "Perhaps I should call for Mama and you should sit—"

"No need, I'm quite steady on my feet." In fact, she was going to be needing them *tout suite.* "Oh, thank you, Wrexford. Thank you so very much. I wish you well in life. I'm sure you and Mama will find the perfect bride for you."

"Actually," he began, his blush deepening into his signature radish red, "Mama has already—"

"Of course she has," Celia interrupted, her skirts in hand and her feet already on the move. She hadn't all day. "I must go."

"But... where?" he called out.

"To seize my happiness," she tossed over her shoulder.

The last thing Celia heard as she flew from the room, into the chapel, and down the aisle was, "Should we should send for a doctor, Your Grace?"

But Celia didn't break stride as she sprinted down the corridor and poked her head into the first room she came to.

No Gabriel.

Nor was he in the next room... or the next.

The man was nowhere.

Panic wanted to seize her. So, she did what she always did when anxiety threatened. She went still—and let her mind settle.

And it came to her.

She knew where he was.

She took two instinctive steps in that direction and came to a sudden stop.

She couldn't go to Gabriel like *this*.

Not dressed head to toe in Wrexford's finery.

But she did know precisely the dress she would be wearing when she asked Gabriel to make her the happiest woman on earth.

If he rejected her, as he had every right to do, she understood something she'd never known before—something Gabriel had shown her.

She could fashion a life on her own.

She didn't need Gabriel for the money and security he could provide her.

She needed him because she loved him and ached for his love in her life.

To make her life whole.

For that, she would be entirely vulnerable to him—and let him decide their future.

If there was to be one.

CHAPTER TWENTY-NINE

*G*abriel had been pacing the mansion since dawn.

Now, he was in the center of the hedge maze, wearing a path in the grass.

It was the only place in London he trusted himself to be.

He'd tried confining himself to his bedroom... the study... the kitchens... the water closet. But all those rooms allowed him to exit easy as he pleased and make his inevitable way to the chapel.

Where Celia presently was.

Where he'd seen her standing at the end of the aisle, dressed in a mountain of white lace, readying herself to say *I will* to Wrexford, and become that man's bauble for the rest of her days.

As it ever did, the thought had the blood scorching through his veins and his hands clenching into fists.

Mountain of lace notwithstanding, she made a beautiful bride. It had been all he could do not to march up that aisle, toss her over his shoulder, and claim her as *his*.

She ever inspired the medieval warlord in him.

But she'd made her choice.

And he'd determined he would live with it.

So, this was him living with it in the only sensible way he

knew how. Really, he should be congratulating himself for his self-restraint.

He snorted. He'd been reduced to the sort of man who paced the center of a labyrinth to keep himself from kidnapping a woman.

But he was here.

That was the salient point.

Even if he found his way out now, Celia and Wrexford would already be well and truly married.

He might have to stay here forever.

Or at least through the wedding breakfast.

And through the afternoon when the marriage would likely be consummated.

A low growl of frustration escaped him.

For the sake of his sanity, it might be best if he remained here until morning.

She'd actually gone through with the wedding.

He couldn't believe what his eyes had clearly seen. *Celia...* standing at the end of the aisle... marrying a man not him.

A flicker of movement caught the edge of his eye.

Or was it the color he noticed first?

Fuchsia.

He half pivoted, and the breath froze in his chest.

There, standing at the boxwood entrance, was...

He blinked. It couldn't be...

He blinked again.

It was.

Celia—dressed in the fuchsia ballgown, her amber eyes bright, her cheeks twin scarlet patches, and her chest heaving as if she'd sprinted a dozen miles.

His heart thudded hard and fast in his chest. Celia... here...

It had to mean something.

But his mind couldn't yet believe what his heart hoped.

"Aren't you a married woman?" he asked into the uncertain air between them.

"Actually—"

She took a step, and he instinctively did the same.

"I think I've been jilted."

An incredulous laugh escaped Gabriel, even as his brow dug a deep groove into his forehead. "Pardon?"

He couldn't have heard her correctly.

A sheepish smile formed about her mouth. "To be fair, *I* was about to jilt *him*, but he beat me to it." She shrugged one shoulder. "It only seemed sporting to let him have the win."

Though the blood jangled through his veins and sweat slicked his palms, Gabriel smiled despite himself. "Ever the honorable sportswoman."

They'd neared the fountain, drinking one another in as if parched, the air dewy and golden. The morning light caught Celia's hair that tumbled about her shoulders and turned the ends honey. Her beauty was indisputable, but it was the nerves that shimmered about her that gave him hope.

Here was a Celia without smile or artifice.

A vulnerable Celia.

Ache pulsed through him as he took another step. He couldn't not be near her. He needed her so badly—not the physical ache, but the one deeper… the one borne in the soul.

The one borne in the heart.

Need.

He needed this woman.

He loved this woman.

The distance between them gone, her head had to tip back at a slight angle so she could hold his gaze. "Celia, why are you here?"

Her tongue nervously swiped across her bottom lip. He followed the motion and immediately tamped down the responding wave of desire.

First came the heart's need—then would come the body's.

"I knew here was where you would be," she said, an emotional wobble in her voice. "And I only want to be where you are."

Hope took wing in Gabriel's chest. "Celia—"

"And," she continued, cutting him off, "I have something to tell you." She exhaled a rough breath. "You were right."

"About?"

Men ever enjoyed hearing such rare words from a woman—and he was only a man.

"I don't need you."

He blinked. "Pardon?"

Unexpected.

"I don't need you to put a roof over my head or food on my table or to provide security for me and my stable. I don't need you to give me diamonds or pearls or silk gowns—although I do love this dress so very much," she said earnestly.

Gabriel had never seen Celia so lacking in composure—and he loved her all the more for it.

"What do you need, Celia?" he willed himself to ask, braving the question—because he must.

For she must brave the answer.

She took his hand in hers, brought it to her mouth, and pressed a kiss to his palm, her breath a whisper against his skin. Her gaze lifted. "I need you, Gabriel. I need your love in my life. I can fashion a successful existence without you, or any other man, for that matter. You made me see that. But I cannot live a life worth living without you."

The hope that had taken wing in his chest... Her words were all the permission it needed to soar. But within her eyes he saw that she hadn't yet given over to the joy that now coursed through him.

"What is it, Celia?"

"Can you forgive me?"

"For?"

"For being a dunderhead and refusing to see what you'd been showing me all along?"

"You were choosing the only path life had shown you. It was all you knew."

As frustrating as that had been for him to accept.

Now, it was time for him to speak from his heart. "The path I knew was also born from need. From the time I learned how to provide, I took to being needed. It was a source of pride for me that I could support my sisters."

"There is so much admirable in that."

"And I made it a point that while others might need and succumb to feeling, I never would. Never would the flesh or the heart dictate my life. It was beyond pride. It was vanity. Then I became a duke—and I met you."

Her eyes earnest and understanding, she observed him in silence.

"I wanted you in a way that held no logic. But it wasn't mere wanting, but rather need in its purest form, a feeling I wasn't prepared for. I thought need was weakness, but, in fact, it's the opposite. Need is a vital ingredient to happiness. If one never opens to need, one can never open to love." He reached out and caressed her cheek. Her eyes drifted shut for the split of a second, and she swayed ever so subtly into his hand. "*You*, Celia, you are my need. You are my weakness. You are my strength. You are my love, forever." Around the lump in his throat, he said, "I love you."

His declaration produced three immediate effects upon Celia.

She gasped, tears sprang to her eyes, and she dropped to her knees before him, silk skirts puffing into a fuchsia cloud around her.

"Celia…"

"I love you, Gabriel," she proclaimed, reaching up and taking his hands in hers. "I don't have to choose money or security. I can choose my heart. I can choose *you*. Would you do me the great honor of choosing *me* for the rest of our lives?"

"On a single condition."

"Anything."

He lowered and sat back on his haunches so their gazes were level. "That you only marry me if you want to."

She blinked, then threw her arms around his neck on joyous impulse. "Yes," she muttered against his throat as she kissed him. "My love."

He turned his head and met her mouth with his, deepening the kiss. "Shall we start our forever now?" he murmured, his hands already answering as he tugged her bodice. Her puckered nipples all but demanded to be set free, and who was he to deny them?

"I believe in—*oh*—proceeding as we mean to go on," was her reply as nimble, talented fingers began working the falls of his trousers.

This wouldn't take long.

But then, they had as long as they needed.

They had forever.

EPILOGUE

ONE MONTH LATER

$\mathcal{T}$hey'd been married that very afternoon.

The special license had taken a couple of hours to obtain, and the wedding only ten minutes. Celia hadn't even needed to change out of her dress.

And that was Gabriel and Celia married.

Society had been shocked to the tips of its satin slippers. The Sixth Duchess of Acaster had begun the day intended to become the Countess of Wrexford and ended it the Seventh Duchess of Acaster. It was simply too delectable a morsel of scandal not to be savored over lengthy tea-infused gossip sessions all over Town.

For their parts, Gabriel and Celia had seen to their London affairs before decamping to Ashcote Hall—well, the cottage— where they'd remained these last four blissful weeks.

Dawn's first rays peeking through the kitchen windows, Celia stood before the stove, trying to remember each step of Mrs. Davies' tea instructions. Celia had given the staff the morning off. Today, on the last day of their Ashcote idyll, she would be preparing and serving her husband his breakfast in bed.

She knew precisely how he took his morning brew. How

brown he liked his toast. The ideal consistency for his boiled egg. The correct density of his porridge.

But how to make them perfect had, admittedly, eluded her.

So, this last week, after she'd spent mornings in the company of her horses and while Gabriel spent his afternoons tending the multiple branches of his business and dukedom, she'd had Mrs. Davies walk her through every step of the morning meal process —from how to stoke the stove fire to a proper heat... to the correct pans and crockery to use... to tea steeping and egg boiling times.

Celia was ready.

Now, being the capable woman she was, she set to work, and half an hour later, she'd done what she'd set out to accomplish— prepared breakfast for her husband.

A less than stellar breakfast, admittedly.

In fact, she was tempted to dump it in the bin and start over.

In fact, that was exactly what she would—

A throat cleared behind her, and she whirled around, still clutching the serving tray. The sight before her nearly had tray and contents clattering to the floor. Her husband... seated at the kitchen table... settled into a straight-backed chair as if he'd been there a good long while... a smile on his face.

"Gabriel," she exclaimed. "How long have you been sitting there?"

"Long enough," he said easily.

"You're supposed to be in bed."

He spread his hands wide. "Yet here I am."

Oh, how attractive was her husband with his sleep-tousled hair and undone muslin shirt and bare feet.

He jutted his chin. "What do you have there?"

She followed his gaze to the tray she yet held. She'd almost forgotten it. "*Erm*, your morning tea." Her sense of dread doubled. "Actually, I was thinking I would just start over."

"I'm certain the tea you've prepared will be lovely."

Oh, her lovely husband would say that.

But he held a determined look in his eye that she knew well.

He would eat this breakfast.

She exhaled a resigned sigh and began arranging the contents of the tray before him. Somehow, the fare looked even less appetizing on the table.

Gabriel didn't seem to notice as he smiled down at the spread before him. "Now, wife, sit."

Hands clutched before her, she only now noticed she was hovering. She lowered into the nearest chair and watched him pour his tea. He glanced up. "We'll need another cup."

"Is that one chipped?"

"For you."

Of course. He wouldn't want her watching him like he was a bear on display at the Tower of London.

Cup retrieved, he poured for her. She took a sip and winced. "It's possible I steeped it over long."

Possible?

A most definite certainty.

Gabriel took another gulp. "A hearty brew that braces a man for the day."

That was one way of putting it.

He began tapping the soft-boiled egg with the back of his spoon. Instead of collapsing in, as it should, the egg held its ground. This was no soft-boiled egg, but rather on the firm side. It might even bounce, if put to the test against pine floorboards.

"Here," she said, reaching for the egg. "I'll peel it for you while you, *erm*, enjoy your porridge."

"Thank you, my love."

My love.

Her heart fluttered in her chest every time he spoke those two words.

As she peeled, she kept half an eye on her husband as he stuck spoon into porridge. She suspected that if he let go, the spoon would remain standing. Still, he managed to wrest a clump free and take a bite.

After he'd been chewing rather longer than one would expect of a bite of porridge, she ventured to ask, "Perhaps it's a bit stodgy?"

He gave his head a shake and spoke a muffled, "Perfect," around porridge that had to be sticking to every surface in his mouth.

She finished peeling the egg and returned it to its little cup. Gabriel picked up a slice of toast. As it closed the distance to his mouth, Celia's stomach dropped, and it was all she could do not to snatch it out of his hand. She'd been deceiving herself that it was merely a dark shade of brown. With black marks on either side, it was obviously scorched.

He took a bite, then another, and another, until he'd consumed the entire slice. Then he ate his egg and finished his porridge and tea. Not a drop or morsel of the meal remained as he sat back in his chair and patted his stomach as if in satisfaction.

Celia only realized she'd been watching him with her mouth slightly agape. "Gabriel," she said, "that had to have been dreadful."

He swiped his napkin across his mouth, then reached out and took her hand, pulling her onto his lap, her arm instinctively curling around his neck. "It was the best meal of my life."

"That cannot be true."

Except she saw something in his direct blue eyes.

Belief.

He believed those words.

"Within this meal was an ingredient I've never tasted in a breakfast before."

"Charcoal?"

He laughed, but she was most serious.

"The love of my wife."

Love... the ingredient that had been missing from both their lives.

Until they'd found each other.

How unlike the fairy tales was true love—*real* love.

And how much better.

The End

ALSO BY SOFIE DARLING

All's Fair in Love and Racing

Odds on the Rake

The Duchess Gamble

Shadows and Silk

Three Lessons in Seduction

Tempted by the Viscount

Her Midnight Sin

To Win a Wicked Lord

At the Pleasure of the Marquess

One Night His Lady

Nell and the Runaway Duke

ABOUT THE AUTHOR

Sofie Darling is an award-winning author of historical romance. The third book in her Shadows and Silk series, Her Midnight Sin, won the 2020 RONE award for Best Historical Regency.

She spent much of her twenties raising two boys and reading every romance she could get her hands on. Once she realized she simply had to write the books she loved, she finished her English degree and embarked on her writing career. Mr. Darling and the boys gave her their wholehearted blessing.

When she's not writing heroes who make her swoon, she runs a marathon in a different state every year, visits crumbling medieval castles whenever she gets a chance, and enjoys a slightly codependent relationship with her beagle, Bosco. Visit her website.

Printed in the USA
CPSIA information can be obtained
at www.ICGtesting.com
CBHW021133181223
2729CB00006B/460